PRAISE FOR
NIGHTMARES FROM THE GRAY

"Powell sets the bar high with this fantastic debut. The story starts with a gripping chapter, and what happens next takes you on one hell of an imaginative ride reminiscent of a cross between *Stranger Things* and Stephen King, when Stephen King's in top form."

-Isaac Nightingale, Author of *Neon Nightmares*

"Joey Powell attacked this material like he was Wes Craven in charge of making a version of *Nightmares on Elm Street* or *Shocker* for teens and absolutely nailed it. Book reads like a horror movie made in the late 90's; unique characters, wildly new premise, a ton of moving pieces. Kind of like if *The Breakfast Club* was made by Behemoth."

-Damien Casey, Author of *The Nine Teeth of the River Styx*

"If *Guardians of the Galaxy* had a baby with *Stranger Things* and that baby happened to wield magic and manifest a dark, coming of age tale of adventure and sacrifice... it might be this book. This is a publishing debut from a wildly creative writer."

-David Washburn, Author of *Devils That Prey*

"Powell brings nightmares to life on the pages of this book."
 -Nadine Stewart, Curator of *Curbside Cursed: The Yardsale Anthology*

"A highly creative, action-packed, wild ride! Powell creates a highly imaginative and vivid world, taking the reader deep into another place and time ... I found myself completely lost in the vivid images materializing from the words on the page."

Julie Hiner, Author of *Thrash Track*

"A truly wonderful debut."

-A.D Jones, Author of *Umbrate* and *Sacificial Waters*

"Entertaining and metal as hell."

-J Flowers-Olnowich, author of *The Three Warlocks*

"A young adult horror story that will blow your mind."

-Rabia Tanveer for *Readers' Favorite*

NIGHTMARES FROM THE GRAY

Joey Powell

MADAXEMEDIA.COM

Nightmares From the Gray

Joey Powell

All rights reserved.

Copyright © 2023 by Joey Powell & Mad Axe Media

No part of this publication may be reproduced, distributed, or transmitted in any form or by any means, including photocopying, recording, or other electronic or mechanical methods, without the prior written permission of the author, except as permitted by U.S. copyright law.

The story, all names, characters, and incidents portrayed in this production are fictitious. No identification with actual persons (living or deceased), places, buildings, and products is intended or should be inferred.

Ebook ISBN: 979-8-9891730-1-3

Paperback ISBN: 979-8-9891730-0-6

Cover Art & Design by Joey Powell

This book is dedicated to my twin brother Josh, who said he'd only read
a book if I wrote one.
Challenge accepted...
And to all you square pegs out there struggling to fit in:
This one's for you.

NIGHTMARES FROM THE GRAY

A NOVEL

JOEY POWELL

PART I.

INTO THE
GRAY WORLD

Chapter One

The steel rungs of the water tower ladder were even more frigid than Ronnie expected on a January afternoon, but it was the height that caused him to shake. His grip had become increasingly unreliable the higher he ascended, coated in the hot sweat flushing from his palms. The steel enclosure behind him, which was meant to catch climbers from falling, was of no comfort, considering the gaps were large enough for his small, skinny body to fit through.

Roughly two stories above ground, Ronnie had a clear view of the downtown strip, the rec center, rows of pop-up neighborhoods, and woods beyond a hundred-yard radius of grass. The Knollwood Pines water tower had the distinction of being the highest point in all of eastern North Carolina, a thought that further compounded Ronnie's anxiety.

A yelp from the ground below prompted Ronnie to glance downward. "Almost there, Ronnie! Don't you dare come back down!" It was the voice of Jack Sutter, looking up at Ronnie with his feet comfortably on the grass at the bottom of the tower. He was a junior at Knollwood Pines High—a grade above Ronnie—and Ronnie's opposite in nearly every way. Jack was magazine-cover-handsome, with piercing green eyes and sharp cheekbones, and an attitude that announced to the world that it was his for the taking. That attitude and the fact that he could toss a football thirty yards down the field off his back foot granted him captain status on the varsity football team, something only seniors were eligible for in previous years.

This was an initiation. A tradition passed on by upperclassmen. Take the wimpiest runt who shouldn't even be handing out water bottles on the sideline of a JV football game and convince him that by climbing the water tower he could hang among the high school elites. Why did Ronnie ever think he could pull this off without freezing in terror? Joining the football team had presented an opportunity to be tough—to not be seen by the rest of the school as a punching bag—yet here he was, still being punched at while two stories off the ground.

To Jack's left stood Therber Windell, a six-foot-six-inch behemoth with a boyish face and arms like an oak tree. He elbowed Gavin Grace, beaming at his side. Gavin always seemed to be smiling, projecting a confidence that Ronnie couldn't possibly possess. While the two of them and Jack seemed positively delighted in Ronnie's horror, Preston Collinsworth's was the only expression Ronnie couldn't quite make out. Within the long, thick hair that surrounded his face like a lion's mane was a stillness that Ronnie could have mistaken for concern if he thought any of his onlookers had the capacity to feel empathy.

Ronnie clenched his eyelids and focused on the task at hand. Make it to the top and earn the acceptance of the guys below, a group that many at Knollwood Pines High referred to as the Blue Jackets, named after their custom matching coats with blue bases, yellow sleeves, and a yellow "KP" embroidered on the chests.

Jack yelled out, "Hey, Ronnie! We're getting a little bored down here... I think we need some reading material!"

Ronnie repositioned his right hand into an underhand grip and rotated his head over his shoulder as Jack lifted the bookbag Ronnie had removed before starting his climb. "No! Don't!" Ronnie screamed. "I'll go faster!"

Jack unzipped the bag and turned it over, dumping the contents out. Binders, textbooks, notebooks, loose-leaf paper, and pencils fell to the ground.

"Jack!" Preston barked. "Don't go through the kid's stuff!"

"What do you think we're gonna find?! Tampons?!" Jack responded, loud enough for Ronnie to hear as he rifled through the contents of the bag. He stacked the notebooks on top of each other and held them at chest level.

"Jack, could you please stop?!" Ronnie yelled, quickly realizing it was pointless as Jack began spreading open the cover of the top notebook.

"Begging's not a good look, bro!" Therber yelled back.

Gavin added, "All the way to the top! We all had to do this!"

"Whoa!" Jack blurted out. "We got us a bit of a sicko!"

Whatever was left to sink in Ronnie's stomach sank even deeper as Gavin and Therber crowded behind Jack. Six eyes looked down at the contents of the notebook.

That notebook.

Jack looked up at Ronnie. "Is this Coach Caine?!"

The three boys laughed as Ronnie visualized the picture he had recently drawn of a muscular man in a leather mask beheading Coach Cain with a machete, his whistle flying in the air.

"Buddy, come down!" Preston called out to Ronnie. "You've gone far enough!"

"It's for an art project!" Ronnie whimpered. But that was a lie. Last year during football season, Coach Caine had made Ronnie's life miserable. Caine thought by reminding Ronnie of his weakness he was toughening him up, but every verbal attack left mental scars. Every reminder of him not being good enough on the field was a reminder that his father thought he wasn't good enough to raise. But whereas Ronnie's father had abandoned him at birth, Coach Caine was an unavoidable presence.

Ronnie had to interact with him nearly every day, five days a week, as long as his sophomore season lasted.

So, he drew vivid images of Coach Caine dying horribly. The catharsis was almost worth the paranoia of his collection being discovered. And now it had been discovered by the very people he was trying to impress. If only he hadn't been so stupid as to leave his bookbag right next to them.

"It's fine! We don't care what's in the book!" Preston yelled as Ronnie began to tremble.

"I don't know, man!" Jack yelled. "I think the responsible thing for us to do would be to show Coach Caine!"

"No!" Ronnie twisted his body even further. This time, he twisted too fast. The sweat on his palms had made the rungs impossible to keep hold of. His right hand slid from its underhand grip and his left couldn't stop the momentum. His body jackknifed through the gap in the cage behind him. His right foot *clanked* against metal on its way out, sending him into an uncontrollable flipping motion.

Sky became grass...

Grass became sky...

Then everything was black.

Color folded into shapes in front of Ronnie's eyes. Once his pupils adjusted, he recognized a translucent overhead light boxed in by acoustic ceiling tiles. The light was dim and barely lit the room around him. No longer was he in plain clothes, but rather a hospital gown, with thick air touching the bare skin on his backside.

He was hovering two feet off the hospital bed, floating with the indescribable notion that it was perfectly natural.

Somehow, he knew he could control it.

He willed his body to the left side of the bed and tilted upright, floating to the window, the view of which was covered by curtains. He waved one curtain aside as effortlessly as fanning a feather.

The earth surrounding Old Knollwood Pines Road was charred and withered, appearing like the aftermath of a firestorm that had blown through and consumed all wildlife and forestry. Ashes of the town he remembered swam aimlessly through the air. The sky above was stark red and moving violently in a way Ronnie could not understand—a swaying motion repeating like a thousand ladles stirring a pot of blood.

Suddenly, from out of the sky, a long piece of metal spun toward the ground and pierced the pavement with an echoing *crash* a football field's length away from Ronnie, jammed in a diagonal position.

Ronnie was in a dream—he knew it—and because he was in a dream, he was unafraid to examine the object further.

He floated inches above the floor through the hospital, its halls caked in a drab shade of gray with an eerie buzzing sound forcing its way through the walls. The buzzing sound became more prominent as he went down the stairs and exited through folded, busted doors in the lobby, finally recognizing the sound for what it truly was.

A chorus of screams droning like radio waves.

Ronnie let his feet touch the pavement, peering up at the red sky above and studying an endless sea of arms reaching down, flailing from the shoulders of screaming humanoid *things* stuck upside down.

He walked forward onto Old Knollwood Pines Road and made his way to the metal fixture jutting from the ground. The street was lined with abandoned cars and crude lumps that he knew to be human bodies as he got closer, their skin gray and withered, their bodies drained of life, their faces stuck in a perpetual state of fear.

"How did you do this?" a faint voice echoed unnaturally from behind Ronnie. Confusion surged through him, as everyone and everything around him was dead.

Rubber soles smacked pavement, tracing the path he had come from. He darted forward, zigzagging through the piles of bodies, becoming increasingly frightened by his unseen pursuer as he closed in on the metal object.

It's just a dream. Just a dream.

Twenty yards away from the object, he marveled at the sheer size of it as his heart pounded in his chest. The thing appeared ten times the length of his small body.

"Stop running!" whoever was behind him said between breaths. "I'm not going to hurt you!"

Before he could get a good look at the object, a rush of flames spat out of the sky and surrounded it with a ring of fire. Ronnie raised a forearm to his eyes, shielding himself from both the light and the heat, momentarily forgetting he was being chased. The flames receded just below Ronnie's eyeline.

Inside the ring of fire, a double-bitted axe lay wedged in the pavement, one blade submerged in the street, the other shining brightly against the fire, showing signs of both polish and wear. The hilt was covered in toughened leather and surrounded by barbed wire, twice the size and thickness of that in the real world, spiraling crudely around from top to bottom. A weapon of destruction far too large for any human to wield.

"You're Ronnie Hendrix..." A girl appeared next to Ronnie, wearing a baggy black dress and combat boots, with jet-black braided hair and black lipstick. She towered over Ronnie, but looked to be around the same age. Catching her breath, she said, "You're Ronnie Hendrix... People think you're dead, but you're... here. Did you create all this?"

Unsure how to respond, Ronnie watched the orange glow of flames dance on her awestruck face, her eyes rising from the bottom to the top of the monument before them. He didn't know what *this* was, much less his ability to influence it.

Ronnie circled the perimeter of the ring of fire, close enough to feel the heavy wave of heat against his skin.

"What are you doing?" the girl said.

As Ronnie rounded to the other side of the axe, a figure came into view, walking from the opposite side of the street, illuminated by flames. A thin man in a gray three-piece suit too large for his boney frame. If not for the buttons, the vest and jacket may have fallen clean off. He wore a gray fedora to match the suit, the stark color accentuating his leathery tan skin and gentle blue eyes, which met Ronnie's stare in a knowing manner. A smile rose over the man's face as he walked closer to Ronnie with his hand extended.

"It's not safe here. We have to go," the girl said.

The image of the man in gray faded from existence, replaced by black again.

He woke up in the hospital with scattered figments of a dream and a name on his tongue to associate with the massive weapon he had gazed upon.

Karnalaxe, Ruler of the Underworld.

Chapter Two

Everyone in Knollwood Pines knew about the sixteen-year-old boy who fell from the water tower and slipped into a coma, but the last place Malleck expected to find him was on a plane beyond consciousness. The boy was a traveler like she was, confused and scared, as she had once been. In Manari culture, some referred to it as the Outer Realm. Malleck, however, called it the Gray World, seeing it as a neutral canvas to fill with her artistic creativity. Inside the Gray World, the Manari could manipulate their own personal environments and invite others in. Ronnie Hendrix, having suffered a terrible accident, filled his with darkness, whether knowingly or not.

Seeing Ronnie in the Gray World made Malleck feel less alone. Seeing the man in the ill-fitting suit, however, reminded her of the dangers of aimless travel. It was her personal duty to watch over Ronnie Hendrix since his trip into the Gray World was like a broadcast signal that was easily intercepted, putting him at risk.

No one in the town was aware of the magic strain woven through Malleck's family tree, connecting her to an ancient race of people with extraordinary abilities, a strain that touched very few descendants. Still, the Manari culture was so secretive that even Malleck's parents remained shielded from the knowledge of her gift. If they knew, they might see her as something other than a disappointment. Then again, her abilities offered pure expression, something they saw as antithetical to success.

So it goes.

Malleck stood on a remote field fifty miles outside of Knollwood Pines next to her Aunt Helga, trying to clear her mind for a training session. She was nearly a foot taller than her aunt, a wide woman in her forties with a permanent expression of anger and jagged mid-length hair that Malleck assumed was self-managed. If Helga's intention was to make herself unapproachable, she succeeded consistently.

It was Helga who first recognized the sensitivity to magic in Malleck, a sense that Malleck had come to know well, like being pulled into someone else's orbit as if their presence threw off the very laws of nature. Malleck had relied on Helga as a mentor figure over the last decade, either by choice or circumstance, since she was the only other person Malleck knew who was sensitive to the power of the Manari.

At least until recently.

A steel target shaped like a human sat thirty yards away from Malleck and Helga as they stood surrounded by dried dirt and shell casings. A natural cluster of boulders with large chunks removed lay behind the target.

"So... is this a... *public* shooting range?" Malleck asked.

Helga shrugged. "Yeah."

Malleck gave her a suspicious look.

"Okay, it's private property," Helga relented. "I'll give us some cover."

Helga's eyes faded into rolling clouds of white. No irises, no pupils, just stark white ovals aimed like headlights in Malleck's direction. Helga held her palms high, concentrating energy into her hands.

She let out a slow breath.

"We're hidden," Helga said, her eyes remaining white.

"How do you know?" Malleck asked.

"We've been over this, Malleck."

"How am I supposed to know an illusion works if I can't test it?"

"An experienced Manari knows."

"If I could go to the Manari village—"

"When you're ready," Helga interrupted, "I will take you. But until then, you know the rule."

"Right." Malleck snapped her fingers sarcastically. "We're forbidden from revealing magic to the outside world. Must've forgotten." Malleck shook her head, rolling her eyes in frustration.

"I can still see you, young lady," Helga smirked.

Malleck smirked back. It was easy to forget that Manari magic didn't blind whoever used it, the whitened eyes a deceptive signifier of senses beyond sight. "What do you want me to do?" she asked. "Shoot a lightning bolt at the target?"

Helga laughed. "That type of magic cycled out of the Manari a century ago. No, I want you to pull that target out of the ground."

Malleck gave Helga a confused look. "Telekinesis? For real?"

"You've done it before."

"Yeah, and you told me to never do it again."

"I said don't do it without my supervision. *This* is supervised. I need to know to what extent you can actually do this."

Earlier in the school year, a group of girls at Knollwood Pines High formed their own coven. It was innocent enough—just kids being rebellious and playing pretend. They practiced spells and dabbled in the occult but had no real abilities. To them, people like Malleck only existed in myths and legends. Malleck joined this "coven" and felt like she belonged, even if she had to keep her abilities suppressed.

Until one day she slipped. A brief display of magic horrified the coven. The girls disbanded and spread the word that Malleck was a *real* witch. Though she was certain no one outside of the group actually believed it, the rumor left a scab on the public consciousness. A scab that kept tearing, tearing, tearing.

Stay away from Malleck. I heard she sacrifices animals and stuff.

I heard she can possess people with like... entities.

She cast a spell on a guy at another school to make him fall in love with her. So sad.

"You think it was a fluke?" Malleck asked.

"I *think* you're different. We just need to see just how different you are."

Malleck only knew of Manari magic based on her lessons from Helga. Most Manari could travel to the Gray World. Some Manari could create illusions of the mind. Others, like Helga, could create mass illusions that spanned a large geography, something the Manari relied on to stay hidden from the world.

It was clear to Malleck that being able to move things with her mind was seen as a bit of a superpower.

"No pressure," Helga said. "A very low percentage of our people can do this."

But there *was* pressure. Malleck wanted to be extraordinary, but instead was a bird placed inside a cage. Not only was she flapping wildly to get free, but her wings were getting bigger, pressing against the cage. She knew that if she carried on like this, she'd lose the urgency to flap those wings. Helga kept telling her to wait until the time was right, and so she kept spreading her wings, but not as far as she desired.

Malleck focused hard on the steel target, separating it from the rest of the world in her mind. She bent her elbows and clenched her hand instinctively. She knew not to clench. Physical strength had no bearing on what her mind could do, but it was so difficult to separate the image of the target being ripped out of the ground from the image of her hands pulling it.

She was holding her breath.

She was straining.

She was failing.

"Gah!" she screamed, releasing all the tension in her body, letting oxygen fill her lungs.

"Be patient with yourself," Helga said. "Remember, this is a process."

A process, Malleck thought. Hearing whispers of the "school witch" as people passed by her locker. Every piece of artwork meaningful to her glanced over by her parent's uncaring eyes. Begging her aunt to remove her from this miserable society and take her to a place where she belonged.

Was *that* the process Helga was referring to?

Anger radiated from her chest as she took another hard stare at the target, this time forgoing any notion of a free mind. Her thoughts ran wild like flames licking her skull. The sudden surge in her hands grew rapidly. A translucent cloud of energy formed around her fingers. *Holy shit.* That was new—the heat of fire and buzz of electricity twirling across her skin.

This was power.

Excitement and anger collided. The spinning clouds around her hands thickened, turning dark red. She visualized the target ripping out of the ground.

"Malleck, stop!" Helga yelled, snapping Malleck's concentration.

The red clouds faded from Malleck's hands, and she dropped to her knees as the world blurred around her.

CLANK. The target slammed to the ground.

Malleck fell to her back, letting out a tired, satisfied laugh. "I did it, Aunt Helga."

When Helga didn't respond, Malleck turned to catch a sideways view of the short woman, standing with her mouth agape. The look on Helga's face told Malleck this wasn't a good thing.

"It shouldn't be possible," Helga said as she pulled the stick shift hard into second gear. Her Dodge pickup truck, once a vibrant red, was now pale pink with rusted edges. Malleck has seen the paint fade through the years, and now it both sounded and looked like it was in a perpetual state of falling apart.

"What's wrong?" Malleck asked. "I moved that target thingy. Isn't that what you—'

"Don't tell *anyone* about this," Helga said. She accelerated and slammed the stick shift into third gear.

"Who would I tell?"

"I was able to protect you from the council once—"

"So what? I made a girl levitate. She barely got off the ground. No one was hurt."

Helga gave Malleck a stern look.

Malleck grunted in retaliation. "Okay, yeah, it was a *mild* concussion, but I still think she faked it."

"If the council finds out that you can conjure dark magic, they won't overlook it. I won't be able to protect you again."

"I can conjure... what now?"

Helga took a deep breath. The percussive rattling of the truck filled the air between them. For Malleck's entire life, Helga had been training her in secret. She always assumed it was to prepare her for joining the Manari commune, but Malleck had grown up with a strong will. It was becoming more difficult to decipher whether Helga was keeping the Manari secret from Malleck, methodically integrating her into their culture, or whether Helga was keeping Malleck secret from them.

She was becoming less certain that it was the former. In her still relatively infantile understanding of Manari magic, she knew that once in a generation a child was born with the power to conjure dark magic.

"The magic in your hands burned blood-red," Helga said. "The color of the Underworld. The kind of magic that's forbidden."

Chapter Three

Nine months was all it took for Ronnie to make a full recovery. The doctors couldn't believe what they'd witnessed in what they called a series of miracles.

Given the way Ronnie's body was reportedly flailing in the air, the fact that he landed on his back was miracle number one. His inertia surely would have caused his body to fold in a grotesque manner had he landed any other way.

Of course, the fact that he landed on his back from two stories up and didn't experience any significant damage to his spine was miracle number two. He could move his legs during the third month of recovery, he was walking by the fifth month of recovery, and by the seventh he could've done a full sprint.

The impact of his head hitting the ground certainly should have caused at least minimal brain damage. At first, they thought their brain scans were incorrect, but the day he awoke from his four-week coma, he immediately began speaking in full sentences. It appeared that his brain, which would have shaken like a crash test dummy in his skull on impact, was completely unharmed. That was miracle number three.

The Hendrix household, consisting of only Ronnie and his mother Cynthia, had never been particularly religious, so it was reasonable that when staff members at the hospital and the rehab clinic discussed Ronnie's recovery as proof of guardian angels it fell on deaf ears. At first, Ronnie just saw it as extreme luck. The universe's way of bringing balance to a life of consistent failures and exclusion. After all, he wasn't built like most boys, and he didn't think like most boys.

He didn't tell a single soul why he really climbed up the ladder or who was with him that day. He told no one of the letterman-jacket-wearing group of kids who had everything and thus nothing left to satisfy themselves but cruel jokes. The same ones who had gone through his bag and found something he never intended to share with anyone. His artwork was deeply personal and particularly macabre. He had no desire to physically harm anyone, only to see his tormentors meet their demise. Being small, athletically stunted, and far beyond what some would call socially awkward, he was an easy target for those looking for someone to abuse. In attempting to join the ranks of a higher social class, he'd been exposed as what he really was.

A freak.

Though he never said a word about the four boys, they were all found out.

Further down the road to his recovery, Ronnie was gifted a leather-bound sketchbook, beautiful in its hand-stitched construction. With nothing but time to recover and blank pages to fill, Ronnie channeled the anger he harbored into the notebook, letting his dark imagination run wild. Written passages accompanied detailed depictions of suffering. Faces sagging with anguish, bodies maimed and bludgeoned. It all just seemed to pour out of him, an uncontrollable urge to keep going, to make his four enemies suffer in ways he was physically incapable of doing. His revenge existed only between the sturdy leather covers of the book.

But this project of his was different from what he'd done before. Ronnie was driven by an unseen force. An energy urging him to create. The drawings were dastardly, but they had to be accompanied by something unifying, something that would make sense of it all in Ronnie's furious mind. Something that would recreate that red sky of screaming souls and the unforgettable image of the axe surrounded by flames.

A vision of Knollwood Pines in ashes.

So, he wrote of rituals. He wrote of chants. He wrote of a circle of offerings removed from their hosts that would please the demon who wielded the axe. He wrote of a spell that would shift the axis of the Underworld and place it in the sky, creating a gateway to the natural world. He wrote of a demon with the power to destroy.

Ronnie had never dabbled in the occult. He wasn't familiar with magic or ritualistic ceremonies. But the comfort he felt while crafting the bullies' demises was more jubilant than he'd ever felt before, and the dopamine purge every time he stopped was nearly devastating. He knew that there was darkness in him now and it made him wonder if a guardian angel was actually watching over him. Or maybe something else.

He grants life to the righteous
And damns evil committed
He gives power to the powerless
And vanquishes the wicked
Provide the severed offerings
And roar into the night
For they who summon Karnlaxe
Control the demon's might

Chapter Four

The sound of lead dragging smoothly against paper helped distract Ronnie from the day ahead. It was the first week of October and the day on which he would return to school. He wasn't ready for the looks he was sure to receive, the sympathetic smiles, the atta-boys from people he'd never met. When he woke up from his coma, his hospital room was filled with gifts marked with names of people he couldn't place, who would want nothing to do with him otherwise. But such was life: Some were remembered for the things they've done and others were remembered for the things that happen to them. Any local celebrity status was the result of a dumb dare he did to impress a group of kids he had no business trying to impress. The same kids he was least looking forward to seeing again.

The leatherbound book was almost full and the last handful of pages were pristine compared to the slightly withered pages before them. A few quick scratches of his pencil provided the finishing touches on a portrait of a young man with long black hair on his knees, naked and hunched over, with his elbows bent and forearms to his chest, his palms turned inward and fingers interlocked. Behind him, a man in a black robe with a hood that hid his face dug both hands into the middle of the kneeling boy's back, struggling to remove the victim's lungs.

"Whoa, that's frickin' gnarly."

Ronnie jumped in his seat and slammed the notebook closed, spinning around to catch a smile from Leslie Masood, her leather biker jacket reflecting the small amount of light in the room.

"How did you get in here without me hearing?" Ronnie said.

"I'm sneaky like a ninja. You didn't know?" She tilted her head, determined to see what Ronnie was hiding. Her wavy hair bounced as she bobbed—the thickened result of it being washed once a week to remain as wild as possible, which Ronnie knew was in service of her punk rocker image. All the better to thrash with.

"I've seen you elbows-deep in that thing," Leslie said, "but I've never actually seen what's in it." She walked toward the desk, reaching for the book.

Ronnie promptly stood, blocking her from getting to it. He opened his mouth to say something, but then realized how awkward the action was and said nothing at all.

"Okay. That can be your little secret," Leslie said with a wink.

"It's just... It's personal. I don't want anyone to see it," Ronnie looked down at the carpeted floor. If he was ever going to share the book with anyone, it would have been Leslie. They'd been friends since elementary school, and if there was a single person on the planet who wouldn't judge him for the weird and twisted things in the book, it might have been her. Still, though, it was only a *might*.

"As you wish, Mister Legend of Knollwood Pines. Get your stuff and let's go be our best selves."

Ronnie's stomach rolled. "Please don't call me that."

"Legend?"

"Yeah, that."

Leslie giggled and circled the bedroom, a room she'd seen many times before. "Like it or not, you're something of a legend, Hendrix." She eyed the twin bed in the corner with monochromatic sheets, an L-shaped bookshelf above it with an assortment of sci-fi and fantasy paperbacks.

"In fact," Leslie said, "We might need to spice this place up a bit. Can't have some lucky lady wanting to spend a night with the indestructible kid subjected to all this."

Ronnie let out a disgruntled sigh and shook his head. He grabbed his bag from beside the desk and eyed the leather book of rituals. Everywhere he went, even during rehab, it was by his side, either tucked under his arm or concealed in a bag. It may have been dependency or shame or perhaps a bit of both. The vengeful rituals got him through recovery, but the thought of someone other than him opening it was cripplingly mortifying.

Even so, he slid the notebook into his bookbag.

"There will be no lucky ladies," Ronnie said.

"We'll see about that." Leslie giggled. "You excited for the big day?"

Ronnie sighed. "What do you think?"

"Leave this all up to me. You'll be reintegrated into society in no time."

"But seriously..." Ronnie said, "how'd you get in?"

"Your mom left the door unlocked. It's Knollwood Pines, Ronnie. No one locks their doors."

The houses lining either side of the pavement on Surry Dale Street were connected by a scattered network of red and orange leaves. Some houses had gotten a jump on Halloween, displaying fake spider webs on bushes, skeletons hung on trees, and pumpkins that were sure to rot before the thirty-first of the month.

Ronnie followed Leslie to the black Toyota Corolla she'd parked on the curb. It was an ugly machine with stripped paint and bare tires, peculiarly on-brand sitting outside Hendrix house, a ranch-style with the odd combination of a light blue base and green shutters.

Leslie turned back to Ronnie as her high-top shoes crumpled the leaves of the front yard. "I know you're dreading this, big guy, but it's going to happen whether you like it or not."

Ronnie sauntered joylessly through the yard behind her.

"I know what you need," Leslie said, sliding into the car.

Ronnie fell into the passenger's seat. As soon as he shut his door, Leslie punched a knob on the stereo, prompting a cascade of death metal loud enough for the next two houses down the street to hear. Ronnie wanted to scream at Leslie to turn the music down, but as her frizzy hair rose and fell in rapid succession, bobbing to the chaotic drumbeat, he couldn't help but grin.

An old woman in a bathrobe walking a Pomeranian waddled next to the parked car and shrieked, "Turn it down!"

Oh no, Ronnie thought as he attempted to hide his face. *Not Mrs. Covington.*

Leslie rolled down the window, not minding the music. "What's up?!"

"Turn that down!" Mrs. Covington grunted. "Don't you know what time it is?!"

"Oh." Leslie hit the dial on the stereo, killing the music. "It's 7:04," she said matter-of-factly.

"What?" the old woman said.

"You wanted the time. It's 7:04... a.m., if that matters to you."

"Do you even *live* in this neighborhood?"

Ronnie rose in his seat. "Oh, come on, Mrs. Covington." Leslie was Pakistani-American, and it wasn't hard for Ronnie to glean the subtext within the question.

Mrs. Covington shook her head and threw up a dismissive hand, carrying on her way with the Pomeranian. Leslie raised a middle finger in return, aimed directly at the back of the woman's head.

She turned the stereo on again. "It took me months to get my after-nine!" she yelled to Ronnie over the music. "As far as I'm concerned, it's a license to shred!"

Chapter Five

T he brisk morning air blew his best friend's hair back as a metal band Ronnie had never heard of serenaded him with guttural lyrics he couldn't discern.

"Okay, enough of the music!" Ronnie yelled as a shiver ran down his back. "And maybe roll up your window?!" Even with the double layers of his black hoodie and jean jacket, Ronnie was still all bones, with very little to insulate himself from the cold.

"Ah, not you too," Leslie replied as she rotated the hand crank on her side door, rolling the window up manually. She shut the music off. "Hey, you think that old lady would leave her dog to me in her will?"

Ronnie didn't respond. He simply held his head against the cold window, listening to the eerie droning of the engine and hum of tires against pavement. Leslie *had* to get new tires soon.

"Just take it one day at a time, okay?" Leslie said. "It'll be fine. A month from now, people will forget all about this."

Ronnie turned his head to her, glaring mockingly.

"Okay... in a year, people will forget all about this."

Ronnie repositioned himself, leaning back in his seat. "I'm a square peg."

"Huh?"

"You know... All last year I tried my best to be... visible. I didn't want to be the guy no one recognized. I wanted people to see me and go, 'Hey, that's Ronnie.' Not, 'Wait, who's that?'... I thought that by joining the football team, I'd get some friends and have something to be proud of. Have my mom come out to games and see me on the field and be proud that her son's a part of something. But it didn't happen. I didn't really make any friends. I suck at football. I thought that I could force my way into a world that I just didn't belong in, but I get it now. I'm a square peg."

"Can't fit into a round hole?" Leslie asked.

"Yeah. That's how it feels at least. But all of a sudden I'm making national headlines for surviving something that should have killed me or at least should've paralyzed me. Everybody in this town knows me. It's exactly what I wanted, but now all I want is to be invisible and find *my* people. People like you."

Ronnie looked over at Leslie and waited for her to look back. He wanted her to know how genuine he was. Leslie returned his gaze and smiled.

"Then that's our project for the rest of the year," she said. "Finding more square pegs. Holy shit... Square Pegs... That could be a good band name."

Ronnie smirked. "It'll be *our* band name."

"For cryin' out loud, man, learn an instrument."

Ronnie had been so caught up in the conversation that he hadn't realized they'd entered the school parking lot. Leslie poked her head over the steering wheel, looking for a free spot. Ronnie tensed, scratching at the cloth seats underneath him. He closed his eyes and focused on his breathing, a technique he'd modified through his physical therapy.

Deep breath... Slowly push out the one.

Deep breath... Slowly push out the two.

He'd visualize the number floating away into darkness, being replaced by the next one.

Leslie let him have his moment as she pulled into an empty spot and put the car in park. She stayed silent as he counted all the way to ten, then opened his eyes.

"Sorry, dude. Still here," she said. "The first step's the hardest. It gets easier after that. Just take one step."

Ronnie tilted his head to the side and cracked his neck. "Let's do this," he said, psyching himself up.

The parking lot led directly to the courtyard of the school, where kids were counting down the minutes before the first bell rang, giving them a five-minute warning. Ronnie flipped his hood up, pulled either side of his jean jacket tight against his back and shoulders, and placed a hand on each strap of his bookbag, his eyes darting back and forth. Leslie, as usual, walked with an exaggerated bob in her step, which caused her loosely-strapped bookbag to flop dramatically against her butt.

As they made their way closer to the worming cluster of students, passing by a group of soccer players kicking a hacky sack and a girl squad recording a synchronized dance, there seemed to be no eyes on the so-called "indestructible kid".

"See," Leslie whispered. "You're still invisible."

As if on cue, some random kid blurted out, "Is that Ronnie Hendrix?!"

Silence swept through the courtyard as a hundred sets of eyes fell on Ronnie and Leslie.

"Uh," Ronnie muttered.

Leslie, who Ronnie had never known to shy away from attention, melted into a smile. "That's right... Legend."

The remainder of the day solidified Ronnie's suspicion that his life, at least in the short term, would not be the life he remembered. His old locker was packed so tightly with handwritten notes that when he opened the locker door it caused a hard splash of colored envelopes and folded paper. It was too much to fit in his bag. The janitor, who happened to be in the hallway when it happened, unrolled a trash bag for Ronnie so he could stuff them in. Ronnie didn't imagine he'd be going home with a bag of notes. This would destroy his goal of staying under the radar.

What surprised him most was the smiles of onlookers he'd never met, and only some of whom he recognized. He wasn't used to the smiles of beautiful girls focused in his direction, but it was something he could get used to, even if it was under these circumstances. Tinsley Oppenheimer, a senior cheerleader who had never spoken to him, found him in the hallway and gave him a hug. "Are you okay?" she said with her brown hair and blond streaks brushing against his face. She asked it the way you'd ask a lost puppy that snuck out, was found, and then returned thereafter. He responded with a soft, "Uh... I guess so," and she told him if he needed anything he could come to her.

He went to his first class experiencing similar stares, smiles, and sentiments. His first period teacher, Mr. Crosby, an older man balding at the top of his head with a donut-style haircut surrounding it, called roll and didn't have Ronnie's name on the attendance sheet. He called out the final name, put a checkbox next to it, and folded the notebook, returning to his desk to file it away. A girl in the corner said, "You forgot Ronnie Hendrix," seemingly to remind the universe that Ronnie hadn't been the center of attention enough that day.

This did not occur in his second class, Arts and Crafts, as Ms. Springle not only had an updated attendance sheet but requested a round of applause for "our newest addition." Ms. Springle was youthful, barely five feet tall, and had an infectious zest for life. While he hated the attention, Ronnie knew this class would be a nice reprieve from the others.

The clapping put a shy smile on Ronnie's face. He looked around the room at the artists-in-training, all staring back with genuine glee. His eyes landed on a face he recognized. A girl with a slim face, sharp features, black lipstick, and straight black hair pulled up into a bun. She stood with her hands in the pockets of her overalls, the bottoms of which were rolled midway up her black combat boots.

Those black combat boots.

The girl from his dream.

When the clapping died down, the girl said to Ms. Springle, "I'd like to help Ronnie get his station set up, if that's okay."

"I think that's a lovely idea," Ms. Springle said. She then announced to the class that the assignment for the day was continuing their work on landscape portraits.

The class broke and the girl made her way toward Ronnie. He wasn't sure how to react. He had to have seen her around school, and that's how he dreamed of her... Right? Why could he remember her so vividly, down to the fact that she towered over him?

"I'm Malleck," she said with a hand extended. Bracelets of several colors jingled on her wrist.

He shook her hand and responded, "I'm Ronnie."

"Yeah." She giggled awkwardly. "We all know."

She held his gaze for an uncomfortably long time. Either she knew something he didn't, or he was just being paranoid.

"Have we met before?" he asked.

She tilted her head. "Have we?"

Okay, she's definitely acting weird, he thought. Her expression was too self-assured, as if she was waiting for him to admit something.

"Let's go get you set up," she said finally.

Ronnie shook it off, telling himself that he was imagining things.

Five minutes later, he had his brushes, his water cup, his paints, and a blank canvas to throw them on. The square tables in the classroom could fit four people, but Ronnie and Malleck were the only two at the table in the corner.

"Is no one else sitting here today?" Ronnie asked while mixing a glob of blue with a glob of white on his pallet. He was going to try for a snowy mountain range.

"I'm usually alone at this table. Which I guess means I suckered you into sitting with me." She had a playful confidence to her that Ronnie enjoyed. "They all think I'm a witch."

Ronnie furrowed his brow. "Like a *witch*-witch?"

"Yeah, like spells and magic and all that stuff. And before you ask, it's not... *not* true. I did make a girl float once." She said it like a joke, but for all Ronnie knew, it could have been completely genuine.

"So you and I have never spoken before?" Ronnie asked.

Malleck's face shifted into something more serious. "I'm gonna go get my portrait. Be right back."

She walked to the other side of the room where the portraits were stored on racks for drying. She carefully slid hers out from a shelf and returned to the table, holding it face up and tilted in a way that Ronnie couldn't see.

"Let me ask you this," she said as she walked around Ronnie and sat her portrait on the easel at her station. "Does this landscape look at all familiar to you?"

Ronnie set his paintbrush on the pallet, stood, and rounded the corner of the table. He stopped at Malleck's side and looked down at the painting. The center of the portrait was blank with rugged streaks threatening to close it in, but surrounding this untouched spot was a long dark street lined with vacant cars and buildings reduced to ash. The sky above was hues of red with jagged off-white streaks, appearing to be limbs reaching down.

All blood drained from Ronnie's face.

"Maybe we should talk," Malleck said.

Once again, Ronnie wanted nothing more than to be invisible. His heart thrashed violently in his chest. He couldn't help but run his thumbs against the pads of his fingers, moisture loosening the friction. All he could do was run, but the last thing he wanted to do was cause a scene.

And so he walked out fast enough that no one could stop him. The image in his mind as he left was the hole at the center of the painting, a blank space where the double-bitted axe begged to materialize.

"Ronnie, wait," Malleck called out after him, probably causing a scene and making things even more uncomfortable.

Ronnie kept walking, hearing the taps of leather boots behind him. He picked up the pace. He grabbed the handle of the classroom door and flung it open, then entered the hall and made a beeline for the exit.

"Ronnie, let's talk about this." Malleck's words had a gentle echo in the hallway, bouncing off the metal lockers and competing with Ronnie's hard footsteps.

Ronnie kept his head forward, nearing the exit door. "I don't know what's happening," Ronnie said.

"Let's pump the brakes for a second," Malleck called out behind him.

Ronnie pushed the exit door open, letting the cool air outside slap against his face and flow through him, helping to calm his nerves. He let the door close behind him, knowing that Malleck would push it open shortly. He closed his eyes and breathed in and out slowly, willing his heart rate to come down steadily.

The door squeaked open.

"Everything's okay," Malleck said. "I know you're confused. I'm a little confused myself, honestly, but I think it's important that we talk through this."

"How were you in my dream?" Ronnie asked.

"I think you know that wasn't a dream," Malleck replied. "It didn't feel like a dream, did it? There was a sense of control to it. Am I right or am I wrong?"

Ronnie's heart rate began to pick up. "What's happening to me?"

"It's okay," Malleck said softly. "This is going to sound really weird, but... there's really no normal way to say this. You accessed another plane of existence—"

"Hey, Ronnie!"

Malleck's explanation was cut short by a jovial shout that came from the opposite side of the courtyard. Preston Collinsworth, looking like a bodybuilder in his thin tank top and shorts hugging his thighs, approached them quickly, his thick hair bobbing behind him.

Ronnie's luck had run out. It was only a matter of time before the Blue Jackets found him.

Preston gave a dorky wave. "Hey, Ronnie! It's good to see you, man!" He sounded too excited, causing Ronnie to think this was a joke.

Ronnie noticed a cold glare from Malleck directed at Preston. She had gone silent, her black lips pursed in an angry expression.

"Hi... Malleck, is it?" Preston said.

"Yeah," Malleck responded quickly, offering nothing else.

"Sorry for interrupting." Preston refocused his attention on Ronnie. "Can we talk, man? I've been wanting to talk to you for a while, but your mom wouldn't let me see you in the hospital."

"You... tried to see me in the hospital?" Ronnie asked.

"Well, yeah. I mean, I get it. I don't fault your mom for wanting to keep me out. I was just so happy when I heard you were doing better and I wanted to see if I could make things right and—" Preston cut himself off.

Malleck, looking particularly unimpressed, turned to Ronnie. "You okay here?"

Ronnie took a moment, then nodded.

"Let's talk tomorrow, okay?" Malleck gave Preston another angry glance and re-entered the building.

Ronnie shared an uncomfortable few seconds alone with Preston, who somehow seemed just as nervous as he was.

"Look…" Preston said, "I've thought about what happened that day every single following day since. I feel like… I could have stopped it, but I didn't. I don't need any kind of forgiveness from you and I don't deserve it. I just need you to hear me say that I am truly, deeply sorry that I had anything to do with it."

Ronnie's eyes strayed, checking his surroundings.

"What—What's up? Are you looking for someone?"

Ronnie finally spoke. "Did they put you up to this?"

Preston's head twitched in confusion. "You think I'm messing with you right now, don't you?"

"Are you… *not* messing with me?"

Preston let out a nervous laugh. "Ronnie, I don't hang with those guys anymore. They ran away the moment you hit the ground. They just tossed your things and left. I don't associate myself with that type. Not anymore."

Ronnie gave Preston an unconvinced glare. All he could muster in response was, "Huh."

"I was hoping," Preston pressed on, "that we could maybe hang out. Maybe you could come to some get-togethers and meet some quality people? Not everyone in Knollwood Pines is terrible. What do you think?"

"Why are you… being so cool?" Ronnie asked.

"Uh… Just being me. I don't know how else to be, you know?"

Ronnie relaxed his face and stood up straight.

"Yeah," Ronnie said.

"Yeah, what?" Preston replied.

"Yeah, I'll hang out with you," Ronnie said.

Preston smiled and bobbed his head in a surfer-bro kind of way. "Nice. Can I get your phone? I'll text you my number."

Ronnie pulled his phone from his pocket and held it up to Preston. Preston sent himself a text, then handed the phone back to Ronnie.

"Sweet, so I should probably get back to class," Preston said. "I'll text you later on this week so we can hang, cool?"

"Cool," Ronnie replied.

"Hey, man..." Preston put a hand on Ronnie's shoulder and looked him in the eye. "I'm really glad you're back. If you need something, call me."

Preston gave Ronnie's shoulder a pat, then turned and walked back to the school gym, the fabric of his shorts stretching against his thighs. When he was at a far enough distance, Ronnie said to himself, "What just happened?"

Chapter Six

Ronnie replayed Preston's hat-in-hand moment in his head. It was something he never thought he'd see. So much of his anger and frustration in recent months had been partially directed at Preston, hoping that he would meet some untimely demise. But even that untimely demise would be less surprising than what he saw earlier that day. That dread that he'd stored for so long flushed right through his body and left him with a sense of clarity.

The bell rang, announcing the end of second period and the start of lunch. Ronnie stood outside Leslie's classroom, leaning against a row of lockers.

"Stalker much?" Classic Leslie burn. She had given him a list of her classes and the buildings they were in a week ago so he could find her.

On their way to the cafeteria, Ronnie recounted his interaction with Preston Collinsworth, still in disbelief at what transpired.

"He's actually a really good guy," Leslie said. "I've heard that since your accident he's been doing a lot of volunteer work with a local church. I'm pretty sure he's not even religious. He just does it to do it."

"Maybe I had him all wrong," Ronnie said. "Maybe he's not like the other Blue Jackets."

"I don't know much about that crowd, so I can't confirm nor deny. I just know he's sexy as hell."

"Didn't think he was your type."

"Oh, he's not. Too clean cut. But I can appreciate a work of art when I see it." She let out a euphoric sigh. "Anything else interesting happen?"

"Do you know that girl Malleck?" Ronnie couldn't let her know the full extent of their interaction—there were some things he preferred to keep secret even from his best friend at that moment—but he could at least gather some background on who the girl was. Leslie was a gossip queen. If anyone knew whether Malleck was bad news, it was her.

"The witch?" Leslie responded. "Where did you run into her?"

Wow, Ronnie thought. *Malleck was right. People do call her a witch.* "She's my... art partner, I guess? Why did you call her that?"

"You're right, I shouldn't, but everyone calls her a witch. Last year she and some other juniors formed a coven, or whatever, and started doing spells and shit. Story goes they were doing that stiff as a feather thing—"

"Light as a feather, stiff as a board," Ronnie corrected.

"Yeah, that. Anyways, one of the girls started floating and everyone freaked out. That's when they all saw Malleck's eyes. They'd gone completely white. She was actually making the girl levitate."

There was no way that was true. Malleck was different, that was for sure, but making her eyes glow and lifting people off the ground? Ronnie would have to get the real story for himself. "People actually believe that?"

"You'd be surprised how bored people are in Knollwood Pines."

They entered the cafeteria, with a standard high school buffet on one side, complete with stacks of plastic trays, sneeze guards, and men and women in hair nets, and lines of tables at the other side. The tables took up a forty-yard space, but the environment looked enormous with all the warm bodies scattered in it.

Their path might as well have been on a red carpet. When Ronnie and Leslie entered, once again, head after head turned in their direction. Ronnie kept his eyes forward, desperately trying to find an empty table, as Leslie did her best Queen of England impression with a playful smile and stiff-handed wave. Every other step, Ronnie looked up and made eye contact with another student, then looked away just as quickly.

He found an empty table and sat on the round bench connected to it. It was as uncomfortable as he remembered. Leslie stood across from him, still performing her queenly wave.

"Could you please stop?" Ronnie pleaded.

"Oh, come on. When are you ever going to get this kind of reaction from a crowd again?"

"I'm really glad you're enjoying yourself." Ronnie put his head down and decided to get on with lunch by himself.

"Um… Ronnie?" Leslie said from behind him. He ignored it, knowing she was never one to spoil an opportunity for attention.

"Ronnie," she said again.

Ronnie unzipped his bookbag, searching for his lunch. "Yeah, I know. Quite the reaction."

"No, um…" Leslie was actually at a loss for words.

A male voice rang like the sudden shriek of an old telephone into Ronnie's consciousness, but only because Ronnie knew the voice. "Ronnie Hendrix, my man." A firm hand grabbed his shoulder, the same shoulder that Preston had patted earlier that day. This, however, didn't feel like a friendly pat. His brain finally placed the voice to a name. Out of his periphery, a figure in a blue jacket with yellow sleeves lowered onto the bench beside him. He turned his head to confirm what he already knew.

It was Jack Sutter.

"I missed you, buddy. How you been?" Jack's hand was still on Ronnie's shoulder in some primal sign of domination. Jack completely disregarded Leslie, who for once in her life was speechless, and kept his attention trained on Ronnie. All Ronnie could do was freeze and hold Jack's mendacious smiling gaze. He was close enough to see the slight breaks in Jack's skin from the morning shave and to have the smell of Jack's strong masculine cologne perched in his nostrils.

Leslie finally came to her senses and broke the tension. "I think you should leave," she said.

"I'm just talking to my good buddy, Ronnie." Jack leaned in closer. "We're just talking. Right, Ronnie?"

Ronnie didn't respond. He was back on the field, hanging onto the water tower ladder, his palms soaked and sliding off the rungs, his heart thumping in his chest.

"Buddy... I'm really sorry about what happened, yeah? That, uh... really sucks. But, hey, you're here and you're all better. And the guys over there..." He glanced over at a table in the distance and gave it a nod. Therber, the enormous bald-headed brute, and Gavin, the pretty-and-I-know-it boy, sat backwards on the table benches facing Ronnie. Gavin had gotten both ears pierced since Ronnie last saw him, with diamond studs that sparkled in the sunlight from the large glass panes of the room. The only thing different about Therber was the jawline full of acne, perpetuated by a sweaty chinstrap and a bad diet. They were surrounded by other football players, some wearing letterman jackets and some not, but each of them giggled like elementary school children when Ronnie looked over. Jack continued, "They're really sorry too."

Ronnie tried to find the best way to respond. "Okay" was what he landed on.

"Okay?" Jack replied. "I come here to apologize and all I get is... okay?"

"It's time to go, Jack," Leslie pressed.

"Was anyone talking to you? Who are you supposed to be, anyway? Some member of an 80s feminist punk band? Halloween's not till the end of the month. Take it easy." Jack chuckled.

"It's a good thing you're here to laugh at your own jokes. No one else finds you funny," Leslie said.

"Aw, that hurts. I'm sure if you spent some time with me, you'd find I'm a really fun guy," Jack said with a stupid grin.

"How much time? Because the word around school is, I'd get two minutes tops."

Ronnie snorted out a laugh.

But Jack wasn't smiling anymore.

Jack rolled his eyes at Leslie, feigning disinterest, and addressed Ronnie. "I'm trying to make amends here. Me and the boys did a lot of community service to make up for that little incident. I lost my shot at team captain. That 'C' on my jersey meant a lot to me, man. Do you understand?"

Ronnie responded shakily, "I'm sorry that happened."

Jack smiled. "Well, look at that... We're both sorry." Jack nodded slowly. "I'll be seeing you around, indestructible kid."

What Ronnie heard was, *We'll see how indestructible you really are.*

Jack finally removed his hand from Ronnie's shoulder and turned to Leslie. "Pleasure." Then Jack walked off, his perfectly cuffed blue jeans hovering over canvas sneakers. Gavin and Therber kept their attention fixed on Ronnie as Jack walked back. When they were reunited, Jack took another look back and they all shared a quiet laugh like they were in on an inside joke.

"What a dick," Leslie said, sitting down. "You should get a restraining order against him. Do you want to file a restraining order?"

"No, no way," Ronnie said. "I don't want to make things worse. I just want to carry on as if everything is normal."

"You know, there was a rumor that you and Jack climbed up together and he kicked you off the top of the tower, Leonidas-style." Leslie's lanky leg did a kicking motion from her seat.

"I'm sure there were a lot of rumors." Ronnie took a bite out of his sandwich. "What was all that about them doing community service?"

"Man, you're really slow on your gossip, huh?" said Leslie.

Ronnie shrugged. "I found ways to keep myself busy."

Leslie moved in closer. "You mean… You didn't tell the police it was them?"

Ronnie swallowed his bite. "Of course not. They're rich assholes. I knew they wouldn't be punished for it and they'd come after me if I snitched."

Leslie looked at the ceiling, squinting. Thinking.

They spoke at the same time.

"Preston."

Chapter Seven

R onnie had to get away. He'd made it through half a day of school and that was more than he expected. He exited the school out of the back lot reserved for school buses. Those yellow tubes were nearly two hours away from being fired up, so no one was back there to monitor the comings and goings.

Just across the street was a wooded area that stretched from Knollwood Pines to the next town over. The land sloped down just off the road and led to a cement drainage opening plastered with graffiti, which spat out a long winding creek that went for miles. The water level was high and flowing at a hurried pace, the result of generous rainfall over the past two weeks.

Ronnie walked along the edge of the creek with his bookbag, now a quarter of a mile away from the school and from the road. The whipping of cars cutting through air had been replaced by the gentle sounds of water and the crunching of dried leaves. He could keep walking for another forty-five minutes and still be back in time to catch a ride with Leslie, but instead, he stopped at the base of a wide tree, slid his bookbag from his shoulders, and took a seat. There he replayed the events of the morning. His strange interaction with Malleck, the genuine kindness from Preston.

And then there was Jack, who made it very clear by figuratively pissing on Ronnie's leg that Ronnie was on his radar and there was nothing he could do about it. He could feel the firm pinch on his shoulder, the knowing stare from Jack's smiling face that read "I own you." It made him sick to imagine what the rest of his life would be like at Knollwood Pines High. If only there was something he could do to make Jack Sutter go away.

But there was nothing he could do. All he had was the air in his lungs and a dark imagination. He unzipped his bookbag and withdrew the leather-bound notebook and a pencil. It was time to indulge once again in Jack's horrible demise. He ran his hands over the leather and sensed all of his darkest thoughts vibrating through it.

There was a crunch in the distance from the direction Ronnie had walked. He turned his head.

Shit.

Therber, Jack, and Gavin, arranged from tallest to shortest, walked down the side of the creek, gaining ground slowly. They were all in crouched positions and taking gentle steps, trying their best to be sur-reptitious. The afternoon sun shot through the many branches that concealed the woods, leaving jagged shadows over their blue and yellow jackets. They knew they had been spotted and stopped. They each grew a wild grin and stood up straight.

Had they been following Ronnie since lunch? The only thing Ronnie knew for certain was that he had been stalked and now he had to run like the prey that he was.

Ronnie closed the book, shuffled it back into the bookbag, and zipped the bag hastily. He shot up to his feet and a second later the bookbag straps were over each shoulder. He gunned it, running away from the gang chasing him, looking for an opening, looking for anything that could provide sanctuary. Unfortunately for Ronnie, he had come here for isolation, and his panicked sprint was only delaying the inevitable.

Gavin was known at Knollwood Pines High for his speed. He was a track star in the offseason, and this year he would likely claim school records for the hundred- and two-hundred-meter dash. There was no one on the football field who could match his speed, and so Gavin would line up wide, sprint down the field, and Jack would throw the ball up as if daring Gavin to catch up to it. And almost every time, Gavin did.

Ronnie knew this and still he kept running. Speedy footsteps shuffled behind him—sporadic stabs of dried leaves crumbling under shoes.

Just inches away, Gavin said, "Hey there, Hendrix." He was barely out of breath.

All it took was sudden nudge to send Ronnie plummeting forward with the inertia of his own wimpy sprint. He landed on his palms, dragging them against the dirt, then rolled onto his back, sandwiching the bookbag between him and the ground.

Gavin, with his stud earrings and high cheekbones, stared down at Ronnie. "Chill out, man. We just wanna talk," he said.

Jack and Therber caught up, throttling down from a slow jog, and stopped next to Gavin. For a moment, the woods were quiet. The adrenaline rushing through Ronnie's body heightened every sound, from the branches twisting in the breeze to a squirrel scratching itself against dried bark. The stream of water flowed through the creek like air being forced through a compressor.

"I need to get back to school in time for fourth period, so I'm gonna make this brief," Jack said. "What happened to you had nothing to do with us. You chose to climb up that tower, but your little wimpy ass couldn't handle it. You fell and you blamed us for it. You took us down with you and ruined our reputations. I find that inexcusable."

"I didn't tell anyone anything," Ronnie pleaded.

"Bullshit," said Gavin. "The same night you fell I had police on my doorstep. They questioned me in front of my parents for an hour."

"I was unconscious, you idiot."

"Too unconscious to speak?" asked Therber with an ominous booming voice that seemed to come from the heavens. It took Ronnie a second to realize that, yes, this was a serious question.

"Do you know what it means to be unconscious?" Ronnie asked with genuine curiosity. He was hoping this wasn't the question that got his face smashed.

"Stand up," Jack commanded. "Seeing you like this is making me sad."

Ronnie slowly gathered himself and stood to his feet.

Jack continued. "Take off the bag."

Ronnie slid the straps off each shoulder and dropped the bag to the ground next to him. Jack took a step forward and peered down at Ronnie. Keeping Ronnie's gaze, he lowered himself, clutched the top of the bag, and stood. He held the bag between him and Ronnie as they stood at a distance that would make a high school dance monitor nervous.

"I recognize this bag," Jack said. "It's the same one you wore that day, isn't it? You got any more freaky stuff in here that me and the boys can take a look at?"

No. The word repeated in Ronnie's mind like machine gun fire. He couldn't let them see the notebook. He should have never put it in his bookbag. It should be at home under his bed. If Ronnie got out of this, he'd make sure there was never any threat of someone finding it. No matter how much he was drawn to the book. No matter how complete he felt with it in his possession, he'd lock it away forever.

For the first time, he truly contemplated exactly what it would mean for the book to be discovered. He had named his bullies specifically in the text. He had drawn them posed in gruesome ways, maimed and brutalized. He had written rituals and chants to coincide with their murders. This would look worse than bad for him.

It would look like a plan.

He had no choice but to resort to begging. "Please," Ronnie said. "Just leave me alone."

Jack took hold of the zipper. Ronnie instinctively clasped his hand over Jack's, stopping it from moving the zipper up. Jack glared at him with a deadly serious look, and it was only then that Ronnie realized he had not only made contact, but he had also made the slightest attempt to defy Jack.

Jack released the zipper. "On second thought... I'm not interested."

Jack chucked the bag into the creek, and it was instantly swallowed by the stream. Ronnie turned to make a run for the bag but was halted by a punch to the gut. His entire midsection collapsed around Jack's fist and all of the oxygen in his lungs released. His body buckled underneath itself. His knees touched the earth just a few feet from the creek as he clutched his stomach, heaving for air.

"Don't get the face," Jack said to his buddies. "Just hit him where no one can see. He won't tell anyone... because he knows what will happen if he does."

Ronnie looked down the stream, tracking his bookbag as it drifted out of view.

"You see, Ronnie. You have to understand that there are consequences for your actions," Jack said.

Ronnie thought of making one final attempt at talking sense into Jack, to beg him to understand that he had nothing to do with whatever punishment he, Gavin, and Therber had received, but it was useless at this point. Ronnie was surrounded by hungry wolves, asking them not to eat.

Everything hurt: His ribs, his stomach, his hips, his thighs, anything that looked like a meaty target to kick. Ronnie stayed on the ground long after the boys had faded into the trees and out of sight. Each breath seized an aching muscle.

Ronnie gathered his strength and crawled to the base of a tree. He turned and propped himself against it, letting the weight of his aching body sink into the base. He pulled his phone out of his pocket. The screen had one rippling crack through the width of it, but the phone was operational. School was still in session, and he had no idea how far down the creek his bag had traveled. He imagined water seeping through the zipper—any opening that might have been left by Jack's uncareful fingers—and the thick pages going limp as they soaked in the stream. If he went looking for it, he'd be increasing his distance from the school and thus anyone who could give him a ride home, and he was in no condition to add miles onto his long trek back.

Ronnie remembered Preston's face, the genuine concern and the desperate attempt to win his good graces, the promise to be there if he needed anything. With his entire midsection aching to the touch, Ronnie needed something now. He'd take Preston up on his offer, considering it was Preston who got him into this spot to begin with.

Ronnie found Preston in his sent messages and texted:

Can you call me when you get this? I need help.

He realized this might be a bit alarming to sweet Preston and followed it up with:

I'm fine. Kind of. No need to worry.

It was better than texting, "I just got the shit beat out of me by your former buddies and can barely move."

With a palm pressed firmly on the ground, Ronnie forced himself to stand. He patted down his jean jacket, releasing leaves and clouds of dirt. He put all of his strength into the first step, then the second, and so on.

A silver Honda pulled off the road at the mouth of the creek. Preston rolled down the passenger's window as a car zipped past him on the other side, its horn pressed down. Not the best place to stop.

"Get in!" Preston called out to Ronnie.

Ronnie hobbled to the door, opened it, and fell in. The cloth cushioning was a cloud compared to the dirt he'd pulled himself up from. As soon as Ronnie was inside, Preston accelerated and rejoined the flow of traffic.

"Thanks for coming to get me, man," Ronnie, every word stabbing his ribs. *They're just bruised*, he thought. *Just bruised.*

"Are you kidding? I'm sorry I didn't get here sooner." Preston said. "I didn't check my phone until after third period. We were breaking down the nuance of Flannery O'Connor's use of Southern culture juxtaposed with dark American history and—" He shook his head. "Jeez, sorry, that's not important. Tell me exactly what happened."

Ronnie recounted the events to him. How he had been stalked by the Blue Jackets. How Gavin had tackled him, how Jack had thrown his bag into the creek, how all three boys had tenderized him like raw meat, taking turns hitting any doughy muscle that could bruise. And of course, he told Preston why they did it.

"They think I ratted them out," Ronnie said. "They think I told the police it was their fault I fell from the water tower." Ronnie looked at Preston, waiting for a confession.

"Crap," Preston said. "Oh, crap, man, I'm... This is all my fault." He looked at Ronnie worriedly, his head shifting back and forth from Ronnie to the road. "Ronnie... I told the police it was our fault. All four of us. When the ambulance came out a police car came with it and I just... What was I gonna say? You just *had* to climb the tower and see the top of Knollwood Pines, but you fell? I had to tell them what happened. We all deserved to be punished. Even me... But especially that idiot Jack." Preston took in a deep breath. "I guess I didn't think that all this time later it would come back to you. I haven't even spoken to those guys since then. Of course they would have thought it was you."

Ronnie sat silently next to Preston as they turned into a neighborhood. The convenience store and body shops were quickly replaced by homes. The car eased toward a stop sign and Preston put the car in park. He squared his shoulders to Ronnie, his boyish face reminding Ronnie of a shamed puppy. "I'm—"

"It's not your fault," Ronnie interrupted. "They were going to come for me regardless."

"Do you wanna press charges?" Preston asked.

"No," Ronnie said. "Whatever lawyer you have, I'm sure their families have more expensive ones that can help them wipe the slate clean. They'd just win the case by saying I have a vendetta and did this to myself."

"Crap... That's a good point," Preston said in response.

Crap? Ronnie thought. *Is he just too pure to curse like a regular teenage human being?*

"I'm going to make this right," Preston said.

Ronnie chuckled and winced from the rib pain.

"You okay? Oh... Dumb question, huh?" Preston said. "Let's pick up some Tylenol and get you home." He put the car in drive and they started moving.

"What are you gonna do?" Ronnie asked.

"Just pay our old buddy Jack a visit and tell him to lay off."

"Or what?"

"Or I'll kick his... butt."

Chapter Eight

A worm of nerves spun through Preston's stomach. The football stadium was in plain view in front of him, sunken in the distance beyond the gated entrance, the freshly painted box office sitting unoccupied next to it. The metal stands on either side of the field looked quaint when they were empty. No attendees lined up at the concession booth. No groups of students huddled in circles near the main entrance chatting and giggling. Come Friday night, this place would be alive. Preston missed the lights and the cheering crowd, but the rubber track that lined the football field was of much greater comfort to him now. The coming months would bring about the start of track and field season, and Preston was developing quite a niche in the events that every other athlete tended to overlook. As a junior just a year ago, after some trial and error, and to the surprise of the track and field coaching staff, Preston was exceptionally good at throwing a javelin and tossing a discus. His hip power mixed with his upper body strength made him a natural.

The stench of body odor wafted out through the field house that stood to the left side of the stadium entrance near the edge of the parking lot. Even at a distance, Preston could smell it, thick and heavy like mud, bringing to mind the brick walls and the metal cages decorated crudely with worn shoulder pads and helmets, kids sitting in metal chairs peeling soaked football pants off their legs and patting themselves dry.

Jack Sutter finally exited the field house, wearing an oversized hoodie and a gym bag slung around his shoulder. He was walking Preston's way, which Preston had intended. Jack always parked his shiny Jeep Cherokee in the same spot, so it was easy to find.

Preston crossed his arms, then considered uncrossing them, but he'd already committed to it and didn't want to reveal any uncertainty. He knew it wouldn't matter, though. This was Jack Sutter he was about to confront. Jack was intimately familiar with Preston's uncertainty.

This was the first time they'd been in the same proximity in months. The comfort that Preston once felt seeing Jack as a kid was gone and left behind a weight in his gut. He kept telling himself he didn't care. He hadn't lost his friendship with Jack. Jack had chosen a different path.

Jack disregarded Preston as he walked to the Jeep and opened the hatch. His unique ability to make someone feel insignificant was like a superpower. After securing his gym bag, he closed the hatch and said. "If you wanted to look intimidating, you should've leaned against the tail light. You just look like a guy I paid to guard my car."

"Hilarious," Preston said dryly.

"What do you want?"

"I want you to leave that kid alone. I know what you and the guys did to him. You should be sitting in a jail cell right now."

"What are you talking about, man? What kid?"

"You know who I'm talking about. Ronnie Hendrix. He had bruises all up and down his body today. Did that make you feel like a big man?"

"Dude, I really don't know what you're—"

"He didn't say crap, Jack. He wasn't the reason the police showed up at your door after what happened at the water tower. It was me. *I* told the police what happened. *I* told them that it was our idea and the only reason you and those idiots weren't there is because you ran. So if you want to take it out on anyone, take it out on me."

Preston stepped up to Jack, his large frame threatening to swallow the smaller guy within it. His size was the only thing Preston could use to intimidate Jack, but from the look on his former friend's face, it wasn't working.

"So you snitched on us," Jack said. "I should've guessed. All that time you spent ignoring my texts, embarrassing yourself throwing that stupid javelin around the football field. You don't deserve to be anywhere near that field."

"I'm going to tell you one last time," Preston said sternly, "stay away from Ronnie Hendrix."

"We got a problem over here?" Therber's deep voice knifed into Preston's ear. The giant peered down from several inches above him, wearing a hoodie that would have engulfed any normal-sized person.

"Oh, it's you," Therber said. "I almost didn't recognize you without your track unitard."

Jack eased up visibly at the sight of Therber. Any edge Preston might have had on Jack was now gone.

"Preston here was just telling me that something bad happened to little Ronnie Hendrix earlier today," Jack said. "But... we wouldn't know anything about that, would we, Therber?"

"Ah, poor kid. He's been through a lot," Therber said with all the enthusiasm and grace of a sentient boulder.

Preston looked from Therber to Jack. "You guys keep doing this and eventually you're going to get what you deserve."

"And what *do* we deserve?" Therber asked.

"You think everyone's afraid of you," Preston told the giant. "I'm not."

"Let's go then," Therber said.

"Go... where?"

"Let's go. You and me."

"Where would you like me to go with you?"

"Let's fight, dumbass."

"Oh, great idea," Preston said. "I fight you in the school parking lot where the only witness is your best friend whom you do assaults with and keep it secret. Very smart."

"Does it ever get exhausting being this much of a boy scout?" Jack said. "Look at this." Jack removed his phone from his bag and shoved it in Preston's face, showing him an image of a beautiful young woman with pouty lips wearing a lacy bra, frozen in the act of sliding one strap down her shoulder. "That's what I'm getting into this weekend. College freshman. She says for every touchdown I score, she'll…"

Preston had already diverted his eyes.

Jack smirked. "Still a prude." He turned the phone to Gavin.

"She's hot," Therber said.

"Hell yeah she is."

"Hey, check this out," Therber unzipped his bookbag and found his phone, then raised it to Jack.

Jack read a message aloud. "'Hey cutie—smiley face. What are you doing tonight?'" He gave Therber a sly look.

Therber grinned triumphantly, but Preston knew this wasn't him. He was simply taking Jack's lead. Preston and Therber had never been the best of friends, but Preston noticed a shift in Therber right around sophomore year when universities began taking notice of him. Therber wasn't desirable in the same way Jack and Gavin were. Seeing girls draped over those two was commonplace. Not so much for Therbrer. But once the headlines surfaced about a sophomore being recruited by Division I schools, Therber had a new attitude. He *deserved* a girl around his arm, so he began doing some recruiting of his own. Still, the acne that caked the bottom of his face like a mountain range further removed him from the circle of girls that flocked to his friends. Preston would have felt bad for Therber if not for his quiet aggressiveness and pompous self-indulgence.

"Any idea who it is?" Jack asked.

"Nope, but she seems ready and willing to climb the mountain. Says she wants to meet up later."

"Oh shit." Jack put his hand over his mouth, muffling his boyish giggles.

Preston was losing patience. "Do we understand each other or not?"

Jack removed his hand from his mouth, his cheeks lowering. "Sure, man. We understand you. Hey, Therber, do we understand him?"

"Stay away from Ronnie Hendrix or you'll kick our asses. Yeah, we understand." Therber stared blankly at Preston.

"Then I think it's time for us to be on our way," said Jack.

Jack got into the Jeep. The fuzzy dice that hung over the mirror swayed as the vehicle shifted. Preston remembered being in the passenger's seat when Jack first hung that dumb memento. A relic of a bygone era.

Jack backed out quickly, nearly swiping Preston, and sped off.

Therber looked Preston up and down and chuckled, then turned and walked away.

Preston was alone in the parking lot again, wondering why he'd even bothered.

Chapter Nine

Ronnie didn't speak much that night. He got home before his mom did, which was typical. She worked until five and they'd usually have dinner at six. Because of this, Cynthia didn't see Preston drop Ronnie off. That was for the better though, as it would be hard to turn her opinion around on Preston.

Her absence afforded Ronnie time to clean himself up, to wash the dirt out of his hair and inspect his bruises in the mirror. Under no circumstance would he tell his mother what happened. The truth would send her on a warpath, and she wouldn't stop until Ronnie's three attackers were arrested. No, he couldn't risk experiencing further punishment. He had to let this pass and carry on like everything was normal.

Ronnie stared at his spackled bedroom ceiling as the hours drained through the night. The darkness eventually swallowed everything in room, with only the streetlamp outside his window to tell him there was still light in this strange world. A world where he had been broken once again for reasons outside of his control. He imagined himself fading into the blackness to join the unseen phantoms of the night, roaming around in their invisible shield of darkness, the unassuming critters and beasts that lived by their own means. With badges of shame covering his chest, ribs, stomach, and hips, he was reminded of his powerlessness. The dread of reliving that day's attack diffused into anger, and into the early hours of the morning he finally fell asleep, wondering if his notebook was lost forever.

Ronnie awoke in his room completely alert. There was no grogginess. Nothing holding down his eyelids encouraging him to rest a bit longer. He was closer to the ceiling than usual, but that didn't make sense unless he was...

Floating.

I'm back, he thought.

The memories of navigating the hospital came back to him as he willed his body to the edge of the bed and tilted into a standing position. A small flurry of gray particles brushed against his face. He trapped a piece of the floating flakes in his hand and it crumbled instantly, its edges disintegrating.

"Ash," he said aloud.

A low buzzsaw hum of frenzied screams poured into his room. He looked over to his window, where the glass pane he expected to be there was missing. Glowing embers floated around the frame and rose gently up Ronnie's walls. The streetlamp outside his window no longer lit the street with an amber glow. The street was caked in a cone of red. He approached the opening that used to be his window. The streetlamp was splattered with blood, still fresh and dripping... dripping... dripping.

He stepped out of the opening in his room, though he didn't feel the resistance of gravity and simply floated onto the front yard. The grass was dead. The oak tree was barren and charred all the way up to its jagged, wiry branches. The houses that lined the street were blackened and caved in, buckled under burnt frames. It looked as if a wildfire had blown through Surry Dale Street, but the only house it missed was Ronnie's.

Arms swayed aimlessly in the sky, churning through a sea of glowing red with hands reaching down to the earth. The distant screams echoed through the night in a way that was emphatic and impossible in the natural world as Ronnie knew it.

Ronnie walked onto the street and headed toward the stop sign. Because the world was so foreign to him, he knew it had to be a dream, and knowing that gave him the freedom to explore. What would he find? Certainly nothing good, but it was a dream after all.

An inhuman roar erupted in the distance, but it was difficult to know how far away. It sent a wave through the neighborhood and rippled through Ronnie's chest. He hadn't heard of an animal that could make such a sound, but it didn't seem mechanical in nature either. For roughly three years as Knollwood Pines was transitioning from a quaint town to a booming familial destination, the construction projects implemented to keep up with the population—housing developments, supply stores, grocery stores, a strip mall—created a series of what the developers called "controlled explosions". It was commonplace to be sitting in school, quietly taking a test, and hear a muffled boom accompanied by a tiny quake in the ground below. The roar was an elongated rumble, but not an explosion. It was emotional—fierce, angry—like a battle cry that had been repressed for months, years, centuries.

And then, instead of lightning, strands of flame shot down from the sky, as if a thousand fire performers were hidden in the sheet of red above and blowing plumes of fire downward. The suddenness of the fire accompanying the roar made the scene around Ronnie feel ceremonial.

A voice pierced the echoed screams and the bursts of fire. "I thought I'd find you here again." It was the familiar voice of Malleck.

He looked past the stop sign and down Carpenter Street, which stretched into the opening of his neighborhood subdivision. Malleck made her way toward him with her signature combat boots slapping against the concrete. With every puff of fire, she came closer into view in shades of red and amber. Her many bracelets clanked with each swing of her arms. She wore cargo pants with the legs tucked into the boots and an open flannel that rattled over a tank top underneath.

Spotting Malleck's wardrobe from afar, Ronnie was suddenly aware of his appearance. His flannel pajamas were sloppy and wrinkled and just a little too big. His stubby legs dragged the bottoms against the floor of his hardwoods and carpets and now against the concrete.

Malleck stopped suddenly in front of Ronnie. "We need to leave," she said.

"What?" Ronnie said.

"I'll explain everything, but you have to trust me," Malleck said.

Ronnie could recall past memories the way he couldn't in a regular dream. The memory that came to him was that of Malleck's painting—her near-perfect recreation of his last vivid dream of an ashen wasteland, the blank center of the painting with a missing axe. Somehow, he was connected to Malleck, but he had no discernable way of understanding how.

Another roar shook the ground, which somehow quieted the screams from above. Ronnie and Malleck looked toward the sky as an opening formed within the sea of hands, leaving behind a dense red fog, rolling wildly. Hundreds of flames burst from the sky and for a brief moment illuminated a shape inside the fog. It was the giant head of a ram, twisted horns flanking its face, with a pair of wide-set, glowing red eyes staring down over its snout. It opened its mouth and let out another fierce and rumbling roar.

Ronnie gazed into the eyes of the ram in horror. He knew what it was. The demon that existed in the pages of his notebook.

Karnalaxe.

"We have to go!" yelled Malleck. "Close your eyes!"

Ronnie did as she commanded. A smooth palm touched his forehead and a second later...

There was silence, save for the hum in his eardrums left by a sudden shift from loud to quiet.

He opened his eyes. They were at the peak of a rounded wooden bridge, staring out into a shallow lily pond. Pink flowers blossomed between pads of green, riding the gentle sway of the water. A dim sun—much larger than it should have been—was halfway down the earth miles and miles ahead of them, casting everything in gold.

A sudden calm came over Ronnie. He looked at Malleck, who removed her hand from his head and looked onward at the sun.

"Did you just..." Ronnie wasn't sure what to ask. He was still dreaming, wasn't he?

Malleck let out a sigh, gathering her thoughts. "I'm really not sure what to say, Ronnie. I don't know if you'll even believe any of this when you come out." She let out another breath, then turned and sized him up. "What's important is you're here... And we have to figure out why."

"What is *here*?" Ronnie asked.

The tall girl pressed her hands against the railing of the wooden bridge and peered down at the lily pads underneath it. "Some might call it different things, but I like to call it the Gray World. I know it may feel like a dream, but it's not. It's something completely different." She turned, putting her tailbone against the railing, and crossed her arms. "Centuries ago, people realized that they could access this plane to create new environments and landscapes. Eventually, they realized they could invite others into their creations. You can imagine the joy that this brought our people in their early days—"

"*Your* people?" Ronnie interrupted.

Malleck grinned. "*Our* people, Ronnie. Like it or not, you have the strain."

"The strain?" Ronnie said.

"That's the second time you repeated me. I'm glad you're paying attention. I'm saying you're... special. Something beyond human."

Ronnie was certain he was dreaming. "One thing I am *not* is special."

"Well, it's not up to me to convince you. You'll have to convince yourself. Why don't you just play along for now as I give you some potentially life-saving information?" Malleck gave him a glazed-over look.

Ronnie couldn't help but smirk. "Be my guest."

"What these realm-travelers didn't expect was that outside parties could use this as a sort of..." She waved her hands in the air, struggling for an explanation. "Out-of-body echolocation. Evil actors would invade the creations of young travelers and capture them in the real world... or worse. Do you remember the man in the gray suit?"

Ronnie thought back to the dream from his hospital bed. "Yeah, actually. It was when I first saw you," Ronnie said.

"I think he was tracking you," Malleck said.

"Then what were *you* doing there?" Ronnie asked, skeptical.

Malleck started pacing, rising and falling with the curve of the bridge.

"It's hard to explain. I just... felt it... I can feel things. Ever since your accident, I've felt this burst of heavy energy surging over the town, and it gets more intense the closer I get to you."

"What does that mean?" asked Ronnie.

Malleck stopped pacing and stood still. "Did something happen recently? Some big event? Something challenging, even traumatic?"

Ronnie let out a defeated chuckle. How else could he say this and it not sound pathetic? "Yeah, I got the shit kicked out of me. It was three guys."

Malleck raised her hands to her head. "That's it."

"What's it?"

"Anger, fear, maybe a combination of both. Your emotions bring you here, and that same anger and fear must be causing these horrifying realities."

"Shit... So that's why I get Knollwood Pines in ashes and you get... this?" Ronnie pointed out to the half-sun, which didn't appear to be moving. It was stuck in a permanent sunset.

"When you first discover your power, it's not something you can easily control. I had to learn to shape it. I think... maybe your Gray World is an expression of your darkest self. If you travel after a traumatic event, I suppose it would make sense that you'd fill the space with some horrific images. It's almost like you're constructing hell on earth."

"Could it not be random? Like any regular dream?" Ronnie couldn't believe he was entertaining this, but while he was there he might as well ask questions.

"A sky full of hands? Twice? That's very specific. It's an expression of you." Malleck waved her hands as if wrapping them around the entirety of the pond. "This was nothing. A blank canvas. *I* filled it with what you see here. It's a place that only I know. If you are like me, then you filled your blank canvas with an absolute nightmare. There's darkness in you."

Ronnie wanted to defend himself, but he knew it was true. Through the twisted knots of anger in his head he'd imagined himself doing unspeakable things to awful people, things he himself believed he would never be capable of doing.

"But it makes sense that there's darkness in you. Look at what you've been through," Malleck said.

"How do I know when I'll enter... the Gray World, is it?" Ronnie asked.

"Let's walk before we can run first," Malleck said with a reassuring smile. "Try to keep those emotions in check. Luckily, you have me to keep an eye on you. It goes without saying but... don't tell anybody about this, okay?" She stepped closer to Ronnie, the shift in the curved bridge once again revealing her height compared to Ronnie's. "It's time to go back. See you in class tomorrow?"

"Uh," Ronnie said. This was *so weird*. "Yeah. See you in class."

Malleck put a hand on Ronnie's forehead. "Maybe you'll have a good dream. An *actual* dream."

In an instant, everything went black.

Then Ronnie woke up with the weight of gravity pressing him into the mattress. The areas that were bruised were no longer soft and sensitive to touch.

But that was impossible.

He pulled down his comforter and lifted up his pajama shirt, raising his head to inspect his ribs. There were no marks of blue and purple. The bruises were gone.

The indestructible kid.

Outside his window, the morning darkness was fading with a faint stroke of sunlight. The grass was dark green, the leaves shown in reds, yellows, and oranges, and the tree was pale brown. No ashes, only the promise of life and Ronnie's expected reality.

As he lay in bed, he grappled with last night's dream. It was unnaturally vibrant, down to the smell of the ash. He recalled the conversation too well, unlike most dreams that he only remembered in fragments. How would he react when he saw Malleck today?

He didn't have much time to figure it out. Leslie would be at his house soon and he had to figure out an excuse as to why he was going to school without a bookbag.

Ronnie got out of bed and went from his bedroom, through the hall, and into the kitchen, where his mom was sitting with a laptop and a steaming cup of coffee. With snakes of red surrounding the edges of her eyes, she said, "Something terrible's happened."

Chapter Ten

Therber Windell was found dead at Lake Forest Park five miles from the high school. An early morning jogger saw his body and called the police. The massive star offensive lineman was easily identifiable, as there weren't many people in Knollwood Pines who shared his stature.

As Ronnie's mom shared the news article with him, his stomach fell to the floor. Sure, Ronnie had thought about Therber meeting a gruesome end, but he didn't actually *want* him to die. Yet, Therber was found dead the morning after Ronnie's notebook was tossed in the creek. To Cynthia Hendrix and the rest of the town, it must have seemed like a random killing. Ronnie's mind went in circles trying to ease his paranoia. He couldn't help but think that someone out there was in possession of his notebook.

Someone completed the first ritual.

The passage in the book clung to his mind—the scattered handwriting, the drawing that provided a window into his imagination that he never intended for anyone to see. The image played in rotation with each bad memory of Therber.

Therber's eyes removed, leaving vacant black sockets in their place.

Therber laughing as Ronnie shook against the water tower ladder.

Therber's mouth open with no tongue between the teeth.

Therber pummeling Ronnie by the creek, the sheer force of his legs an extension of his gargantuan, terrifying power.

Ronnie has yearned for revenge, but was content in settling for the notebook, where his vengeance would lay dormant, never to emerge. Until now. He wanted to ask his mother whether the news report included any mention of Therber's eyes and tongue, but was too frightened to do so.

He wrote it off as an absurd notion. He had to. Otherwise, he wouldn't make it through the day.

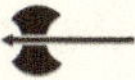

An announcement came over the courtyard intercom before first period. The Knollwood Pines High principal addressed the student body: "I know there's been a lot of talk about it this morning and I want to address this before your classes begin. Your fellow student Therber Windell has tragically passed away. Some of you knew Therber as a friend or a teammate, and I know for many of you this will come as an immense shock. I want to encourage each and every one of you to seek out your guidance counselor at any time if you need to express your feelings on the matter. Instructors should be prepared to allow students to be dismissed temporarily for this reason. I'm asking that you all keep the Windell family in your thoughts and prayers. Please know that I am thinking of all of you during this difficult time."

Tragically passed away. That made it sound like Therber died in his sleep.

Silence fell over the students in the courtyard.

Until one particularly dumb kid muttered awkwardly, "Well... that sucks." The phrase caused Ronnie's entire body to clench. Shortly after the anonymous kid said it, a scuffle broke out around the flagpole as a swarm of people worked in unison to hold back a Blue Jacket, some benchwarmer offensive lineman that Ronnie only knew of from his short time during tryouts. The Blue Jacket bucked like a bull, his scalp red under a short buzz cut, as several other smaller players held him back. Leaning against the flagpole, the kid below him, presumably the one who broke the silence, ran his hands over the concrete, searching for a pair of glasses scattered just out of reach. There were no excited shouts egging on the fight, as it was so obviously one-sided.

"Jesus," Leslie said quietly at Ronnie's side. Whether it was Therber's death or the sudden assault she was reacting to, Ronnie couldn't be sure. She ran over and scooped up his glasses, then handed them to the boy. The Blue Jacket choked down his tears and power-walked out of the courtyard.

Everyone at Knollwood must have known that Therber was partially to blame for Ronnie's accident. On his first day back, Ronnie was uncomfortable in his own skin. The attention from onlookers feeding his newfound celebrity status made him want to disappear back into the crowd. Now on his second day, every stare from a fellow student was alien and strange. His mind twisted his perception of these looks, making them appear as scowls of suspicion. An immense fear sat heavy on his chest, fear that everyone would see the image Ronnie drew of Therber and blame him for the death.

He feared that the students at Knollwood Pines High would see the drawing of a large boy stripped naked in front of a wide oak tree with his body fixed in a prayer pose, his shins against the ground and his hips resting on his ankles. His head tilted down in a bow and his wrists nailed to either side of the tree. His chest propped up by wooden stakes stuck into the ground inches away from the puddle of blood formed below his empty eye sockets and mouth.

They'd think Ronnie was disturbed and deranged. He'd bring shame to his mother, who worked so hard to build a life for him in this safe, quiet community. As hard as he tried to shake these thoughts, his bookbag floating down the creek was a stain on his memory, and one that he was helpless to remove.

If there was any silver lining to Therber's sudden death for Ronnie, it was that he was now just as invisible as he used to be. His celebrity capped out at twenty-four hours the moment Therber's death was announced. Numbers blurred into shapes on the chalkboard as his mind raced during first period Algebra. As the students remained mostly silent, there was a sense that everyone was simply getting through the day. The announcement failed to give the details the students already knew, and that weight festered in the classroom, the hallways, and down every dusty pit of Knollwood Pines High.

Therber hadn't simply passed. He'd been murdered.

Ronnie entered the art studio and sat on the stool at the opposite side of the table to Malleck, who already had her painting supplies ready at the table. He smiled weakly as Malleck mixed her paints together. They had only interacted—*really* interacted—once, but the conversation from last night's dream was still fresh in his mind. He remembered it vividly, not in fragments like he usually recalled a dream.

"Good morning," Malleck said as she swished a dab of black paint inside a splotch of red.

"Yeah... Good morning to you."

Without looking up from her paint, Malleck said, "I know what you're thinking. Did it happen?"

Ronnie moved in closer. "Did... what happen?"

Malleck lowered her voice. "Did you and I walk through a hellscape and then jump over to a lily pond together?... Yeah, man. All that happened." She spoke comfortably as if existing with another person in a fabricated dream realm was perfectly normal.

The rhythm of Ronnie's heart picked up. Two rapid breaths came in place of one. *Not a panic attack. Not here.*

"Everything's fine," Malleck said. "You're okay."

But Ronnie's breathing maintained a rapid cadence.

"Ms. Springle!" Malleck stood from her seat, grabbing the teacher's attention. "Ronnie and I need to visit the guidance counselor. That cool?"

It only took a moment for Ms. Springle to recognize the panic on Ronnie's face, likely mistaking it for sadness.

"Absolutely," Ms. Springle said. "Take all the time you need."

Jagged rows of naked pine trees cluttered the wooded area behind the football stadium. The vast bed of scattered pine straw gave a mild crunch under the muffled pressure of Ronnie's sneakers and Malleck's boots. The fresh air had opened Ronnie's lungs, and though he was sick to his stomach, his panic had subsided.

"I felt something this morning," Malleck said to Ronnie as she clung to a skinny pine tree and shifted her weight to the side. "I felt it like how I felt you last night. It was like a... big burst of energy, if that makes sense."

Nothing really did make sense to Ronnie in the moment, but he resisted the urge to interject.

Malleck continued, "Like a shockwave, but traveling slowly. I think it had something to do with what happened to Therber Windell."

Ronnie's stomach sank again at the very mention of Therber's name. Ronnie had been on edge the entire morning, like a thief concealing a bag of jewels, trying to convince himself he had nothing to do with what happened.

"Why do you say that?" Ronnie said with a crack in his voice.

"It's day zero, so the police aren't going to be sharing a lot of details, but people talk. People like me."

Ronnie's stomach twisted even further, a gigantic knot being pulled into the ground.

"Some are saying it was a ritual." Malleck moved her hands from tree to tree, spinning herself whimsically in a figure eight motion.

"Uh... What? What are they saying?" Ronnie stammered.

"You really don't wanna know the details."

"No, I do. Please. I have to know."

Malleck stopped spinning and faced Ronnie. After a silent moment—maybe out of respect for the dead, maybe because she feared the words were too awful to say—she spoke.

Her words formed images in Ronnie's mind, his drawing morphing into a full color tapestry, whether he wanted them to or not. She described the pose that Therber was found in—on his knees with his wrists nailed to the tree, chest propped up wooden stakes. With every detail, a cold wave shot up Ronnie's spine, flooding Ronnie's eyes. Then, finally, "They took out his eyes and tongue." That was it. Ronnie was finished.

"Who would do something like that?" Malleck said.

Ronnie's knees wobbled and failed him, causing him to stumble and fall against a tree.

"Oh shit," Malleck said.

It's okay, Ronnie thought, *she doesn't know. How could she?*

"Uh... Just a little squeamish is all," Ronnie recovered.

"I'm sorry to upset you with all this. It just... feels wrong. This was premeditated and painstakingly executed. People don't just pose their victims like that."

But that's exactly what Ronnie did. Not literally, but it was a death of his own design. Someone had seen his work, had seen Therber's name in the book, and had followed every detail like an instruction manual.

"I've heard of similar rituals before. If I had to guess, I think Therber's eyes and tongue are going to be used as some kind of offering."

Provide the severed offerings.

And roar into the night.

Ronnie's words.

"Why are you telling me this?" Ronnie asked.

"I'm sorry," Malleck said. "I just have this feeling that… what happened during your accident, that blast of energy, you traveling to the Gray World and Therber's death happening just hours apart… I think it's all connected somehow. I just haven't figured it out yet. I think you might have, uh…" She spun her hands in circles, searching for the words. "Released something. Like an invitation of sorts. I'm not saying any of this is your fault, but if I can feel the wave, then a worse version of me can feel it too."

"You mean, like… someone who snatches children in their sleep?"

Malleck nodded. "Yeah, someone like that, but maybe even worse. Take this headline I saw before class." She pulled her phone out of her pocket, thumbed at the screen, and turned it over to Ronnie. "This happened just twenty miles from here."

The headline on the screen read, "Server Accepts Napkin from Guest, Claims It Was $100 Bill".

"This just looks like clickbait," Ronnie said.

"Or maybe someone actually made that woman see something that wasn't there. How do you figure a near-three-hundred-pound lineman gets lured out to a park in the middle of the night? How many people do you think it would take to overpower him?" She shook her head. "This must sound crazy. It probably is. But we need to stay in communication.

Put your number in my phone. If you see anything... I don't know, weird or out of the ordinary, just tell me."

"And if that happens, what exactly would you do?" Ronnie asked. "I mean, I know you can crash my nightmares and all..."

Malleck paused and did a quick sweep of the woods, scanning cautiously. "I wish I could tell you more, Ronnie. Maybe someday I will. Right now, just like I said last night, I need you to trust me. Do you think you can do that?"

Ronnie nodded, his brain still having a hard time accepting Malleck's extraordinary gifts. He put his number into her phone and handed it back.

"I'm skipping," she said. "You wanna come with?"

"Probably shouldn't. Last time I skipped..."

"Didn't turn out so well. Got it." She backed away from Ronnie. "Promise me you won't get into any high-stress situations? You seem to have a knack for finding trouble."

Before she was out of earshot, Ronnie said, "Hey... so did you, um... Did you actually make that girl float?"

Malleck's cheek rose. She shrugged playfully, turned, and kept walking. Ronnie wished the grin had any influence on his mood, but Malleck didn't know that someone had his book.

Someone was following his plan.

For they who summon Karnlaxe.

Control the demon's might.

Chapter Eleven

M alleck arrived at a quaint diner just outside the city limits of Knollwood Pines. The shiny silver tube and neon OPEN sign appeared like a relic of old-folks stories.

Back in my day...

As far as she could tell, there were no good back-in-my-days for people like Malleck. In the 1600s she would have been burned alive. Even in the modern world, she had to live in such damn miserable secrecy. It made her wonder why the magic gene, through some strange cosmic equation of chance, had found her.

She parked her SUV and walked up the steel ramp, leading to a door with a metallic exterior to match the rest of the diner. The savory smell of butter and pancake mix greeted her as she opened the door. Eight booths in total lined the front side of the diner facing the road.

A woman in an obvious Marilyn-Monroe-style wig smiled at her from behind the bar area. Over the taps of silverware against plates, she said, "You can sit anywhere, sugar. I'll be with ya shortly." *Sugar... Retro wig...* Malleck grinned, admiring the commitment to the vibe.

Malleck eyed two empty booths at the right side of the entrance and began walking. A couple, probably in their late twenties, took forkfuls of food off each other's plates in the first booth, giggling while they did it. The second booth showed remnants of a sandwich, the tomato-and-lettuce-filled corner left next to a dirty napkin on a plate.

The third booth was empty...

But Malleck was pulled toward it in the same unexplainable way she was drawn to Ronnie, causing her to backstep. Some invisible orb of energy pulsed like the heavy base of an amplifier. Someone had been there.

Someone like her.

The force grew stronger as she slid into the booth. This all could have been a terrible cause for concern, but she couldn't help but feel giddy that her theory may have been correct. *Malleck: Paranormal Investigator*. She touched the table and focused. Never in her life had she struggled to project images into people's minds. For reasons she couldn't explain, that ability came naturally. She was, however, still weak in her ability to track others. It took a seasoned and powerful Manari to do so. She knew this, but it seemed a cruel act of her own biology that she would be able to summon dark magic but not track a person using the items or surfaces they touched, like she'd jumped ahead in line without buying a ticket.

She closed her eyes and fought hard, trying to pull the images into her mind—*Who the hell sat here?*—but knew not to strain too hard. Strain could mean another slip of dark magic, and that was something she couldn't afford.

A few seconds passed as she invited the images in, requesting access to a memory from the booth itself. Something was forming in the clouds of her subconscious.

When she opened her eyes, her hand was still her hand...

Except for her pinky finger, which had been replaced by someone else's. It sat there at the edge of her hand with bronze skin, long and bone-slim, with a dry, cracked knuckle.

Just as soon as she'd seen it, the alien finger was gone, and her pinky was her pinky again. The jolt of Malleck's surprise had scared the vision off, forcing it to flee from her eyesight.

Damn. So close.

"What can I get started for you?" the woman in the blond wig said at Malleck's side.

Malleck removed her hand from the table. "Hi, yes, uh..." She'd gone over it in her head but was suddenly struck by how ridiculous she knew it would sound. "A woman here recently was... given a napkin, and—"

The woman grunted. "You another one of them reporters?"

"Uh, no."

"An Internet kook then? We've seen 'em all here in the past day, honey."

"No, I just... I study supernatural phenomena." The lie, unrehearsed, fled quickly from her lips.

"Like for a TV show or somethin'?"

Why not? "Yep, for a TV show. We're interested in an interview."

Somehow, that seemed to one-eighty the woman's skepticism. She turned her head to the kitchen, the wig's bright strands trailing closely behind. "Kimmy! There's someone from a TV show wants to talk to ya!" She turned back. "Should be right out. Just warnin' ya, she's gone eight days without a break, plus with the unwanted attention from that damn article I doubt she'll be in the peppiest of moods."

The woman named Kimmy exited the diner kitchen, tying the straps of her apron in a bow around her back. Malleck guessed she was around fifty, with long, voluminous brown hair graying at the roots. Fatigue was evident from her forehead to her chin, and so, the first thing Malleck said was, "Take a seat."

Kimmy did so, looking disinterested in Malleck's company. "So you work for TV?" she asked with a thick Southern drawl.

"Yeah. Just wanted to hear a little more about—"

"You think I'm nuts."

"No no no," Malleck said. "I think you saw what you saw."

"Yep, saw somethin' I wasn't s'posed to see. No wonder why nobody believes me. I pulled back the curtain on somethin' not of this world.

Any minute now, the men in black or whomever else is gonna come back here and wipe my brain clean. Just the way these things work. I been workin' at this diner back and forth goin' on sixteen years at this point. Back before that street out there became a highway. Let me tell you, this ain't the friendly neighborhood diner it used to be. We get some very strange folk in here."

Kimmy seemed relaxed, almost secure in knowing that she'd experienced something supernatural. It didn't bother her that no one believed her. After all, she hadn't actually lost a hundred dollars. This was a cheap diner, and she was probably out twenty bucks tops.

"Could you tell me about the person who gave you the money?" Malleck asked.

Kimmy looked out the large windowpane, squinting at the sun-kissed scene of speeding cars on the highway. "It's a crime to dine and ditch, right?"

It may have been a rhetorical question, but a long silence prompted Malleck to respond. "I... I'm not sure."

"Ah, it's probably not. But I gotta think someday the universe'll bring the guy back around to me. I got some words for 'im." Kimmy turned back to Malleck. "You want some coffee? I'm about to pour myself a cup. I'll get you one too." Her teeth appeared under her lips in an unexpected smile. "Don't make me drink alone, now."

Malleck let out an awkward laugh as Kimmy left the table. She came back with two empty mugs clanking in one hand and a carafe in the other. The woman poured coffee into her mug, then slid the carafe over Malleck.

"Not much to say, really. I see this man sittin' in this here booth—this *exact* booth. Probably about two in the afternoon. He asked me how the coffee was. I told him it was the best in all of North Carolina." She laughed into her mug and took a loud sip. "Our coffee's not very good." She licked the not-very-good coffee off her lips. "He asked for a cup and got some steak and eggs. Rare and sunny side up. I know that's not really important, but it's this thing about me. I just remember orders really well.

"Took about fifteen minutes to prepare the steak and eggs and that man sliced through it in half that time. Had the corner of his napkin tucked inside the collar of his dress shirt. It's a good thing he did because them threads weren't safe against the meat juices with how fast he was eatin'. It wasn't that he was in a rush. He couldn't've been. Normally when people eat in a hurry, they ask for a check with their food. This was just... instinctual. A polite gentleman maskin' a hungry lion."

"Polite gentleman?" Malleck repeated.

"Oh, he spoke kindly enough, but he had a suit on. Like a... suit with a vest. And an old-timey hat. Kinda like Frank Sinatra, if you're not too young to know who that is."

"He was wearing the hat inside?"

"Yeah, I thought it was weird. The hat was gray to match the suit. Looked pretty sharp, if I'm bein' honest."

Gray hat and a gray three-piece suit.

Kimmy continued, "He was starin' out into the sun when I walked over. Didn't look like he was a stranger to the sun though. He had really tan skin. Might've been Greek or somethin'. His skin was tough, kinda like overcooked meat. Could've been forty-five, could've been sixty-five."

The description took Malleck all the way back to nine months ago, to the day she met Ronnie in the Gray World around the ring of fire. She remembered the man standing on the other side of the axe.

"Was he skinny?" Malleck asked. "Like, *really* skinny. Almost like he was wearing a bigger person's suit?"

Kimmy tilted her head curiously. "Yeah, actually he was. Have you... seen 'im?"

"No, just trying to paint a picture. That's all."

Kimmy took another sip of her coffee, apparently content with Malleck's explanation. "Anyways, I asked him what brought him to Knollwood Pines. Just a lucky guess that he wasn't from 'round here. Said he was here on business, but didn't say what kind. So I went to grab the check and when I came back—Surprise!—got me a one hundred dollar bill on the table. Over four times the cost of his meal. Hell of a tip. Looked out the window and saw him drive off in an Oldsmobile. A pretty old model. Somethin' a man who hands out hundred-dollar bills at diners wouldn't drive, but I didn't think much of it.

"I put the money in the cash register and calculated the change. Next person who opened it saw the napkin right where I put the hundred. Explain that, sis."

Kimmy went on to describe her confrontation with the manager, how she'd had to explain why she accepted a spare napkin from a man just to watch him drive away. She'd been accused of "seeing things" when she swore up and down that it was, in fact, a one-hundred-dollar bill when she first held it in her hand.

Malleck may have been one of the few people who would ever believe her.

Chapter Twelve

Ronnie waited beside Leslie's car in the school parking lot, hood up, hands buried in his jean jacket. He needed his best friend now more than ever, but even though he knew her better than anyone, he couldn't imagine how she'd react to what he was about to tell her. Would she think he belonged in a straightjacket? Would she curl up into silence and never speak to him again, the tension of the secret between them growing like a tumor until one day she spoke up and outed him? Would she tell him he was imagining things, reminding him that he's not as special as he thinks he is? Would she tell him that imitation is the greatest form of flattery and no one in all of Knollwood Pines was looking to flatter little Ronnie Hendrix?

A ball of bobbing black hair emerged from the crowd of Knollwood Pines High students as Leslie rocked out to a song trickling in through her earbuds. She spotted Ronnie and took the earbuds out.

"What's up, fam?" she said.

"Can I hitch a ride home with you?"

"Well, of course, kind sir," she said playfully, doing a waving motion as if presenting the car. "Your chariot awaits."

Okay, this is it. Ronnie speedwalked to the passenger's side and put his palm on the door handle, waiting for the door to be unlocked.

"Another bad day?" Leslie asked, unlocking the car doors.

Ronnie slid into the car and waited for her to join him. Once they were both inside with the sound of the school crowd isolated from Ronnie's heavy breathing, he spoke quickly. "Okay, I gotta tell you something. You have to promise to not tell anyone, and you have to promise you won't think differently of me."

Leslie gave an exaggerated "yikes" kind of look with her eyes bugged out. "What's goin' on, man?"

"You have to promise," Ronnie insisted.

"Okay, chill out. I promise. What's up?"

"The thing that happened to Therber Windell... I think it was my fault," Ronnie said, pushing the words out from deep inside his chest.

"What?!" Leslie exclaimed. "That's impossible, Ronnie. Stop being crazy."

"Yesterday I didn't ask you for a ride home because I skipped third period and..." Ronnie struggled to get it out.

"And what?" Leslie asked.

"Jack and Gavin and Therber, they... kinda jumped me."

"They what?!" Leslie exploded. "Oh, I got somethin' for their asses. Except Therber. He died... My bad."

"You remember that notebook? The one you said I've been elbows deep in and never let you look at? I've been putting passages in it since my accident. I had it in my bookbag when they got to me. Jack threw my bookbag in the creek and I have no idea where it went."

"So you lost your notebook. How does this have anything to do with Therber dying?"

"That book *had* his murder in it," Ronnie said, realizing how wild he must have sounded.

"So you wrote a story about Therber dying?"

"No, I'm saying that the way he was found, it fits what I wrote. It matches what I drew. It's Therber's ritual *exactly* how I created it. It's like someone used it as a blueprint. I wrote his damn name in the ritual and drew his likeness and everything."

"How was he found?" Leslie asked, clearly knowing far less than Ronnie did at that moment.

As they drove to his house, Ronnie described the details that Malleck had given him. Unbelievable as the story might have been, Leslie agreed that there was only one way to find out whether everything Ronnie was saying was a total coincidence or if it was true. They had to go back to the creek and find the bookbag.

She knew Ronnie had a vivid imagination, Leslie told him, saying human beings always want to feel like the protagonist of a story more exciting than real life. At least she hadn't decided to abandon him outright. The one possibility Ronnie hadn't considered was that Leslie would actually be excited for a little mystery. "Leslie and Ronnie, trekking through the woods, in search of a mystical book of rituals," she said in her best Australian accent, which wasn't saying much.

They agreed to go searching for the bag just as they passed through Ronnie's neighborhood. Ronnie spotted something odd on Surry Dale Street and told Leslie to stop.

"Whose car is that?" Leslie said. "Looks like your mom has some afternoon company."

It was Preston's car parked in front of the Hendrix house.

Ronnie entered the kitchen, where Preston and his mother sat at opposite ends of the table. This was pairing he never expected to see.

Leslie came in behind Ronnie and closed the door hard. "Hi, Ms. H!" she yelled out.

Judging by the look on his mother's face, Ronnie could see he'd stumbled in on a pleasant conversation.

"Uh... You're home early from work," Ronnie said.

"Yep," Cynthia replied. "I took a half day. It turns out that Preston's mom was looking for a property in my neighborhood." Ronnie was always weirded out by his mom referring to the neighborhood in which she was assigned to sell properties as *her* neighborhood. "We got to talking and it turns out you and Preston have a few things in common."

Eh, I doubt that, Ronnie thought.

"She also told me that Preston gave you a ride home yesterday," Cynthia looked from Ronnie to Preston. "Thanks again, by the way."

"Oh, don't mention it," Preston replied.

"Right," Ronnie said. "He gave me a ride home after school. After I got out of fourth period. After we both got out of fourth period. Separately." *Stop talking*.

Ronnie shot a look at Preston and gave him a sneaky nod.

"Anyways, I was very rude to Preston after your accident. I made some assumptions I shouldn't have, and I just wanted to clear the air," Cynthia said.

"As did I." Preston smiled at Cynthia.

"Well..." Ronnie said. "I'm really glad you two were able to hash things out."

Leslie butted in. "We were just about to go back to the school. Ronnie here forgot his dumb bookbag—I mean, the bookbag isn't dumb. Obviously, you bought him a good bookbag, Ms. H. Ronnie is dumb for leaving his bookbag at school."

"Oh," Preston said, "I was actually about to head that way too. I can help you look for it."

Leslie and Ronnie looked at each other, then back at Preston. "Yeah," Leslie said. "We could use all the help we can get... I guess."

Chapter Thirteen

Leslie didn't have a chance to confer with Ronnie as to how much they wanted Preston to know. In quintessential Ronnie Hendrix fashion, he remained tightlipped himself as to why exactly they were looking for the bag, careful not to reveal the spooky implications to Preston. For a kid who wanted out of the spotlight, he could be such a drama queen. He had a weird imagination for sure, and he was definitely a good artist, but thinking that some weirdo serial killer was out there following his gnarly ritual plan? Straight-up, bonafide madness.

But scavenger hunts were fun. And madness, well... that was kind of Leslie's Mansoor's jam.

She walked down the mouth of the creek with Ronnie by her side and Preston by his. The mash of leaves beneath their feet began to have a certain rhythm to it, muffled by the gentle rush of the stream to their right side. Leslie's musical mind kept trying to follow the steps into a beat, but she was constantly pulled out of her internal sound design every moment the steps got out of sync. She had to keep the conversation going between the three of them to keep from going insane.

"So, Mr. Preston," Leslie said, looking over Ronnie's head, "according to Lady Hendrix, you and Ronnie have a lot in common. Here I am looking at two strapping individuals who couldn't be more different. Sooooo, what about you two is the same?"

Preston laughed. "Sure, we may not *look* very similar, but our up-bringings aren't that different. We both grew up with single moms."

"Oh, so your parents are divorced?" she said a bit too quickly.

"We really need to work on your filter, Les," Ronnie said.

"Damn. My bad." He was right. Leslie really didn't have a filter. Her mouth would often move faster than her brain.

"It's cool," Preston said. "I'm not sensitive about it. My biological father walked out on me and my mom when I was six. I never knew the guy, so why should I be upset? My mom's pretty awesome. Kinda like Ronnie's mom."

Leslie held up an authoritative finger. "Don't you get sweet on Ms. H, okay? I'm very protective of her. Also, I'm pretty sure she doesn't date younger men."

Preston laughed again. That smile of his never seemed to fade. "She's not my type."

"What *is* your type?" An elbow stabbed Leslie's rib—Ronnie telling her to chill. "Ah, sorry. The filter thing. You'll get used to it. Is it just the two of you, then? You and your mom?"

"She remarried a couple years ago. My stepdad lives with us. I like the guy. He's good to her and I like seeing her happy." Preston turned his head to catch Leslie's glance. "What kind of stuff are you into?"

Leslie couldn't hold the look for long. She was a hard-ass when it came to boys, having made a habit of keeping her feelings to herself, but *damn*, he was fine. It was one thing to see Preston Collinsworth, but to have him see you—really *see* you—was something else entirely.

"I do some music," Leslie said.

"She's in a punk band," Ronnie added. "A pretty good one."

"No way!" Preston said enthusiastically. "What's your band called? I can't believe I haven't heard you play. I love live music."

Leslie giggled. "I don't think you'd like our music."

"And why not?"

"No offense, but you seem like a Christian soft rock kinda guy. You know, music with a message or whatever."

"Ah, fair enough. I'd still like to hear it though. When's your next show?"

"We were supposed to have one this Saturday night, but we're having trouble with our venue."

"Oh…" Preston took a long pause, thinking. "Maybe I could help you out. My uncle owns The Rambler downtown."

"The bar that lets kids under eighteen in but throws them out if they try to get alcohol?" Leslie grinned ear-to-ear. "I love that place."

"They're looking to do more live shows. I'm sure I could get you a gig. Especially if you're a *really good* band."

"That would be… incredible." This time, Leslie held his stare.

"Great. I'll let you know what my uncle says," Preston replied.

Was this flirting or was he just being nice? Leslie had never been a particularly smooth or romantic girl. She was mostly awkward as shit around boys. She'd had one boyfriend back when she was a freshman. The boy was a junior and very, very goth. He wore these baggy black pants with the bottoms all tattered and was always caked with make-up—black lipstick and eyeshadow. Looking back now, she wondered what the hell she was thinking. The guy liked music but seemed to take pleasure in depression, which suppressed Leslie's wild charisma. When she conjured her perfect partner in her mind, she saw someone who could roll with her weird sense of humor, liked rock, and hated just about everything else. Someone who'd rage against the machine and anything else that sucks. Preston didn't rage. At least, that's what Leslie had gathered after knowing him for all of twenty minutes.

She was beginning to think she'd had her "type" wrong this whole time.

The conversation between her and Preston would have been even better if Ronnie wasn't acting completely off his damn rocker. She knew how much this meant to him, but the guy had no chill. The three of them were out there looking for a bookbag and Ronnie's head was zipping around frantically like he had parachuted into an enemy warzone and everything was out to kill him.

Ronnie stopped suddenly, breaking the line.

"You okay?" Leslie asked.

Ronnie took a deep breath. "This is where it happened." He was reliving the beating he took yesterday. "You know, it's funny. When I heard Therber was dead this morning... Just for a few seconds, I felt happy that he was gone. Does that make me a bad person?"

Leslie stepped up to Ronnie and rubbed his shoulder. "No, Ronnie. You're not a bad guy."

"The way he died... He didn't deserve to die like that," Ronnie said, and for a moment Leslie thought he might cry. For all she knew, that girl Malleck was lying about this whole ritual thing just to screw with her friend's head. If she ever found out that was the case, Malleck would have to unleash some serious magic to keep Leslie from whooping her ass. Ronnie was more distraught than she'd ever seen him.

"We need to keep looking." Ronnie walked toward the stream. "Jack tossed my bookbag here. I say we go down another mile and if we can't find it, we turn back."

Ten minutes of speedwalking later, they spotted the bookbag down the stream, propped up against a natural dam of branches and mud that bottlenecked the running water's pathway.

"Holy shit. I can't believe we found it," Leslie said, trying to keep pace with Ronnie, but falling quickly behind.

Ronnie snatched up a large branch as Leslie got a closer look at the bag. It was unzipped. Whatever remained inside was likely waterlogged to hell. She imagined the relief on Ronnie's face when he found the notebook soaked, its pages smeared with bloated lines of text and penciled shapes forming indiscernible blobs. The book would be ruined, but Ronnie could finally calm his ass down.

"Awesome, we got it," Preston said with his hands on his hips.

"Yep, it's a total win," Leslie said, but she knew Ronnie wasn't convinced.

Ronnie stuck the branch out and slowly guided it through the top loop, careful not to push it away and send it back down the stream. He got the branch through the loop, lifted the bookbag out of the water, and rotated it away from the stream. He sat it down on the ground and took a second to breathe. The front end of the bag was flopped open, displaying a wet collection of binders and papers. Leslie stepped toward it.

"No," Ronnie said. "Let me check."

Ronnie crouched over to the bag and widened the opening, looking inside. He pulled out the wet contents. Nothing that flopped onto the ground resembled a leatherbound notebook.

"Is it…" Leslie couldn't finish. The horrified look on Ronnie's face said it all.

"What's wrong?" Preston asked, clueless.

Leslie thought Ronnie might scream. She finally began to consider the validity of Ronnie's ludicrous conspiracy. That book had all of the evidence of premeditated murder. They had to find out who the sicko was that had it and fast.

"We should go," Leslie said.

"Guys," Preston said in a panicked tone, "something's wrong."

The rustle of the stream was constant, but the unmistakable snap of a twig and the rustling of leaves entered Leslie's orbit from beyond the slope she stood on. It was too heavy and slow, almost calculated.

"You guys hear that?" Preston whispered.

"Yeah," Leslie said back. "What is that?"

Leslie turned to walk up the slope and have a look, but stopped suddenly. Her breathing became rapid and broken.

"What is it?" Ronnie asked.

But he'd have to be blind to ask that.

The sky went dark—almost black—past the trees. The stream beside her glowed red. The trees that lined the path ahead erupted into flames. Fire split the creek in half between the path they could continue down, fully ablaze, and the path they came from, dry and untouched. The heat waves pounded against her skin.

Leslie looked at Ronnie, who was still crouched over his bookbag and staring at her and Preston with a confused expression.

"Are you not seeing this?!" Leslie called out.

He was dumbfounded. As Preston raised his arm to shield himself from the massive twisting beams, Ronnie sat still, contorting his face like he was watching circus clowns.

But he was the closest one to the fire.

It was as if he didn't see or feel a thing.

Chapter Fourteen

L eslie and Preston shielded their faces, reacting to something that wasn't there.

"We have to go!" Preston yelled amidst a trickling stream and into the silent woods.

As Preston and Leslie began to back away toward the direction they'd traveled, Ronnie spotted a figure on the slope leveled above him standing underneath a tree. The figure wore a black robe, giving its body a rectangular shape, and a mask of crooked twigs that were pulled together by twine. Ronnie couldn't make out any discernible features. Even the eye holes of the mask were cast in shadow under the shade of tree limbs.

Ronnie zipped up the bookbag and slid his arms through the straps. He rose from his crouched position, eyes fixed on the robed figure, cautious of what it might do. Footsteps filled the air and several more robed, masked figures come into view, shifting from behind the tree and stepping toward the top of the slope.

"Ronnie! What are you doing?!" Leslie cried out.

Ronnie took a step back.

Every robed figure took a synchronized step forward.

"Run!" Ronnie turned and sprinted for his life, following Preston and Leslie as they sprinted as well. *Don't look back. Don't look back.*

He disobeyed his own orders and looked back. What must've been a dozen people were sprinting toward him with their robes flapping against the wind. Their faces were square and expressionless, hidden behind the handmade masks. In the small strokes of sunlight, he could make out their eyes contained inside the twigs. Glowing white orbs.

Ronnie caught his foot clumsily against a tree root raised in the ground. He crashed hard on the dirt and leaves, catching himself against his palms. He pivoted and crab-walked backward. A familiar sensation came back to him. Once again he was on the ground cowering, staring up at his attackers. This time they didn't wear puffy letterman jackets. This time he couldn't see their smiling, laughing faces. The figures, each in their layer of concealment, were stripped of any humanity. They slowed to a stop a few feet before him and began walking ominously, the sides of their robes coming together to hide the frames beneath. One particularly tall and looming figure stepped forward. Another robed figure, feet planted in the ground, reached inside their robe and removed an object with a leather spine, a leather cover, and pages with yellowed edges. The figure raised it high, the front cover facing forward.

Ronnie's notebook.

"Ronnie, come on!" Preston yelled, lifting Ronnie to his feet.

The masked figure stood roughly six feet five inches tall. Preston might have been a match for this guy, but not for all eleven-or-so behind him.

Then came a high-pitched *shink*.

A blade emerged from underneath the robe, smooth and wide. A machete with a black handle.

"Come on, man!" Preston yelled to Ronnie.

"Guys! Move your asses!" Leslie yelled.

Ronnie backpedaled. The figure raised the machete. What should have been pupils and irises were instead rolling clouds, stark white. Those smoky eyes weren't trained on Ronnie. They were fixed above his head, eye-level with Preston.

The machete rose to the sky, and the figure started advancing again.

"Oh shit!" Ronnie howled as he put his hand against Preston's side.

But then the figure stopped.

It's okay, a girl's voice hummed in a low whisper between his ears. *They can't see you now. Run.*

Ronnie didn't have time to think about it further. The last thing he saw before he turned and sprinted again was the robed figure lowering the machete as the rest of the goons in robes all stood like stalled-out vehicles.

It wasn't until Ronnie reached the opening of the creek that he realized the voice in his head was Malleck's.

Chapter Fifteen

Ronnie dove into the backseat of Preston's Honda Civic, panting wildly. Preston shuffled the keys in his shaking hands, trying to find the one with the fat "H" on it. From the passenger's seat, Leslie put a hand on his shoulder.

"Guys, look..." Leslie said as a sudden calmness came over her.

Preston looked straight ahead toward the trees. "No smoke," he said. "No fire. No... anything."

"What are you talking about?" Ronnie asked, gasping for air. "What did you think you saw out there?"

Preston turned to Ronnie. "Are you serious? The... the forest fire. All those trees burning? The creek was..."

Leslie, looking just as confused, finished Preston's thought. "The water turned into, like... lava or something."

"You saw it too?" Preston said, desperate for validation.

"Dude, of course! I thought it was about to singe my damn eyebrows off!"

"You didn't see the people in robes?" Ronnie asked.

They both stared at him, with only their heavy breaths filling the silence between them.

"Let's get out of here," Ronnie said.

As they drove, Ronnie explained to them what he saw. No flames, no black sky, just people in robes and masks. He explained how close Preston had come to catching the wrong end of a machete. Preston was in no condition to drive. He was gunning it from stop light to stop light and Leslie kept having to tell him to ease off the gas. He told them he could still feel the heat on his skin and hear the crackling of charred branches, that his brain was scrambled and broken, and it took all of his concentration to stay in a straight line on the road.

Leslie told them she tripped on mushrooms once and the things she saw scared her shitless. If what she had just experienced wasn't real, then it was the closest she'd ever come to that bad trip.

Ronnie pondered why only he could see the people in robes. Did they plant those images in Preston's and Leslie's minds? Their eyes... It wasn't an effect you could achieve with lenses. There was movement. What if they chose to reveal themselves only to him?

"They have the notebook," Ronnie said. "They wanted me. You couldn't see them, but they were there."

"What notebook? There's a notebook?" Preston said, speeding up again.

Leslie sighed and nodded at Ronnie. "We should tell him."

Ronnie jerked forward as Preston's car braked in the driveway, returning them to where they'd started that evening. Preston sat sullen and exhausted, keeping the engine running, quietly processing the information dumped on him during the car ride.

After a tense few seconds, Leslie turned to Preston. "Are you doing okay?"

"You think they killed Therber because of your book?" Preston asked with his head forward, frozen in place. Ronnie anticipated judgment, abandonment, maybe even righteous indignation. Preston and Therber had once been friends. Ronnie remembered the machete raised high, knowing he had put Preston's life at risk. Preston deserved to know the truth, even if it meant the end of whatever friendship they could have had.

"I think so," Ronnie finally said.

The silence on Preston's end was nauseating.

"Preston, I'm sorry."

A *ding* chimed, prompting Leslie to wrestle her phone out of her pocket.

"Uh... Ronnie?" she said into the screen. "Those dudes in robes... Is this what they looked like?" She turned the phone to Ronnie.

The screen displayed a message board with a video in the middle of the screen. Inside the video, Ronnie could make out a group of people in black robes and twig masks.

"Holy shit," Ronnie said. "That's them."

Outside the car, the front door opened and Ronnie's mom motioned for him to come inside. It wasn't a jovial greeting. Something was wrong.

"I gotta go... I'm really sorry," Ronnie said. "I wish none of this ever happened. I should have never made that book."

"We should get on LiveChat tonight," Leslie said. "Talk through this some more."

"Okay, I'll talk to you later tonight then," Ronnie said, addressing Leslie only. He clutched the handle of the backseat door.

"Ronnie," Preston said.

Ronnie stopped and waited for Preston to speak. It could have been the last exchange they ever had.

"None of this is your fault," Preston said. "You know that right?"

A wave of relief shot through Ronnie. It was something he desperately needed to hear.

"You were angry and wrote a book," Preston continued. "A lot of people would've done a lot worse. You're not responsible for Therber's death. Whatever's happening... I got your back."

"Me too," Leslie added. "These bitches don't know who they're messing with. We're gonna figure this out together."

Getting out of the car was like leaving the comfort of a warm blanket on a cold night. The world around Ronnie was incredibly, achingly cold.

Cynthia gave a quick wave and a faint smile to Preston and Leslie before ushering Ronnie into the house, not even bothering to ask why his pants were soaked. Careful not to dampen Preston's backseat, he'd been holding his newly found and very wet bag atop his lap.

Cynthia marched him into the kitchen.

"What's goin' on, Mom?" Ronnie asked, trying his best impression of normalcy.

"I made you some dinner," Cynthia said. "Go ahead. Sit."

Ronnie went to the sliding glass door that faced out to the back deck and opened it, setting his bookbag out to dry. The somewhat peculiar action should have warranted even the slightest line of questioning, but when Cynthia stayed silent, preoccupied with fixing Ronnie's dinner, he knew she had something serious on her mind. He sat in a chair on the long end of the kitchen table. Cynthia sat a plate down in front of him with baked salmon, rice, and steamed broccoli, then surrounded the edges of the plate with a fork and a knife. Ronnie could feel the nervous energy radiating off of her with every movement. She sat at the chair on the other side of the table and stared at Ronnie quietly.

"It looks great, Mom. Thanks." Ronnie picked up his fork and poked at the broccoli.

"I can heat it up if you'd like," Cynthia said.

Ronnie rested the fork on the side of his plate. "What's got you so... rattled?"

Cynthia took a deep breath. "From now on, at least for a while, I don't want you venturing out by yourself. And keep your cell phone close."

"Uh, yeah. I can do that," Ronnie said.

"There's a video that's getting viral," Cynthia said.

Ronnie experienced a full-body cringe at the phrase "getting viral". The olds could never get the terminology right. Viral wasn't something you *get*—it was something you *go*.

Cynthia continued, "The news posted about it. There's a group taking credit for the murder of the Windell boy. They're wearing—"

"Black robes and stick masks," Ronnie interrupted without thinking. The words just came to him, accompanied by the image of white eyes closed within a mask.

"You've seen it?" Cynthia asked.

"Oh, um...," Ronnie stammered, pushing out the memory of the robed figures running toward him. "Leslie got a message on her phone right before we left the car."

"Have you seen the video?" Cynthia asked.

Ronnie shrugged his shoulders. *I've seen the real thing*, he thought. "No, haven't seen it."

Cynthia insisted that they watch it together since she knew he'd see it eventually. She brought out her laptop and pulled up the website of a local news outlet on her browser. It was the top story, which was no surprise to Ronnie. A murderous cult targeting children was adult catnip in a town full of helicopter parents. This would dominate the news cycle for weeks.

The video showed the robed, masked figures arranged in a V formation with a leader in front, framed in the video from the chest up. They stood in a dark room with a single source of light facing them. What looked like twenty could have been thirty or more as the lines on either side receded into darkness. Nothing distinguished the leader from the group other than the position at the head of the formation. The room surrounding them was large, like a vacant warehouse, with the far corners distant and untouched by light.

A deep digitized voice said, "Citizens of Knollwood Pines... You are no doubt reeling from the loss of a young member of your community. You may take solace in knowing that his sacrament will benefit a greater purpose."

His sacrament, Ronnie thought. *Therber's eyes and tongue.*

"We are the Neverwells," the digitized voice continued. "It was us who took your young. We will soon take another. Their glorious purpose will be fulfilled by us. We serve Karnalaxe. His will be done." The playback stopped.

A heat wave slithered up Ronnie's spine. He took the mousepad and backtracked a few seconds from the end of the video. He replayed it. "We serve Karnalaxe. His will be done." *Karnalaxe.* These weren't merely psychos out to murder kids. They actually believe they were serving a higher purpose, offering severed body parts to the demon Ronnie made up after recovering from a coma.

"Does that mean anything to you?" Cynthia asked.

Ronnie knew what she was asking. Was it some kind of social media trend? Urban legends centering around child sacrifice and death had existed in the public consciousness for decades, but in the social media age it was now easier than ever to launch a stupid and sadistic viral hoax that targeted the one thing parents cared about more than anything else.

"No," Ronnie replied quickly. "It could all be fake. I mean... It looks like a bunch of kids in Halloween costumes." The memory of a machete rising from the middle of a robe flashed through Ronnie's mind. These were absolutely not a bunch of kids in Halloween costumes. They were dangerous. But Ronnie had to hide what he knew from his mother.

After a talk about the importance of being cautious, which lasted far too long for Ronnie's state of mind, he forced the rest of his meal down and watched some TV with Cynthia. They landed on a comedy film that they had watched together several times over. Cynthia laughed at the jokes she knew were coming and looked at Ronnie often to see if he was laughing as well. He chuckled haphazardly. All he could think about was the digitized voice replaying in his head: "We serve Karnalaxe..."

As they watched TV, Ronnie created a group text with Leslie and Preston and texted:

Watched the video. LiveChat at 8:30 tonight.

Ronnie joined the virtual chat room right on time. His video feed displayed his bed and the L-shaped shelf of paperbacks in the background. Preston was already there, and the posters, jerseys, medals, and trophies Ronnie had expected to line his walls were nowhere to be found. Instead, Ronnie laid eyes a wide room that was relatively undecorated. A caramel-colored bookcase stood prominently over Preston's left shoulder. The case stretched close to the height of the ceiling and was filled with rows of books of all shapes and sizes—fat paperbacks, long hardcovers.

"You're a reader?" Ronnie asked as he stared at both his and Preston's feeds side-by-side.

Preston laughed, "Yeah, man. I'm kind of a sucker for sci-fi and fantasy."

Ronnie grinned. "I am too, but as you can see..." Ronnie waved his hand toward the shelving over his bed, "my collection is nowhere near as impressive as yours."

"You should come over and grab some of my books then," Preston said. He turned in his chair to look at the bookcase. "I've read most of these. A lot of them are just decoration at this point. Here..."

After a few quick clicks of a keyboard, a chat message popped up showing Preston's address.

"Come by any time," Preston said.

"Deal."

The square of Leslie's video feed came on screen. Leslie's background was a hodgepodge of posters with proudly weird metal bands, men with long curly hair and leather outfits strumming electric guitars wildly, tongues out, holding up their index and pinky fingers in a rock-and-roll salute.

"Whoa," Leslie said, "book nerds of the world unite."

"You makin' fun of me?" Preston said playfully.

"No offense," Leslie replied, "but you don't strike me as the reading type."

Preston laughed. "What do you imagine me doing in my spare time?"

"Slamming weights, chewing dry protein powder, beating your chest like a Neanderthal in a cave." Leslie's smile grew.

"Valid." Preston chuckled. "I do that too."

"Guys." Ronnie truly hated to break up the banter, but there was something in his gut, crawling around his insides, that he had to get out.

"Right. We should get to it," Preston said. "I watched the video."

"I did too," Leslie said.

"My mom made me watch it with her," Ronnie added.

"Damn. That must've been awkward," Leslie said.

"They mentioned serving something. Or someone? It was hard for me to understand." Preston squinted, putting his brain to work. "Does anyone know anything about this... Karnalaxe guy?"

A stabbing pain shot into Ronnie's gut again, a bundle of thorns spinning and ripping its way through him. "This is all gonna sound crazy..."

"Crazy's kind of our baseline now, Ronnie," Leslie said.

"Right after the accident," Ronnie said, "I had a... dream. Or at least I thought it was a dream. I was walking through a version of Knollwood Pines that looked like it had been wiped out by an atom bomb. The sky was red, like... blood-red. And there were people screaming up there like they were in pain. This axe fell out of the sky and it was right in the center of Old Knollwood Pines Road. It was huge, though. Way too big for any normal person. And it was covered in barbed wire. In this dream, I kept thinking, *What would use an axe like this?* And when I woke up in the hospital, I had this name in my head..." Ronnie paused and looked down at his desk.

Preston jumped in, "Karnalaxe?"

Ronnie nodded.

"So..." Leslie said, "you wrote the name Karnalaxe in the book?"

Here it goes, Ronnie thought. *If they don't think I'm a psycho now, they definitely will in a minute.* Ronnie fidgeted in his chair and spilled it. "I gave life to this idea in my head. This giant mythical creature from the Underworld with the head of a ram and glowing red eyes. I drew him covered in leather with these muscley arms all bulging with veins. Hooves for feet. Each time he wielded the axe, the barbs would catch the skin on his palms. He would always be a bleeding mess. Even when he wasn't using the axe, a trail of blood would follow closely behind him."

"Far out," Leslie said.

"So you wrote this... demon thing into your notebook?" Preston asked.

Ronnie sighed. "It's not just that I wrote him into the book," he said. "I told you both that I wrote a series of rituals in the notebook... Well, in that book, it's not all strictly random. It's a sequence of offerings. Tongue and eyes, hands, feet, and lungs. According to what I wrote, those are the things needed in order to..." Ronnie paused, hearing what he was about to say in his head. It sounded ridiculous. "Those are the offerings required to summon Karnalaxe." Ronnie looked at his screen as Preston sat back in his chair, astounded. Leslie was still perched forward.

"So you're telling me," Leslie said, "that those jackasses are murdering kids because they saw in goddamn handwritten chicken scratch that if they collect hands and feet and shit, they'll be able to summon a giant demon with an axe?"

"Yyyyyyeeeessss," Ronnie said slowly as if trying to replace the word with something else, something that would make this all a bit less ludicrous.

"I mean, that's..." Preston was trying to wrap his head around it. "That's just... That's absurd."

"It's next-level bullshit," Leslie said, then caught the look on Ronnie's face. "Oh, not your story, dude. It actually seems pretty badass. But the idea that they think they're actually going to bring a flesh-and-blood demon to life... Yeah. Bullshit."

"I know. They're full of shit," Ronnie told both Leslie and himself, wanting to believe it, "but they have *my* notebook. If they're caught, what happens to me?"

"There's no way you'd be held accountable for what happened to Therber," Preston said. "It's not like you... Well..." A thought popped into Preston's head. "You did actually write Therber's name in the book."

Ronnie swallowed the small amount of moisture that was left in his mouth. "Yeah, I did."

Preston looked up at the ceiling. "Well, that... does cause a bit of a problem."

Leslie interrupted his thought process. "We're talking about an investigation, a court appearance. Even if he's found of no wrongdoing, his reputation in Knollwood Pines would be ruined. He and Cynthia would have to up and leave town and start over. No police. We have to find these assholes before they do and take back the book. No book, no sacrifices, no murder."

Ronnie gave the thought some room to breathe.

"Sorry... I listen to a lot of true crime podcasts," Leslie said. "Ronnie, you put together the roadmap to summon this demon, right? These Neverwells—dumb name, by the way—say that they're going to kill the next kid soon. Who is it?"

Ronnie worried that saying the name out loud was like a death sentence to the boy, but the wheels were already in motion. "Gavin Grace."

"Ew, that guy sucks," Leslie said. Ronnie and Preston each shot judgmental glances her way. "My bad. I meant to say, 'Oh no, we must save him. He's so young.'"

"He's not perfect," Preston said.

Leslie nodded in an exaggerated manner, mocking Preston. "Oh yeah, totally, because he's done so many right things in his life. I wouldn't call a guy who drugs girls not perfect, but you gotta cover for your boy, right?"

"He's not my boy," Preston said defiantly. "And those are just rumors. He doesn't deserve this. No one else dies if we can help it. Are we all in agreement?"

Ronnie nodded his head. "You guys have to know... I never wanted anyone to die. I was just, you know... writing stuff. I didn't think any of this would happen."

"I know, Ronnie," Preston said.

"I was just being a dick," Leslie said. "I don't want that tool to die, but I might take some pleasure in him knowing that this tiny little bitch saved his stupid life." She pointed at herself.

"I think I know someone who can help us," Ronnie added. "Malleck."

"The w—" Leslie caught herself. "The person who practices witchcraft?"

"I think she was in the creek with us," Ronnie said. "I, uh… I heard her voice in my head. I think she made the Neverwells see something that wasn't there, just like the Neverwells did to you."

Leslie's mouth hung open and a word formed slowly and dramatically in her throat. The word that came out was, "What?!"

"Yeeaaahhh," Preston said skeptically, "I don't think—"

"You don't have to believe me now," Ronnie said. "Let's meet behind the football field after second period tomorrow.'

"In the pine trees where people go to make out?" Leslie asked.

Ronnie pursed his lips. "Yeah."

"I'm in, chief," Leslie gave Ronnie a salute.

Preston took a moment to respond. "I'm in."

Chapter Sixteen

Ronnie woke up to his alarm, groggy and irritated. It had taken him a while to fall asleep, as he was afraid of where his mind might take him. To his surprise, his dreams were actual dreams. There was no bleeding sky, no ashes, no demons. He took comfort in barely being able to remember the loose remnants of images and sounds his unconscious mind had woven together. The sunlight at his window was like a blanket removed from a sleeping town, promising a few hours of Wednesday morning calm.

Preston's words ratted through his head: *No one else dies if we can help it.*

When Ronnie hopped in the car with Leslie he was immediately greeted with, "Don't you have anything else to wear?" He had, in fact, gotten a lot of mileage out of the black hoodie and black jean jacket, but he just liked how they fit. Jean jackets had a way of upping one's ruggedness a few notches, even if that someone was Ronnie Hendrix.

"I could say the same for you," Ronnie said to Leslie.

"You look like death." Leslie always knew how to make a friend feel special.

"I feel like it too," Ronnie said. "I didn't sleep much after that conversation last night."

"I was pretty wired myself," Leslie said, but with a hint of excitement rather than dread. "This is, like, some crazy shit, right?"

You have no idea, Ronnie thought. Leslie still didn't have the full story. If only she knew that Ronnie could go into an interdimensional plane between dreams and reality, which he could manipulate to look like his unconscious mind's interpretation of hell.

Ronnie walked into Ms. Springle's art classroom just as the bell rang, signaling the start of second period. Students were already at work bringing brushes and pallets to their desks and finding their unfinished landscape portraits from the cabinet countertops that lined either side of the room.

"Oo, just in the nick of time," Ms. Springle said from the corner of the classroom as she fastened an apron around her midsection.

Ronnie smiled shyly and found Malleck at the table in the corner. She greeted him with a half-smile, peering over the top of her canvas. Her puffy sweater and army green cargo pants appeared as Ronnie rounded the table. Malleck's style was a hodgepodge of mismatched items that looked legitimately effortless—as in, she had actually put no effort into selecting them—but it seemed intentional in a way that shouted, "Screw you, this is me."

"Maybe you can help me decide," Malleck said to Ronnie. She waved Ronnie around to the front of her painting.

Ronnie stopped at her shoulder and looked at the canvas displaying the city in ashes, a red sky, and a blank space of unobstructed canvas directly in the middle.

"Obviously I've stalled on this. I'm thinking... Maybe I need some help?" Malleck looked up at Ronnie, who was thankfully less affected seeing the painting this time.

"Are you trying to get me to do art therapy?" Ronnie said dryly.

"Wouldn't be the worst thing for you, would it?" Malleck said back.

"Given recent events, I actually think it might." Ronnie's eyes locked with Malleck's. Her playful expression faded. The look they shared told Ronnie everything he needed to know, but he had to put it into words to be sure. "That was you in the woods yesterday. In my head."

Malleck nodded slowly.

"Can we go outside and talk after class?"

Malleck nodded again.

Ronnie could make out two figures pacing beyond the first line of pine trees about fifty yards away from them. The small amount of pine needles remaining on the trees did little to obscure the boy in tight jeans and the tiny girl in a biker jacket.

"Ronnie," Malleck said, slowing her pace. "What have you told them?"

"Not everything," Ronnie said.

"This is a bad idea." Malleck stopped.

"Look," Ronnie said. "They're in this just as much as I am now. If you can help us understand what's going on, maybe you can prevent the next murder."

"How could I possibly do that, Ronnie?"

"Because I know who the next target is."

"How?"

"I'll explain. Come on."

Malleck gave him a dumbstruck look. Ronnie stepped across the border of the woods delineated between grass and browned pine straw, waiting for Malleck to follow.

She stood ponderously for a moment, lightly shaking her head. Ronnie could only imagine what she was thinking. "Screw the doctrine," she said, then stepped forward to join the group.

"How's it hangin'?" Leslie asked. "I'm Leslie."

Malleck waved and did a slight bob with her knees. "Hi, everyone. I'm Malleck."

"Your boots are sick," Leslie said.

That got a chuckle out of Malleck. She looked at Preston. "I'm very sorry about your friend."

"He's not my..." Preston paused, likely thinking better of disowning a dead kid. "Thanks."

Malleck looked to Ronnie. "So..." she said awkwardly. "This is starting to feel like a blind date."

"You could be so lucky," Leslie joked.

"Ronnie thinks you might be able to help us," Preston said, getting down to business. "Yesterday we experienced somewhat of a... phenomenon you might call it."

"You encountered cultists in masks and they made you see things that weren't actually there," Malleck said casually.

Leslie and Preston traded glances at each other.

"Uh," Preston said, caught off guard. "Yeah, but how did you—"

"I told you, she was with us," Ronnie said. "Or at least with me. Inside my head."

"It's a bit more nuanced than that," Malleck said, like an artist entering a circle of theorists criticizing her work.

"Can you help us understand what happened yesterday?" Ronnie said.

Malleck gave Ronnie a hard stare. "There could be serious consequences for me telling you all this. If anything gets out, I'll basically be imprisoned."

"A little dramatic," Leslie said.

"You don't understand," Malleck responded. "How could you?"

"Listen, lady," Leslie puffed out her chest, staring up at Malleck. "Some idiots are after my friend because he wrote a book about a demon, and we're going after them, with or without your—"

Malleck's face got deadly serious as she turned to Ronnie. "*You* created the manual to summon Karnalaxe?"

"I'm not super proud of it."

"This is all happening because of you?!" Malleck's voice was getting higher.

"Hey," Preston said in a controlled manner. "Ronnie didn't give the Neverwells this book. They stole it. I don't know if you can do the things he says you can, but they're not going to stop. They're going after Gavin."

"Gavin Grace?" Malleck said, easing up. "How do you know?"

"He's the next sacrifice," Ronnie said.

"Oh, Ronnie..." The judgment and shame oozed off of Malleck like a viscous puddle engulfing Ronnie.

"Are you going to help us save Gavin's life or not?" Preston said. "I know you two have your history—"

"History?" Malleck cut him off.

"History?" Leslie repeated.

Malleck stepped toward Preston, staring him in the eye. "What kind of *history* do you think we have?"

"I, uh... I just... heard that you two..."

"You said you were skeptical," Malleck said. "You wanna see what I can do?" Her pupils faded into rolling splashes of white. "Just wait."

Chapter Seventeen

Preston stared into Malleck's eyes, which rolled like swirling clouds. What started as a stare of curiosity became a trance he couldn't break free of.

Malleck faded from his view until his entire field of vision was devoid of any color. "What... What's going on?" Preston said. Though he could feel the vibration of words in his throat, the voice that came out was different. It was more delicate and high-pitched.

There was a stench in the air that Preston recognized. Old, worn cloth cushions from a broken-in couch. His vision began to materialize in front of him. He looked down the length of his arm, which was flung over top of the stale furniture, but wasn't his arm at all. It was slender and lighter, moving in the air with a swiftness foreign to him, ending in a callus-free hand and black fingernails. Draped over his bony knees was a thin floral dress.

This wasn't his body.

The rest of the room faded quickly into view like a subway rushing forward in a tunnel. Everything set in place in an instant. A sudden splash of color followed by mundane quiet.

Preston studied his surroundings. He knew what this place was. He was sitting in "the shack", a tiny one-story house that Jack's grandparents owned and never got rid of. It sat at the far side of a field that the town used for little league baseball games. In middle school, Preston would go with Jack and any number of friends they could fit inside to play video games and ping pong. Starting freshman year, the shack became a little less innocent. It was a known make-out spot. If you wanted to be alone with a girl, all you had to do was book a time with Jack and he'd give you the key. Eventually, it became more than a make-out spot, and any girl that entered instantly developed a reputation. Whatever happened inside was other people's business as far as Preston was concerned. He was more focused on school and athletics than getting laid.

The summer after freshman year, the ping pong table became a beer pong table. Upperclassmen came to the shack to party, bringing twelve-packs and joints to share. The innocence of the shack became something Preston could only reminisce about. The Playstation controllers were sticky with beer. Marijuana smoke took forever to air out.

Preston eyed the entertainment stand in front of the couch, which held up a boxy VHS-compatible TV and a pair of Playstation controllers, the thumbsticks of which were worn down from years of use. The controllers were still plugged into the console with the connected wires wrapped around them. At Preston's feet was a white rug that was so old and had seen so much traffic that the fabric had become rough like wool. Brown stains covered the floor. Old-fashioned wood paneling lined the sides of the living room. Pink drapes hung over the sides of two windows that faced out to the baseball field with the blinds closed.

"How did I get here?" Preston said, again hearing a voice that was not his own.

"I drove you here," a deep voice said from the other side of the shack.

Preston looked past the ping pong table, which had red SOLO cups in a triangle formation at either side, and into the opening of the kitchen. Gavin Grace came into view, with his perfect smile and perfectly faded hair. He wasn't wearing his letterman jacket, but rather a seafoam green sweater that clung to his body in a way that wasn't too tight, but with fabric that was thin enough to show the outline of his shoulders and his chest. He was holding two SOLO cups.

"You feelin' okay?" he asked as he offered a SOLO cup.

Preston took the cup in his slender hand and caught a whiff of a concoction that nearly lit his nose on fire. He looked at Gavin's confident face and noticed the unpierced ears. They hadn't looked that way since a year ago. "Okay, what's going on?" Preston said, hearing his actual voice this time, and stood from the couch, losing his grip on the cup. He fully expected Gavin to move and give him space, but Preston had to wiggle his way around Gavin, who stayed still like a rock, not following Preston's motion.

Instead, Gavin's eyes were focused on the couch, where Malleck sat in a floral dress, her black fingernails pinched against the red SOLO cup.

"Wait, was I just..." Preston said. There was no acknowledgement from either Gavin or Malleck. Preston snapped, snapped, clapped his hands. Nothing.

"I hate to ask this, but..." Malleck said to Gavin, hesitating to trust the contents of the cup. "Could you switch with me?"

Gavin laughed. "You don't trust me? I told you, I'm not like how people say I am. I'm not like Jack and all those other guys."

"So then... switch drinks with me," Malleck gave a playful smile. "Unless... you put something in this?"

Gavin puffed out his chest. "Just drink it, Mal," he said. "It'll help you loosen up."

Malleck's posture stiffened. She sat the cup down on a wooden side table next to the couch. "I think I need to go," she said.

"Don't be like that," Gavin said. "We're just havin' fun, right? Everything's okay. Here." Gavin held out his drink. "You can have mine. I'll make another one."

Malleck waved the cup aside, causing it to spill, and stood up. She actually had an inch on Gavin. "So this is how you do it?"

"Do what?" Gavin said coyly.

"Dammit," Malleck said to herself. "What the hell was I thinking?" She marched toward the door with a wide step. Gavin caught her wrist with his empty hand.

"Come on, Mal," he said, using her nickname to earn a bit of good will. "Just stay a little while. We can watch some TV…" Gavin sat the drink down on the coffee table and got closer. He cupped her hand with his. "We could talk a little…" He moved in with his lips circling hers.

"Get off me," Malleck said. When she tried to raise her hands, she couldn't. They were locked in place against Gavin's grip.

"Hey!" Preston yelled instinctively as he watched the scene play out. He tried to spring forward, but his feet were unconnected from the ground. He was running on an invisible treadmill, like an apparition stuck in place.

"Oh, you don't mean that," Gavin said to Malleck, his arrogant smile inches away from her face. He pressed his lips into hers.

Malleck whined in disgust as Gavin's head jerked away from her. He gripped his shirt collar and raised it to his bleeding upper lip. Malleck spouted a mixture of spit and blood at his feet.

"You bitch!" Gavin yelled out.

"Who's the bitch now?" Malleck said in a low, controlled voice.

Gavin laughed. "Oh, I get it. Girl power. I just figured you were a freak with all your wizardry and shit. The guys told me I couldn't turn you out, but guess what… Come tomorrow, they'll think I did."

"You tell them whatever you want," Malleck said. "Just stay the hell away from me." With that, she walked out the door and slammed it closed behind her.

The slam of the door caused a ripple of soundwaves that rattled the walls surrounding Preston. Everything in his vision shook until the walls were replaced by pine trees, the rug was replaced by pine straw, and the stench of old cushions drifted away. The shape before him molded into Malleck, whose eyes turned from milky white back to brown irises.

"Dude…" Leslie said in Preston's periphery. "What was that?"

"He just saw the *history* he was referring to," Malleck said.

Preston stepped back with his hands raised, questioning his grip on reality. "What… She… She got in my head. Made me see things. Just like them. You're like the Neverwells."

"Not exactly like them. They seem to practice the same magic as I do," Malleck said.

"So you *are* a witch!" Leslie exclaimed excitedly.

Preston shook his head, an aftershock streaking through him similar to what he'd experienced after the woods. "How did you do that? It's like I was there."

"Mind manipulation," Malleck said. "It's magic."

"Is he gonna be okay?" Leslie asked. "Can I go next?"

Preston's brain twisted like a rag being wrung out. His eyeballs tightened in his skull, adjusting to the view in front of him. It wasn't some fun trip. It was disorienting and terrifying, like being a quiet passenger in your own mind.

"He'll be fine. Reality warping isn't something the mind easily comprehends. And I shouldn't do it again. Every time my magic's used, it's like a flare in the sky to others who are sensitive to it. I only expended a small amount of energy just now, but the display the Neverwells—"

"Dumb name, right?" Leslie said.

"Yeah," Malleck said. "Pretty dumb. The display they put together with the two of you locked in… It was like fireworks. That's how I was able to reach Ronnie."

"What did you do?" Ronnie asked.

Malleck shrugged. "I erased you from their sight. It's a pretty simple alteration, actually."

A pretty simple alteration, Preston repeated to himself in awe. How long had Malleck been exposed to this to reach a point where she was unphased by her own extraordinary abilities?

"How long have you been able to do this?" Preston asked.

"Since I was eight years old," Malleck said. "I was road tripping with my parents, sitting in the backseat of their SUV and staring up at the sky. We'd hit a traffic jam going through Atlanta and were moving, like, an inch per minute. Mom and Dad were up in front. Dad was throwing a fit about arriving late to Grandma and Grandpa's house. I remember *really* wanting him to stop yelling. Not because it was scaring me or anything like that. I just didn't like seeing him upset.

"I spotted a flock of birds flying above us, way up in the sky, and I imagined myself floating out of that metal box and into the sky with my parents, soaring through the air toward our destination, brushing clouds off our faces, feeling the wind ripple in our clothes." She smiled for just a moment. "I didn't realize I was extending my vision to them. I heard them screaming and it shook me out of my daydream. The next thing I heard was our car smacking against another bumper."

Preston wasn't sure how to respond. Even after experiencing her magic himself, he couldn't wrap his head around her abilities. "That must have been scary," he said. "For you and your parents."

"They wrote it off," Malleck said. "To this day, they have no idea what I can do... I've only ever told that story to one person. It feels... nice, you know... having you three listen. I haven't had a lot of people to talk to recently."

Preston could hear the pain in her voice.

"Did you actually make that girl levitate?" Leslie asked.

Malleck rolled her eyes. "That was just a slip-up. I didn't even know I could do it. It was the only time I did real magic with that group. We were just having fun pretending to be witches. It was my kind of normal."

"Hiding in plain sight?" Preston said.

"Yeah. Now they and everyone else at this school is afraid of me."

"We, like... need you," Leslie said. "Really, really bad. When we come across those guys again, who knows what they'll put in our heads."

Malleck looked down. "I'm sorry... I wish I could help you, but... I can't. I'm prohibited from interfering." She looked at Preston. "I'm sorry for the violation. I shouldn't have done that."

But Preston was glad she did. He had made assumptions he had no right making. "I'm sorry too."

"You didn't do anything wrong," Malleck responded. She addressed the group. "If there is one thing I can tell you, it's that a trance isn't permanent. It can be broken with a very loud sound. Mind magicians, though, can be very deceptive. As you've noticed, they'll place a sound in your ears as real as anything you've experienced, so any sound that's going to break you free will have to be loud and obnoxious."

"Like an electric guitar solo?" Leslie smirked.

Malleck thought, then nodded. "With a loud enough amp, sure." She walked back toward the school, then turned to face Preston, Ronnie, and Leslie. "Don't try to go after the Neverwells."

"Therber's death is on me," Ronnie said. "I can't just let them kill Gavin too."

"You can warn Gavin, but I'm not sure what difference it will make. He's stubborn and arrogant and won't believe a single word you say. I'd suggest you keep any knowledge of the notebook to yourselves. I'm sorry I can't do more for you." Malleck turned and started walking.

"Wait," Preston said. He sprinted to Malleck. He couldn't let her leave without knowing how sorry he was. "If I had known that about Gavin, I..." Preston paused. "I'm sorry he spread that dumb rumor."

"Water under the bridge," she said ineffectually. She walked past Preston and gave him a pat on the shoulder.

"Well, this blows," Leslie said.

Chapter Eighteen

A blue-tailed dart stabbed the dartboard inside The Rambler, joining three more just like it clustered near the bullseye. Red tails lined the outer rim of the target. With a plume of sharp blue plastic raised between his eyes, Preston focused a little too hard, taking the match a little too seriously. He had a strange urge to impress Leslie, but probably just looked like a dork. He tossed the dart and just nicked the metal surrounding the bullseye.

The nine-inch windows stretched nearly to the ceiling, covering the hardwoods in bright cones of afternoon light. The bar area was about twelve feet long with stools that wouldn't be filled for another couple hours. A half-wall divided an area for booths and tables and the "play area".

"Wow. You're really good at this, huh?" Leslie said. She gave a quick toss and missed the dartboard, causing the pointer to bounce off the brick wall.

"Just takes practice," Preston said as he raised another dart. "When my mom and I moved to North Carolina, we didn't have much. My uncle owned another bar before this one with a similar layout, fancy that." He waved the dart forward and back, forward and back. "When my mom couldn't find a babysitter, she'd drop me off at the bar so Uncle Bob or one of his employees could keep an eye on me. There wasn't much for me to do besides play pool or throw darts." He tossed the dart. Bullseye. "So I got pretty good at darts." He wanted to pump his fist but kept it cool.

Leslie cackled in her throat. "And now you throw a javelin for sport."

"I think I could be fairly accurate with a javelin," Preston said. "I'm pretty good at axe throwing."

"Okay, creepy," Leslie said, holding up her last dart.

"Oh, yeah..." A sting of nervousness shot through Preston. "That was weird. I'm sorry."

"Loosen up, man. I like making you sweat." Leslie tossed her last dart and hit the brick wall again. "Maybe we should play pool?"

"You think we could get Ronnie involved?" Preston motioned to Ronnie, sitting with arms crossed.

"Nah, he's doing his moody thing," Leslie said. "You'll get used to it."

A server sat a basket of cheese fries on the table in front of Ronnie, who waved them over.

"That's our cue," Preston said.

"You owe me a game of pool," Leslie responded with a smile.

His stomach leapt as he smiled back. "You're on."

Preston and Leslie took the stools on the side of the table opposite Ronnie.

"Can you even eat this stuff?" Leslie asked Preston. "Or is this going to ruin your six-pack?"

"I think my six-pack will be fine," Preston said, scooping up a cheese-covered fry.

"Oh my god," Ronnie said. "Would you two stop flirting?"

Preston froze. "Oh, we weren't..." He looked at Leslie.

"What?" Leslie laughed. "Us? What are you even—"

"Just having a little fun is all," Preston said. "Trying to, you know… lighten the mood a bit." But that's exactly what they were doing—flirting.

"Yeah, well, my six-pack isn't going to be affected either in case you were curious," Ronnie said.

"Do you lift?" Preston asked. "You have good bone structure for it."

The look on Ronnie's face told Preston that he'd never in his life been told he had good bone structure.

"No, but I can survive a two-story drop," Ronnie said. "So, what's the plan with Gavin?"

Preston swallowed down a cheese fry and straightened his back, getting serious. "He'll be at practice now and that doesn't let out for another couple hours. I can't imagine what the locker room's like today. One thing you have to realize is that any night of the week could be a party for these guys, and Gavin's house is *the* party house."

"I hear his parents travel for work constantly, so he basically has no supervision," Leslie said. "Is it true that the housekeeper basically takes care of him?"

"That's right," Preston said. "I've met Sharon. Sweet as can be. Whatever she's making off that family, it's not fair compensation for having to deal with Gavin. I'm not convinced the guy has ever done a load of laundry."

"And you used to be best friends with these people," Leslie said.

Preston shrugged.

"How do we ensure he stays safe if we don't know when the Neverwells are going to attack?" Ronnie asked.

"All we can do is tell him he's in danger. It's up to him whether he acts on it," Preston said.

"We should go to his house after practice," Ronnie said.

"No," Preston interjected. "I'll go alone."

"Too dangerous," Ronnie said.

Leslie chuckled. "And what are you gonna do, short-stuff?"

She does have a point, Preston thought.

"We all go together," Ronnie said. "If it means we have to sit idle while you go knock on the door, so be it."

"We'll need something loud and obnoxious just in case," Leslie said, nudging Preston' arm. "It feels like a heavy metal kind of night."

Chapter Nineteen

The Glendale Senior Living Facility sat just behind a strip mall in Knollwood Pines. It had the appearance of a mid-level hotel, which it most certainly was. There were three stories of rooms that the elderly residents could decorate to match their living spaces back home. In the memory care unit, that familiarity was an important piece to a confusing existence.

Malleck had already spent an hour restocking toilet paper and cleaning the public restrooms reserved for visitors. Cleaning the facilities was a thankless job, of course. It paid better than nothing, and about two months in she had gotten numb to cleaning the many, many messes. She found the secret to keeping her sanity was to take a break every hour or so and walk around what was a very well-decorated facility. The artwork on the walls was nothing special besides being larger than anything she had painted before, but the colors were comforting in an algorithmic sense, as if some highly paid interior designer with an eye for elderly care facilities had consulted on best practices for ambiance. Malleck had offered to donate some of her more traditional artwork to the facility, but after a couple okay's from the managerial staff, she dropped it.

She walked through the memory care unit in her pink scrubs, her naked hands soggy after being hidden for an hour under rubber gloves.

Beatrice Bernadette, a seventy-three-year-old resident of two years, sat at one of the tables in the buffet area with her husband Joe. Malleck always greeted Beatrice by saying her full name. *Beatrice Bernadette* was so old-fashioned and cozy that the name itself elicited memories of watching old sitcoms with her parents as a child. Beatrice was a sweet woman with Alzheimer's and had a tendency to wander with no clear direction. This was quite common with seniors living with memory disorders. More and more frequently, Beatrice's brain would shift between months, years, and decades. When her husband visited, Beatrice often didn't recognize the man with a bald spot at the top of his head, with skin that sagged from years of natural aging and a stomach that protruded in a way that her husband's didn't when he was running marathons at thirty, forty, and even into his fifties. On several occasions, Malleck had overheard Joe relaying the last fifty years of their marriage together, all while Beatrice looked at a man she didn't recognize with a skeptical eye.

Malleck approached the couple mid-conversation, but the interruption didn't matter to Joe. Though he came to visit his wife, sometimes Malleck was the friendliest face he'd see.

"How are we doing today, Joe?" Malleck asked. She gave Beatrice a smile. "Beatrice Bernadette. Good to see you."

Beatrice looked at Malleck, confused.

"Honey, you remember Malleck," Joe said to his wife. "Malleck works here."

"Oh, right," Beatrice said. She would oftentimes accept the information she was given rather than question it.

"I'm doing well, Malleck," Joe said. "I was just reminding my beautiful wife of the restaurant we used to visit in the Outer Banks each year."

Malleck looked at Beatrice and responded with an exaggerated, "Wooooow." She looked back at Joe. "I'd like to hear more if that's okay."

A warm smile formed on Joe's lips. "Pull up a chair," he said.

Malleck took a chair from another table and pulled it up. She sat with her attention fixed on Joe.

Joe continued, "There's a place we used to go called Fisherman's Cove. There was an outdoor area that was built to look like the hull of a ship. It was so impressive, I have no idea how they did it. And it was right on the marsh, so when the water level was high enough you could look out and see water for miles. Every Saturday they'd play beach music. You know, the old stuff." He gave Malleck a wink. "Nothing like what you kids listen to now. You can't dance to anything now without it being choreographed. This here was smooth and rhythmic and just cool. It was *cool* music. We'd get there just before sundown and enjoy our meal in that last hour of light and then... come nighttime... we'd dance to the music." His shoulders swayed as he reminisced. "We loved dancing to beach music. We weren't ever any good at it. We just moved to the rhythm."

"Oh, okay," Beatrice said blankly. It was clear she couldn't remember.

"I know what beach music is, Joe," Malleck said with an exaggerated eye roll and shake of her head, playing along. "Tell me more about Fisherman's Cove."

"Uh... Well, there was a bar area with a steering wheel fixed on it. We weren't big drinkers, but the bar display was quite impressive."

"Was there a bartender stationed at it?" Malleck asked.

"Oh, yeah. It was usually a male and they had him in a cool Hawaiian shirt," Joe answered. "Always a Hawaiian shirt."

"How'd they light the place when the sun went down?" Malleck asked. "Just curious, since you said it was outdoors."

"String lights," Joe replied. "They had wooden posts set up around the outdoor seating area and they'd hang these bright string lights from the posts." He took his pointer finger and drew downward arcs in the air, tracing a path of invisible strings around the room. He gave Malleck a grin. "Is that enough to go off of, dear?"

Malleck smiled back. "I think it is." She winked at Joe and checked her surroundings, then looked at Beatrice. "Hey, Mrs. Beatrice Bernadette. This is going to seem a little strange, okay? But I promise you're safe."

"What are you saying, honey?" Beatrice said. "Wait, what's... What's happening?" Beatrice looked curiously along the room, from the buffet to the hallway, slowing fading from confusion to realization. "I... I know this place."

"What's it called?" Malleck said.

Scanning between the corners of the ceiling, Beatrice replied. "It's Fisher... Fisherman's Cove."

"And who's with you?" Malleck asked.

Beatrice smiled at her husband as if she hadn't seen him in years. "Joe, they're playing our music."

"Then I think we'd better dance to it," Joe said. "Just one song, darling." His eyes shifted to Malleck as Beatrice came out of her chair. He mouthed, "Thank you."

Joe Bernadette never questioned how Malleck did what she did. She encouraged him not to question such things, but to rather give the unexplainable room to breathe. To question the existence of such power would be to diminish it, and he had such precious little time left to spend with his wife.

Revealing her power made Malleck a hypocrite, but witness the way Joe met Beatrice on the dancefloor, taking her hands in his as they swayed to a rhythm only she could hear, Malleck was content being a hypocrite if it meant giving them five minutes to cherish.

The sun was halfway down outside the facility. Malleck bussed the mop into the storage closet and pulled her rubber gloves off with two loud slaps. A buzz hit her thigh from the flip phone her parents didn't know about. She bought it at a gas station nine months ago when she began receiving cryptic text messages from an unknown number. She needed an untraceable way of communicating.

The person on the other end only referred to themself as Nu. They claimed to have the same magic strain as Malleck. Something bad was happening in Knollwood Pines, they said, confirming to Malleck what she had already intuited. They felt the same surge of energy, which now only Malleck knew coincided with Ronnie's accident, and they needed someone with their ears to the ground. Malleck wasn't sure she could trust them, but, then again, the only one who knew of her abilities was Aunt Helga, who encouraged her to keep them hidden. For the first time in her life, she could be a part of something greater. Malleck had lived her teen years in the shadows of a dormant war, told to never reveal her abilities and to never interfere. If Nu was who Malleck hoped they were, they could open up infinite possibilities to use her power for good.

Malleck closed the door of the storage closet and locked it, then removed the flip phone from her pocket and flicked it open. She read the text message on screen: "New intel. We need to talk." Malleck picked up the pace and charted a course in her head: down two flights of stairs, toward the lobby, out the front entrance, to the side parking lot. She would get in her car, lock the doors, and have a conversation in a way only she could. A request to talk was an invitation from Nu to join them in the Gray World.

Malleck walked to the border of her Gray World creation, piercing the thin film that encased her environment. Her hand disappeared into the landscape, the nub of her wrist hanging against the pastel colors of a sunset. She pushed through, tearing a hole in her pocket creation of lily pads and dim sunlight, opening a black and infinite orbit, with distant globes radiating energy in a dark void—other creations fully formed. Malleck's body went weightless as she drifted. The pocket creations existed in the proximity of their creator, but movement in the Gray World was quick and untiring.

She viewed the environments from the outside through slowly spinning, translucent fields revealing the environments within. The more detail, the greater the energy output, and the brighter the orb.

What she was looking for wasn't bright at all.

Whereas Malleck meticulously created an environment of serenity that she could escape to, Nu's environment was dark and featureless, which wasn't to say that it was made that way. It simply wasn't made at all. It was a temporary, secret space that expelled the least amount of energy possible. You couldn't find it unless you were looking.

Nu presented themselves as featureless. A walking pitch-black mannequin, smooth and undressed. The appearance, they had said in the past, was for Malleck's safety. They would reveal themselves in due time.

The voice, for one, was high-pitched and delicate. A voice of concern. It was because of the voice that Malleck wasn't afraid of the black mannequin that floated before her as she approached it from a colorless void, which only spared the smallest amount of light to orient them. Light, after all, was energy, and their energy footprint had to remain minuscule. The space was left unoccupied even by gravity, and so Malleck hadn't noticed the sudden shift of her weight when entering through the void of the Gray World. Instead, she floated weightlessly, controlled only by her will, an astronaut with a jetpack, until she slowed to a stop.

"So… Nu… if that is your real name." Malleck waited for the figure to speak.

"For now, you can continue to call me Nu," the figure said. "I do have a real name, of course, but—"

"I get it. I have some secrets of my own. But you should know that all this secrecy makes it really hard to trust you." Malleck had an urge to position herself. To lean against one hip. To sit cross-legged. Floating was so unnatural, yet oddly so comfortable. There was no compression of her spine or ache in her knees. It was a degree removed from floating on water. No fear of sinking.

"Then trust in this," Nu said. "We have an associate who has infiltrated the Neverwells. They do seem to carry the strain, but have certainly rejected Manari principles."

"I felt it myself," Malleck said. "They used mind manipulation on two individuals yesterday. I think it's likely how they lured out their first victim."

"Yes," Nu agreed. "While most have only low levels of magic capabilities, they are a dangerous group. They might look like they're cosplaying as sorcerers, but they absolutely believe in their mission of summoning the demon they call Karnalaxe."

"With their combined energy… Is it even possible?"

"It's only possible with dark magic. It's something that they've studied but haven't been able to replicate. Somehow, they got their hands on the ancient texts—"

"The chaos scrolls? How? I thought the Manari locked them away."

"We don't know. But we do know they've tried to summon other demons from those texts and failed. But Karnalaxe is new territory. They think by following the sequence they'll be able to grant him passage."

"If you have this person on the inside, why aren't you doing anything to stop the Neverwells?"

"Their actions now are less important than the text that guides them. We need to find this book and destroy it, as well as the person who created it."

There it was. Ronnie was presumed evil for creating something wretched, but Malleck knew better. She knew of a scared boy who had endured bullying and abuse. A boy who shook with anxiety when he entered a room. A boy who stumbled through the Gray World unaware of the immense abilities his psyche possessed. This was no evil conduit of dark magic. Ronnie was angry and confused and wanted nothing more than to stop the bloodshed.

Nu continued. "As far as we can tell, the Neverwells don't randomly target individuals. They're fueled by what they believe to be some glorious purpose. You said you've seen them use their magic. Do you know who the targets were? It might lead us in the direction of the creator."

Malleck thought hard and fast about what she said next. "I didn't know them," she lied. "They looked young. Probably around my age. But... isn't it a little outlandish to think a high school student could materialize a new flesh-and-blood demon?"

"You of all people should know that abilities can manifest at an early age."

Malleck was caught off guard. "What do you..." She knew nothing of the being before her, but they seemed to know about her history. "How did you know that?"

Nu stayed silent—a still, black figure appearing lifeless. No one besides Malleck's aunt had knowledge of Malleck's past. The two of them made sure of that.

"Who are you?" Malleck asked.

Nu spoke. "You should know the Neverwells are planning something tonight."

"I can't interfere... The elders—"

"You already have. And the elders know."

PART II.

Chapter Twenty

Preston was a rule-follower and only drove at or below the speed limit. As he sat in the backseat of Leslie's car, moving fast through Shephard's Ridge, his entire body tensed up. Leslie's hair was wild and frizzy from the wind, her head angled forward in concentration. Something metallic was rattling from the left rear end of the car near the wheel, a rattling that would get louder the more she pressed down on the gas pedal.

"What's that clanking sound?" Preston asked.

"Old car," Leslie responded.

"She refuses to get it looked at," Ronnie said from the passenger's seat.

"Take a left up here." Preston pointed past Leslie's head. "It's the last house at the end of the road."

A cluster of massive three-story homes circled around them as Leslie turned. "Holy shit, what do people do with all this space?"

Preston's stomach shifted with the momentum of the car. "Let's slow it down. I don't want Gavin to know you two are here. Especially you." He patted Ronnie's shoulder. "Stay covered behind the bushes up here."

Leslie lowered her speed. "But I won't even get to see the fountain." She stopped just short of the Grace's driveway, with shrubs standing at the height of the Grace's metal fence.

"It's not that great. He only turns it on for parties." Preston opened his side door.

"Be careful," Ronnie said. "If you run into trouble... scream or something."

"It'll be fine." Preston tried to reassure himself as much as Ronnie and Leslie. He was dreading his reunion with Gavin, an infamous d-bag who was sure to be unhappy to see him. "Just stay here."

The Grace house was the crown jewel of Shephard's Ridge, the most prestigious neighborhood in Knollwood Pines, with a plot of land large enough for two football fields and a driveway that could fit two dozen monster trucks. Preston walked through the open gate and toward the roundabout driveway. As expected, the fountain wasn't on.

He walked up the steps, rang the doorbell, and waited.

The door opened, revealing the Grace's housekeeper on the other side.

"Hi there," said Sharon, wearing a sweater and jeans. Preston had been to this house when Gavin's parents were there and when they weren't. If they were home, Sharon would have been wearing an expensive-looking business suit. A look of recognition sparked across her face. "Preston, is it?"

Preston smiled, relieved that it was Sharon who answered the door. "You remember me."

"I never forget a face. I think Gavin's just getting out of the shower." She called up in the direction of the staircase. "Gavin! You have a friend here to see you!" She looked back at Preston. "Why don't you come on in?"

Preston entered, placing his feet on the marble tile of the home's entrance. The open layout was reminiscent for him, recalling memories of large gatherings—maybe twenty-five people—tucked into the living room watching R-rated movies, everyone giddy at what they were getting away with. It was a simpler time.

"He's having some trouble," Sharon said. "Did you know the boy who was..." She caught herself before she said it, as if there was a sensitive way of saying someone had been murdered.

"I did," Preston said. "I'm not on the football team anymore, but I played with him."

"I think he needs someone from outside the football team to talk to. He hated practice today. He feels like the team rallying around Therber is... disingenuous."

Preston wasn't sure how to respond. He didn't know that Gavin had much of a heart, but he was saddened to know that Sharon seemed to be his only shoulder to cry on.

"Oh, I'm sorry, I shouldn't be telling you all of this," Sharon said.

"No, it's fine. It's a difficult thing."

A rumble of footsteps gave way to Gavin Grace, wearing a set of pajamas—probably silk, if Preston had to guess. One look at Preston and Gavin's brows lowered. "What do you want?"

"Gavin!" Sharon barked. "That's no way to treat a guest."

"He's not welcome."

"Gavin..." Sharon gave him a maternal look, likely the only one he'd seen in some time. She then addressed them both. "Well, I'm going to go finish folding laundry in the basement while you two—"

"It's getting late," Gavin said. "You can go home now."

"Are you sure?"

"Yeah."

"Excuse me?"

"Yes, ma'am," Gavin corrected himself.

"No parties, okay?" Sharon waved a finger from Gavin to Preston.

"Come on, Sharon. You know I don't party," Gavin responded with a twist of a smile.

Thank goodness he's lightening up, Preston thought.

"What's the rule?" Sharon asked. "Say it."

"If someone throws up..." Gavin paused.

Sharon nodded, spinning a wheel with her finger.

"I have to clean it up," Gavin finished.

Sharon put a palm on his cheek. "Good man." She walked into the kitchen, leaving Preston and Gavin in an uncomfortable stare-off, which continued as she walked past them, purse in hand, and left the house through the front door.

"She's lovely as always," Preston said, breaking the silence.

"What are you doing here?" Gavin asked.

Preston shuffled his feet nervously. "There's something serious I need to talk to you about."

"Not really in the mood, buddy. I'll see you out." He headed toward the door.

But Preston held his ground. "I'm sorry about Therber, man. I know he meant a lot to you. I know we're not friends like we used to be, but I really need you to hear me out."

"If you don't leave, I'm calling the police. They come quick in neighborhoods like this, but I wouldn't expect your poor ass to know that."

The Collinsworths weren't poor. Preston's mother had made darn sure of that. But since Gavin lived in such boring luxury, Preston supposed that everyone looked lesser-than by default. "Why do you have to be such an insufferable jerk? I'm trying to save your life. The same people that got Therber could be out to get you too. You have to trust me."

"Trust you?!" Gavin yelled. He marched to Preston, peering up with his chin to Preston's chest. "Says the guy who sold us out? Yeah, Jack told me. He also said you were warning him not to go near that little weirdo who fell off the water tower. Sounded like a threat to me. So why shouldn't I be ratting your ass out to the police? It's because I know your little pansy ass wouldn't hurt a fly, unlike me. So, either remove yourself or get removed."

"I've seen the type of person you beat up, man, so spare me the tough guy talk. Cast all that dumb rhetoric aside for now—"

Gavin interrupted him with a mocking tone, "'Cast that rhetoric aside.' Cool, we get it. You read books—"

"Would you just listen to me?!" Preston was beginning to lose his cool. "Just the fact that I got to your doorstep is very bad for you. It means anyone can get to you. You need to lock this place down. Close that darn gate and activate your security system."

"I don't even know the passcode, bro," Gavin said defiantly. "Besides, if anyone's comin' for me, let them. You'll see what happens. Matter of fact..." Gavin took his phone out of his pajama bottoms. "I'm gonna take a picture so that, in case of my untimely demise, everyone knows you were the last person to see me alive." Gavin turned and stretched out his arm, holding the phone above his head. He snapped a picture just before Preston threw an arm up to block his face. Gavin lowered the phone. "Well, it's been real buddy. Now get off my property and don't walk on my very expensive grass."

"Look..." Preston said in a last-ditch effort to get through to Gavin. "If you see or hear anything out of the ordinary, call me. Got it?"

"Aw, thanks, Preston. Really appreciate that, buddy," Gavin said sarcastically.

A sloshing sound tickled Preston's ear. It was faint enough that he would have missed it had he not been standing still. He turned head to the sound. "Do you hear that?"

"Hear what?"

Slosh... Slosh... Slosh. Something was being forced in a circle like a ladle in a thick pot of soup. Preston eyed the door to the basement. It was turned open, obstructing his view through the hallway. He didn't remember it being open when he walked into the house.

"Gavin... Could you come down here, please?" It was Sharon—or, rather it *sounded* like Sharon. To Preston, it seemed more like an imitation. A monotone recreation of Sharon's voice.

"Sharon?!" Gavin hollered. "Are you down there?!"

That wasn't possible, though, as Preston had seen Sharon leave.

"She must've come in through the back," Gavin said to himself.

This was all wrong—Preston could feel it. "We have to go."

"Gavin," the voice called again, this time stronger, with more authority. "Come down here."

"Don't let the door hit you," Gavin said, turning away from Preston.

"Gavin, don't..." Preston grabbed Gavin's arm. Before he could react, Gavin's fist collided with his jaw, washing out his vision and causing him to fall backward.

Preston writhed on the ground in a daze, his vision fuzzy. It was the first time he'd ever been punched. His elbows throbbed from the impact on the marble floor, but he considered himself lucky that he hadn't hit his head on the way down. "See yourself out," Gavin said as the distorted outline of his body glided toward the basement entrance.

Preston shook his head, trying to regain his sight, seeing the colors in his view sharpen. He crawled up to his feet and stumbled to the basement door, peering around to a wooden stairwell enshrined in the light of a single overhead bulb. Darkness engulfed the bottom of the steps as the sloshing echoed beyond it.

One-by-one, the steps *creaked* under Preston's weight.

Creak. Step. *Creak*. Step.

The sloshing sound became more pronounced with each step.

The overhead bulb at the top of the stairs went out with a whimper. The glow that lit Preston's path faded and left his view in darkness. He looked back up to the top of the stairs. Light was coming in from the hallway. Just barely, but at least it was something.

"Gavin!" Preston called out. He took out his phone and touched the flashlight button on the main screen. He held it above his head and descended down the remaining steps with a new cadence of creaks.

Once his feet touched the concrete flooring, the sloshing sound was met with a thud. He turned his light to the source of the noise and put a spotlight on the cleaning room area with the washer and dryer sitting next to each other. The washer bucked violently, flailing side-to-side, corner-to-corner. Gavin came into view of the light, clutching the toggles on the machine.

"Told you to get lost," Gavin said.

Preston walked toward the washer, which seemed to bang harder with every step he took, like something thick was punching at the sides.

The banging stopped.

"Hell yeah. Must've fixed it," Gavin said, stepping back.

Silence surrounded them. There wasn't a wind down from the cycle inside the washer, no transition from rocking to steady. It had gone completely still.

A chill went down Preston's spine. "We have to go."

A thick liquid rose up from underneath the lid and poured down the front of the washer.

Dark red streaks.

Before Preston could process what he was seeing, a puddle began to pool at the front of the machine like a dark red sun growing larger. It touched Gavin's bare feet and he sprang backward.

Preston inhaled a terrible copper smell that he knew too well. If he didn't leave that room then and there, he'd be seconds away from standing in a pool of blood.

"Look at the mess you made!" a voice called out from the other side of the basement.

Preston whipped his flashlight around and found Sharon standing in the corner. No longer was she in the casual sweater and jeans. She was in a full business suit that appeared to be ripping at the seams of the shoulders.

"Sharon?" Gavin muttered.

The woman's head bobbed up and down with every heaving breath she took. Her eyes were bloodshot and wide—impossibly wide—like they had been forced open.

"What do you have to say for yourself?!" Sharon screamed. Then she was gone from the light, strafing—*Crawling?*—around the wall in a flash.

Preston tried to follow her with the light, but everywhere he pointed was blank space surrounded by foreboding darkness.

"What the hell?" Gavin said.

Preston could hear his breath rising. "It's not real."

Gavin backed up, stopping beside Preston.

Without warning, Sharon fell from the ceiling in front of them, landing hard on her feet. "What's our rule?!" she yelled.

Preston stumbled backward, losing the phone in his grip, and fell onto the cold, hard concrete, splashing against a sheet of blood. He sprang onto his knees and crawled to the phone. He shined the beam of light in front of him. Sharon stood in front of the washing machine, panting quickly like an animal. Her back bulged under the ripped suit jacket with each heavy breath. She clutched the lid of the washing machine as blood spurted from within it, flowed down, and splashed against her ankles.

Gavin stood frozen on his feet in front of Preston. "Sharon..."

The housekeeper's fingers pressed against the lid, shaking from the tension. The first joint in her index finger snapped loudly. Her middle finger snapped in an even more nauseating crunch. Sharon gritted her teeth and wheezed, as if breathing out the pain.

"Sharon! What are you doing?!" Gavin backed up toward the stairs.

Preston rose to his feet. "It's not real, Gavin!"

Sharon stopped wheezing. "Where do you think you're going?" she asked in a calm voice. She lifted the lid and plunged her free hand inside so fast it made the blood splash against her face. She grabbed hold of what was inside and turned her head to Preston and Gavin slowly.

The blood stopped flowing from the washing machine. All Preston could hear was his breath mixed with the heavy breathing of Sharon as her veiny, hateful eyes stared angrily at him. His mind tried to make sense of seeing the caretaker, someone who practically raised Gavin for several years, now looking at him like a rabid animal.

"You need to clean up your mess," Sharon said.

Her face curled into a smile. Her cheeks shifted upward higher than they should have, revealing large, jagged, browning teeth.

Sharon pulled her hand out of the washing machine and clasped within it a blood-soaked shirt collar, followed by a head bent lifelessly at the neck. An arm flopped against the side of the washing machine, propping the body up by the armpit. The head clanked against the top of the machine's opening. Sharon put her hand under its chin and lifted the head.

Even through the thick layer of dripping blood, Preston recognized the face of Therber.

"Oh my god," Gavin whimpered, stumbling backward, then spun around and ran past Preston up the stairs.

Preston followed quickly behind, racing up the stairs and out of the basement, shutting the door behind him.

Gavin ran through the hallway and into the kitchen, grabbed a chair, ran back to the basement door, and jammed the top end against the knob, propping the chair between the door and the hardwood.

"Let's go, Gavin!" Preston yelled.

"Hey, guys," a light voice said behind the basement door.

Preston knew that voice.

"Let me out," Therber said behind the door in a soft whisper. "It's dark down here."

Screw this, Preston thought. There was only one way to end this.

He left Gavin and threw open the front door, jumping down from the porch to the driveway. "Play the music!" he yelled, but was unable to release the sound from his lungs. He tried to scream louder, but couldn't.

A deep growl, low and steady, whipped his attention to the side lawn, where a rottweiler inched its way toward him, head down, stalking its prey.

This could have been an illusion as well, but Preston couldn't be certain. A memory of his six-year-old self encountering a dog just like this one flooded his brain, reminding him of how it felt when its jaw clenched his forearm, tight enough to break the skin.

With the dim house lights splashing on top of the rottweiler, the animal's teeth were on full display, a cruel growl bursting through them.

Something cold and mushy pressed against Preston's fingertips. He was no longer holding his phone, but rather a bone with soft fur and flesh hanging off of it. He dropped the bone and brought his hand up to the light. A cold layer of blood lined his palm. He wiped his hand frantically on his shirt, then looked again at the rottweiler, still prowling with foamy saliva dripping from its mouth. It appeared spring-loaded and ready to pounce.

It's not real. It's not real.

Preston walked sideways slowly, making his way past the fountain and down the driveway, staring the dog down as it crept forward, matching step after agonizing step.

The rottweiler charged.

Chapter Twenty-One

onnie looked through the windshield at the intricately displayed Halloween decorations strewn about the houses on the other side of the street.

"How do you think it's going in there?" Leslie asked him.

"Well, he's not back yet, so... I guess it's going good?" Ronnie answered.

"What do you think about the guy?"

"Who, Preston?"

"Yep, that guy."

"What do I think about Preston..." Ronnie paused. "He's full of surprises."

"That's for sure," Leslie said.

Ronnie's phone buzzed against his leg. He answered it. "Hello?"

"Ronnie, it's Malleck," said the voice on the other end. "I shouldn't be telling you this, but the Neverwells are planning something tonight. If you're anywhere near Gavin Grace, it's not safe. Where are you?"

"Uh..."

"Oh my god, you're with him, aren't you."

"Not exactly."

"Leave, Ronnie. Leave now."

A scream shot from behind the gates of the Grace house. "Uh... I have to go. Thank you, Malleck. Really." He hung up and yelled, "Drive!"

Leslie cranked the engine and gunned it forward, swerving into the Grace's driveway and revving toward the fountain. Preston came into view as they entered the roundabout driveway, flailing on his back with his arms extended.

"I got him. Hit the music." Ronnie opened his door and jumped out before the Corolla had come to a stop.

A stab of death metal burst into the air. Drums and electric guitars disrupted the peacefully quiet suburb. A very aggressive man sang or growled or yelled or some combination of all three as the tempo of the drums increased.

"Preston! It's me!" Ronnie yelled.

Preston bench pressed Ronnie off of him, causing Ronnie to stumble back on his feet. Preston rose, swiping the air and shaking his head, his eyes wide like a boy lost in a dark cave.

Leslie walked past Ronnie, taking small steps toward Preston. "It's okay," she said softly. Even as the music overpowered her voice, it seemed to give Preston comfort. He stood still and wrapped his arms around himself, shaking. Leslie cupped her hands under his.

"Leslie," Preston said faintly. He lowered his body, falling against the stone driveway. Leslie followed him down, swinging around to his back and wrapping her tiny legs and arms around his broad frame.

"Where's Gavin?!" Ronnie yelled to Preston.

Preston pointed a shaky hand toward the house.

Ronnie left the two of them sitting there entangled in the driveway, serenaded by the throbbing battle cry of death metal.

He climbed his way up the steps to the front door. He tried to push it open but couldn't make it budge. He ran down the steps and around the side of the house, checking every window he could for signs of Gavin.

Living room: Nothing.

Kitchen: Nothing.

Family room: Nothing.

He dropped down from the last window on the side of the house, then turned the back corner to a broad wooden deck that matched the width of the entire house. It featured a closed-in jacuzzi and sets of porch furniture anywhere they could fit.

The back door popped open, and Gavin step onto the deck.

"Gavin!" Ronnie yelled. If Gavin was in a trance, Ronnie hoped the music from Leslie's car was loud enough to snap him out of it.

Gavin scanned the backyard and met Ronnie's gaze through the deck railing. Whatever he saw in Ronnie's place was frightening enough to make him sprint. He jumped down the entire flight of steps from the porch and landed with a roll, then dashed through the backyard.

Ronnie was already sprinting when Gavin hopped the wooden gate that separated the yard from the woods that isolated Shephard's Ridge. It was effortless and impressive and something Ronnie could never do. He thought about taking his chances at running through the fence like a wrecking ball until he got close enough to guess that the height was doable. He would just need a big jump.

He hit the fence with his foot, using whatever friction he could to propel himself upward and caught the fence with one hand. He set his other hand beside it, rocked his legs to one side... then the other... then hoisted a leg up and caught a pillar with his ankle. The edge of the wood dug into his skin so much that he figured he would see a bloody gash when he finished his foot chase. No time to think about that now.

Ronnie pulled his body sideways over the gate and fell to his side, breaking the fall with his right arm. A burst of pain shot through his shoulder and he cried out like a wounded dog. When he wiggled up to his feet, he knew his arm was out of the socket.

He had to press on.

There was no way for him to know how far he was trailing Gavin. The inability to use his right arm killed the momentum of his run and every rise and fall of his body caused another stabbing twinge of tendons being pulled in ways they weren't meant to be. The darkness of the woods made it so that he couldn't run faster if he wanted to, not unless he wanted to break the rest of his body against the base of a tree.

A shrill cry shot through the air, distant and horrifying.

Gavin.

He remembered the look on Gavin's face when he thrust his sneaker into Ronnie's gut, over and over again. Gavin was so pleased with himself then, and Ronnie didn't even have the ability to scream. All the air had been kicked out of his stomach and he could only gasp, hoping it would be over soon.

Ronnie wasn't like Gavin, no matter how much joy he took in illustrating Gavin's lifeless body with his hands removed. The hands that caught touchdowns. The hands that made the crowd cheer. The hands that kept Ronnie down and didn't pick him up.

Ronnie willed himself forward, hobbling through the darkness, his rotator cuff aching with every movement.

"Come forward," said a gruff voice, distinct enough that it could have been from someone standing next to him. His head zipped around, scanning the area, but could only make out trees under the night sky.

"This way," the voice said. "We have so much to show you."

Chapter Twenty-Two

Malleck's parents were home when she stepped through the front door, still wearing her pink scrubs. They sat in the living room in an unusual manner. It was strange for them to be in the same room together—on the same couch, no less—and even more strange to find them facing her in such an attentive way.

Regardless, her main priority now was getting out of her scrubs and heading to Gavin Grace's house, Manari bylaws be damned. She'd have to find a way to slip out without them asking questions.

But her parents looked off. The faces of her mother and father appeared to be stuck in a perpetual state of bliss. Deep smiles curled at the top of their cheeks. They were both nearing sixty, having had Malleck later than most couples, and the smiles did their part in accentuating the wrinkles of their aging skin. Noticing their strange stupor, Malleck feared for the worst. That is, until Aunt Helga walked from out the kitchen and into the living room, holding two mugs of coffee as if *she* were hosting *them*.

Helga's thick hair shimmied over an open wool cardigan that Malleck certainly would have asked to buy from her if this situation wasn't so odd. Her eyes widened in surprise when they met Malleck's.

"Great. You're home," Helga said with a smile, feigning glee. She finished her trek into the living room and sat the steaming mugs on the coffee table.

Malleck's parents picked up the mugs gently and blew against the steam, smiles still pressed against their faces.

"What did you do to them?" Malleck demanded. "You told me this was forbidden."

"Mally," her mother said, using a nickname she hadn't used since Malleck's preteen years, "don't be so rude. Your aunt traveled here from... Oh, where was it, Helga?"

"Doesn't matter," Helga said.

"Right," Malleck's mother said. "It doesn't matter. Of course. Why should it? She's here to pick you up."

Malleck watched her mother blow on the tea, smile, blow on the tea, smile.

"Here to pick me up?" Malleck said. "And take me where exactly?"

"I think it would be a good idea if you stayed with me for a while," Helga said with a look of regret.

"And we think it's a wonderful idea," Malleck's father said, but it hardly sounded like him. He never spoke about anything being wonderful.

Malleck shook her head at Helga. She was putting the pieces together. "Aunt Helga, I'm not going."

"You know you don't have a choice," Helga said.

Helga gave Malleck a few minutes to pack up her things in a moment of mercy meant to give Malleck the illusion of normalcy. Malleck knew where they were going, and when they got there, she wouldn't have much of a choice in what she wore.

It was a brief moment of isolation as well, one that Malleck took to send a text to Ronnie in warning: "Neverwells planning attack tonight.

Going off for a while. I'm sorry." She deleted the text from her phone immediately after.

"How would the council feel about you controlling my parent's emotions? Does that not break the sacred doctrine?" Malleck said, sulking in the passenger's seat of Helga's pickup truck as Knollwood Pines disappeared in the side view mirror.

"Silver lining, niece. You wanted to see the Manari commune. Now you will," Helga said.

"Do you know what's happening here?" Malleck asked.

"Of course I know," Helga said. "I felt it just like you do. As soon as I was within a stone's throw of Knollwood Pines, I felt the shift. When you're sensitive to this power, there are times when you will feel evil forces among you and you'll have to make a choice. Follow the doctrine and don't interfere... or reject it and do."

Malleck was put off by Helga's casual attitude. Shouldn't she be scolding her? "You know they would have killed that boy if I didn't stop them at the creek."

"I know," Helga said.

"They're going to kill again tonight. You can turn this car around now. We can stop them together."

"The elders have been watching us like hawks since your little levitation incident. You're lucky they sent me after you. If we interfere, they'll send far worse people than me."

"Do they not care about what the Neverwells might do?"

Helga sighed. "There have been others before. The Neverwells are just the latest in a long line of those who get a taste of dark magic and become intoxicated. They've failed before and they will continue to fail."

"What if this time it's different?" Malleck pleaded.

"What if, what if, what if, what if," Helga said sarcastically. "Our responsibility is to react to threats against the human race or to our people." She was ineffectual and expressionless, as if she didn't believe her own words.

"And two dead kids is, what... An acceptable loss?" Malleck asked.

"Not a threat against our people," Helga corrected her. "Just punks in masks abusing their gifts to get some publicity."

Malleck sat back against her chair, realizing that this conversation was pointless. "How long is the drive?"

"Ten hours, give or take. You should get some rest."

Malleck stayed awake with her heart pounding in her chest knowing that in ten hours, give or take, she'd stand before the elders of the Manari and await her fate.

Chapter Twenty-Three

The voice led Ronnie through the wooded area and onto the neighborhood greenway, with lampposts spaced out in wide gaps, creating a checkerboard of light and dark on the trail. The voice was deep and scratchy, sounding like an old, weary man.

"This way," it said. Ronnie stared across the paved trail, which sloped downward into a high tunnel under a bridge. Translucent lights flickered inside—pops of light illuminating the circular concrete structure.

"That's it," the voice said.

Ronnie marched forward, feigning toughness, with his arm useless by his side, pain stabbing his shoulder like a knife. "Where's Gavin?!" he demanded. "What did you do with him?!"

He descended toward the mouth of the tunnel as it shifted from a gaping black hole to an off-white opening with each flicker of light.

One second, a dark void to fill with nightmares.

The next, an empty tunnel.

"Come closer," the voice said.

"What do you want from me?!" Ronnie yelled into the tunnel, his voice shaking with fear. He had to be brave. For himself. For Gavin.

To get that damn book back.

He stopped at the edge of the tunnel, his mind creating shapes in the darkness as the lights flickered on and off.

"Ronnie Hendrix," the voice said. "I'm so pleased to make your acquaintance."

A tall figure appeared at the other end of the tunnel, disappearing and materializing seconds at a time, the bright lights punching against his mask and black robe. The Neverwell moved closer to Ronnie, his robe hovering an inch off the ground, giving him the illusion of floating.

Ronnie stood his ground. "Where is he?"

"With us," The man's voice echoed in the tunnel. "The ritual is being prepared as we speak."

The Neverwell got closer. Ronnie took a step back.

"Ronnie," the Neverwell continued, "we don't mean you any harm. It's because of you that we're here now."

Ronnie's stomach tightened. "I don't even know who you people are."

The Neverwell began to pace from one side of the tunnel to the other. "Allow me to introduce myself. My name is Anson. I come from an... archaic race of people with a very limited vision of our future. Years ago, I and others like me rejected their practices and mobilized, yearning to fulfill our self-directed legacies. The problem is... we've lacked direction. We dedicated our lives to learning the magic of our ancestors, magic that's now forbidden, all in service of creating a new order in our race, one free of arbitrary laws that stunt our progress. We needed the demons of old to unleash their magic and make us even more powerful. Dominant.

"But the ancient texts all failed us. Miserably. Who knew there was an expiration date on spells? Everything we tried yielded no result. The demons wouldn't respond to our summons. We had all but given up. Complacent in our ability to alter minds. It's a nice trick, but it only goes so far."

The Neverwell who called himself Anson stopped pacing and looked at Ronnie. "Then we felt your energy. Such... dark, rich, angry energy. It was something different, indescribable. You weren't like us... You were something else. We came to this town and waited patiently... Until we felt that dark energy again. When we came across your book, we knew we had gotten our hands on something special. The answer to our question. A new ritual. With a new god." He stretched his arms out wide with his palms to the sky in worship. "We serve Karnalaxe."

Ronnie let a moment pass between them, gathering his words. He opened and closed his mouth a few times in false starts.

"This is one big mistake," Ronnie said finally.

"Oh, it most certainly isn't," Anson responded.

"I made it all up!" Ronnie yelled in frustration.

"Careful," Anson said. "You don't want to draw any attention. What if you're found here around the same time the boy goes missing?"

"I don't know anything about demons and gods! I never wanted to kill anyone! Gavin's made my life a living hell, but I don't want him to die. It was just words on a page. Just some stupid drawings. You're killing kids for no reason. Don't you get that?!"

A deep laugh emanated from under Anson's mask. "I can feel your energy now. You may deny your gift, but that denial doesn't supersede your potential."

"Yes, it does," Ronnie pleaded. "I'm not what you think I am."

"A boy who can fall from a great height and yet stands on his own two feet before me. No, you're part of a plan that you can't even fathom. We will do your bidding. And once it's done, you'll see how special you truly are. You'll see what you're capable of. And perhaps then you'll be ready to lead us."

Ronnie's eyebrows quirked upward. "You want *me* to lead you?" he asked in disbelief.

"Well, of course," Anson said. "We're acting at your behest."

"Then... I'm ordering you to stop."

For a long moment, Ronnie could only hear the buzz of translucent bulks. With each second, he grew more fearful of what Anson might say.

Anson spoke. "You deem us unworthy? Do you mean to sabotage us from carrying out your plan?"

Anson's tone shifted into something frightening and primal, like he was preparing to strike.

The scraping of steel echoed in the tunnel as a machete appeared from underneath Anson's robe.

"When we summon Karnalaxe," Anson said, "this world will be under our control. Imagine what we could do together. You, Ronnie... You will be the architect of our prosperity... Whether you're with us or against us." He stepped forward. "Are you against us?"

Ronnie prepared to turn and run, knowing that he wouldn't get far, knowing that the pain in his shoulder would set his body on fire, thinking that this might be the end for him.

He spun, ready to break into a mad dash before stopping at the sight of a man panting under a nearby lamppost, his oversized three-piece suit and fedora bathed in a cone of white light.

"I'll take it from here, son," the man said with the slight twang of a Southern accent, his words broken between quick breaths. White glowing eyes appeared under the brim of his hat as he lifted his head.

Ronnie turned back to Anson.

The tall man palmed the side of his head, emitting a gritted yell. "Get out of my mind!" He ran forward and swiped the machete left, right, left, right. "Get out!" he yelled again, barreling toward Ronnie.

Ronnie ran toward the man in the gray suit, staring back at the white eyes that tracked his movement.

"Are you hurt?"

"No," Ronnie responded.

"Good." The man in the gray shifted his eyes like gun barrels toward Anson. "Hey, boy!" *Huff.* "You ever wonder—" *Huff. Huff.* "—what it's like to have six hundred volts of electricity runnin' through your body?"

"I'll kill you," Anson said, picking up speed. "Show yourself!"

"I'll show you something," the man in gray said.

Anson stopped. His machete fell to the ground. He threw his head back. His entire body seized and vibrated uncontrollably. He let out a horrible, painful, gurgling sound.

The man in gray's breathing became heavier, his body straining. "The thing about the conscious mind is—" *Huff. Huff.* "—it can make perception and reality indecipherable." The man raised his hands as if reaching for Anson. "You would lay hands on this child—" *Huff. Huff.* "You won't lay hands on anyone ever again."

The man's hands brightened, then sparked into swirling red clouds. He couldn't believe what he was seeing.

Anson's feet rose off the pavement and dangled in the air.

The man in gray gave a final grunt and collapsed.

Anson's body flew backward down the slope, rolling until it stopped at the mouth of the tunnel.

The man in gray heaved on the ground like he'd sprinted a marathon. "Goddamn. That almost killed me." He worked his way up to a crouch.

Anson writhed on the ground, then struggled to get to his feet. The thick fabric trailed behind him as he vanished into the tunnel, bobbing side-to-side like his entire body was broken.

The man beside Ronnie vomited purple bile under the lamplight. "Damn. I used too much."

Ronnie turned his head away from the vomit. "Who are you?"

The man pulled a handkerchief out of his back pocket and wiped his mouth, then rose. He was rail-thin, his cheekbones sharp, with olive skin and pale blue eyes. "Davion Stivert. I'm an ally. I've been searching for you for years. I finally found you." He smiled.

The hat, the suit, the tan skin. The memory of Ronnie's journey through a decimated Knollwood Pines came back to him. He remembered the massive axe stuck in the ground. He remembered rounding the side of that axe and seeing a man in a gray suit standing on the other side of it. "That was you in the Gray World," Ronnie said. "After my accident."

"Ronnie!" Leslie's high-pitched voice rang through the woods behind Ronnie.

Preston's voice followed hers. "Ronnie! Where are you!"

Ronnie turned to the woods, the relief of hearing familiar voices overwhelming him.

"Leave them out of this fight," Davion said. "Trust in me."

When Ronnie turned back around, he was gone.

Leslie emerged from the woods, slapping cobwebs out of her hair. "Ronnie! What are you doing?"

Preston leaped out behind her, running toward the greenway. "Did you see him? Did he come this way?"

Ronnie didn't know what to say. He looked down at the machete lying inches from them and realized how close he had come to death, seeing the danger that he had put his friends in again.

Preston grabbed his shoulder—the bad shoulder. Ronnie shrieked.

"I'm sorry, I'm sorry," Preston said frantically.

"It's out of the socket, I think," Ronnie said.

"We'll get you help. Where's Gavin?"

Though Preston was drowning in uncertainty and panic, there was no use in hiding the truth. They'd failed.

"He's gone," Ronnie said.

Ronnie trekked back through the woods with Preston and Leslie by his side. They knew what was coming next and they couldn't risk being seen on Gavin's property on the night of his death.

Preston wept, saying he shouldn't have left Gavin alone.

Leslie tried to console him, telling Preston that it wasn't his fault.

Ronnie was a wanderer in his own body, the events of the night consuming him, every twinge of pain in his shoulder reminding him that it was all real. Of course, it wasn't Preston's fault. It was his. And he alone was responsible for solving this.

Chapter Twenty-Four

Malleck's face rubbed against the harsh surface of a burlap bag, the stench heavy under her nostrils. She'd been asked—though it did not feel like a request—to wear it for the last two hours of the car ride. It wouldn't matter either way, seeing as how the highways were cast in darkness, lit only by the headlights of oncoming vehicles. She'd become accustomed to the barnyard smell of the sack, so much so that she was eager to breathe in fresh air regardless of the setting.

The truck came to a stop. The metallic screech of Helga's rusted car door preceded a scamper of footsteps around the front of the vehicle. A hand grabbed hold of Malleck's arm and pulled her out of the truck. The motion was firm, but oddly gentle—not too rushed. Just as soon as the cold morning air hit her skin, the thick fabric of a heavy jacket fell atop Malleck's shoulders.

"Let's try to keep you warm," Helga said.

A click created a bright circle of light at Malleck's feet as the scents of browning leaves and tree bark seeped in through the bottom of the burlap sack. Below the thin opening at her chin, her boots alternated positions along a dirt path—manmade, from what she could tell. She was being led deep into the woods.

"I hope you're ready to stretch your legs," Helga said. "It's about a three-mile walk."

Malleck wished she'd been able to take that nap.

The burlap scraped against Malleck's nose as it slid off her face. The friction had left the tip of her nose raw, but any discomfort was erased by the image before her. Nine elderly men and women sat at a jagged wooden table. They were not particularly well-groomed. Their aged white hair was puffy and rough. They all wore long fur garments that covered them from head to toe and crowns carved from wood. The old man in the center, appearing to be in his seventies, stood from his position and smoothed his fur coat delicately. He wore the largest crown, which came to a point two feet above his spotted scalp. The hair on the sides of his head hung low and still, as did his long white beard. His skin sagged downward with years of world-weary experience.

Malleck understood him to be Elder Prime of the Manari Council.

Small brick chimneys sat at each end of the hut, which stood ten feet tall. The warmth of the flame wafted against Malleck's face, offsetting the chill behind her.

"You know why you have been brought here," Elder Prime spoke. "Tell us your sin."

Malleck's first instinct was to snap back. She found Helga in her periphery, who knew her too well and gave her a subtle head shake.

"One count," Malleck said. "I inserted myself into dangerous activities that are not the concern of the Manari."

Elder Prime nodded. "Is that all?"

Malleck sighed. "A second count. I revealed my magic to a non-sensitive being."

"You have revealed your power to many. And we have stood by, writing off your transgressions as those of an immature girl. But we can no longer tolerate your actions. To these crimes, what do you say?"

"I'm... sorry," Malleck lied.

"You understand you must be punished," the elder Manari said in a manner that was ambiguous. It could have been a statement or a question.

Malleck took another long look at Helga.

Elder Prime began a slow walk around the table, looming behind the heads of his fellow elders. "For centuries, the Manari have existed as a peaceful people. We are free from violence and hate. We remain pure of heart. While there are those who would damage the world around us, we, the Manari, know that our gifts position us with vast potential. We alone can channel the power of the gods and thus it is our responsibility to preserve the Earth as they intended." He sluggishly made his way to Malleck, his seven decades weighing against his knees. "We do not fight the wars of this world, for the earth is not a battlefield." He stared Malleck down, standing a few inches taller than her.

"Forgive me," Malleck said to Elder Prime, "but are we to simply sit back as lives are ruined by others who were granted the same gifts as us?"

"The doctrine is clear in its direction," Elder Prime said. "What others do with their gifts is not our—"

"Not our concern," Malleck cut him off. "Got it. But why shouldn't it be? You all sit here isolated from a world that's changed. You think you've created an environment free from evil, but all you've done is given evil the freedom to reign unobstructed. There are those who would use their gifts to *kill*, do you understand? Yet you seek out *me*? For what? You call it interfering. I'd say I didn't interfere enough. Another kid died in my hometown because our people are forbidden from conflict. The doctrine is three centuries old. It was created as a guide for peace on

Earth, not peace for one people. You want a clear direction, elders? Burn the doctrine and create a new one. Don't hoard your power. Use it."

With a deep inhale, Malleck quieted. Out of the corner of her eye, she could see Helga's head hung low. The elders sat stone-faced at the table. Malleck looked back up at the elder before her and awaited her fate. She knew what she said would make no difference, but *damn* it felt good to go off on them.

"Do you understand your punishment?" Elder Prime said.

"I *know* the punishment, sir... But I do not understand it."

Early morning sun warmed the woodland ground, which was scabbed over with frost from the night before. The setting had the appearance of a nineteenth-century community. The homes were made of clay. Hand-sewn garments hung from strings between branches. Animal noises livened the many acres of land—cows, roosters, chickens. There was no sign of electricity, and one freshwater well.

Malleck stood on a smooth circular wooden stage in a long white dress, worn leather boots, and a grayish fur coat. Underneath everything, her upper and lower body was covered in a material that, while not the most comfortable, was warm enough to bear the cool morning weather.

She thought many times of making a break for it, though she didn't know how well the boots on her feet would hold up in a sprint. There was also, of course, the not-insignificant matter of her having no idea where she was. She could search for hours for the truck, but being this tucked into the forest and not knowing her way, she'd risk branching off in an infinite number of directions, none of which led to that vehicle.

As per the custom for crimes against the doctrine, Malleck would be stripped of her power by what the Manari called the Affliction, a prolonged illness that affected the body's ability to produce magic, and sentenced to a year of service with this Manari commune. Her natural life would be put on hold for twelve months until she reintegrated, with her parents none the wiser. She'd resume her schooling and probably invent some story about traveling abroad for a year. She'd tell it so many times that she'd come close to believing it. Anything to numb the thought of a year of her life wasted because she used her gifts in a way the Manari deemed careless.

No. She would make it out. She would beat the Affliction and she would be better than this passive group of cowards, even if it meant she had to hide from them for the rest of her life.

The inhabitants of the community—men, women, and children in hand-sewn garments and heavy coats—gathered on long wooden benches, forming a horseshoe of an audience. Malleck, on full display, eyed the crowd silently, their breaths splashing and fading in the cool air. The lack of sleep was causing her body to sway, so much so that she expected her knees to give out at any moment.

The nine elders walked slowly from their hut, wearing their signature crowns and fur coats. Helga appeared at the back of the line, cupping a steel chalice between her hands with her shoulders hunched against her neck, careful not to spill. They formed a line in front of the stage, standing below Malleck between her and the crowd.

Elder Prime addressed the crowd. "You see before you a fellow Manari who has sworn an oath to the sacred doctrine."

Malleck tilted her head, squinting. *When exactly did I swear an oath?* she thought.

"She is your sister under the Manari custom," Elder Prime continued. "Though her sins against the doctrine are apparent and unchallenged."

I do remember challenging them, actually...

"For her sins, she must now succumb to the Affliction. It will be administered by her guardian of the Manari way, Sister Helga."

Sister Helga? What is she, a nun?

Helga stepped onto the stage with more effort than Malleck expected. There were no stairs leading up and so her plant leg required a bit of a hop to make it up. She spilled a drop of liquid in the process and looked horribly embarrassed.

"Smooth," Malleck said to Helga as she regained her posture and straightened out the chalice. "Is there anything left? I was really looking forward to drinking that."

Helga walked up to Malleck and whispered closely, "Malleck... I need you to trust me."

"That's a pretty tall task, all things considered," Malleck shot back.

"Just trust me." Helga winked.

Malleck cupped the chalice in her hands. She had once begged Helga to bring her to this place, hoping to embed herself in the practices of her people. She never expected her introduction to the commune to be like this.

She put the lip of the chalice to her mouth and recoiled at the cold bite of the steel. She downed the liquid in four gulps. The taste lingered on her tongue so strongly that she scrubbed it vigorously against the roof of her mouth to grind the sourness out. She handed the chalice back to Helga.

"It'll all be fine," Helga whispered. "I promise."

"Let us all be silent as the Affliction takes hold," the elder Manari said to the crowd.

The words dragged through Malleck's consciousness. Her knees, which were weak before, vanished from under her. Her field of vision lowered until she was flat against the stage, staring up at the face of her aunt.

Her fragmented memories of the following minutes were a blur of a passing sky and the ceiling of a clay hut. The Affliction would affect her power, but it would not affect her spirit. As soon as she could regain her strength, she'd begin her plan to escape.

Chapter Twenty-Five

R onnie woke up after a restless night's sleep, positioned on the shoulder that he last remembered being out of the socket. With his entire body weight pressed against it, he didn't feel the slightest hint of pain. His shoulder was fully healed.

His bedroom was alive with morning sunshine. The promise of a new day. He wished the light could wash away the failures of the night before, but his heart dropped with the realization that the town would soon know what he knew.

Ronnie took his phone off the nightstand.

At 5:01 AM, Leslie messaged the group:

Gavin found dead.
Dammit.

Ronnie came out of his room and found Cynthia in the kitchen, preparing the coffee maker for a fresh batch—not the first of the morning, he figured. She sat a bag of coffee on the counter and walked toward Ronnie with her arms wide.

Ronnie took a long look at Cynthia before she held him tighter than she had in recent years, tight enough that his ribs compressed. Purple pouches of skin sagged under her tired red eyes.

He played dumb. "What's wrong, Mom?"

Unlike the initial reporting of Therber's death, the reporting of Gavin's murder was incredibly detailed. There was a fifty-yard field in an undeveloped area outside of Knollwood Pines. Some person or a group of people had carried Gavin through the waist-high grass and smashed a wide circle down to create a clearing. A fixture of sticks, all sharpened at either end were placed methodically in the ground to form a chair in an inclined position. Gavin's naked body had been laid over top of the stakes. His arms were raised to the side and upward, with his forearms stuck against tall stakes on each side. His hands had been severed at the wrists and were nowhere to be found. Torches were placed around the circumference of the circle in five-foot increments. The splash of fire in the darkness was enough to cause a late-night driver to slow down for inspection. It didn't take the driver long to notice the body and call the police.

Therber was a dry run for Gavin, Ronnie thought.

The Neverwells *wanted* Gavin to be found. They were proud of what they'd done.

And now they had a set of severed hands for their offering.

Ronnie took the passenger's seat of Leslie's car. They were quiet at first, a stirring silence hanging over them.

Leslie put the car in reverse and backed out of the driveway.

"So," Leslie said to him, "what do we do now?"

As if Ronnie had any plan whatsoever. "We just... try to act normal."

"We need her, Ronnie," Leslie said. "Whatever you have to do to get Malleck to help, do it."

Ronnie thought better of sharing his encounter with the man who saved him. Malleck wasn't his only weapon against the Neverwells. Davion Stivert was out there somewhere, and Ronnie hadn't the faintest idea how to get to him.

Ronnie put his head against the window, the cool glass chilling his skin.

"Don't go quiet on me, Hendrix," Leslie said. "We got a book to find."

After what she'd been through, she still wanted to help Ronnie. She was the greatest friend he could have asked for, probably the best he would ever have. That's why he couldn't put her life in danger again.

"Hey," Leslie said, "we're going to figure this thing out, right?"

"Yeah, we'll figure it out... together," he lied.

They rode to school, preparing themselves for a somber Thursday morning at Knollwood Pines High, dreading the announcement on the loudspeaker that another fellow student had tragically passed.

Malleck wasn't in the art classroom when Ronnie entered. He waited patiently for her, poking mindlessly at his canvas, carelessly filling in the outline of a snowy mountain range over a thick blue sky.

Ms. Springle bounced over Ronnie with a smile nearly pleasant enough to dull the dread in his stomach.

"How are we doing with our canvas, Ronnie?" Ms. Springle asked.

"I think I have a good, uh... foundation, I guess you'd call it?" Ronnie said. "Just need to start filling in the details."

Ms. Springle giggled. "You can call it a foundation. That seems appropriate. That's the great thing about art. It can be whatever we want it to be." She sat at the seat normally occupied by Malleck. "How's everything going? You know…"

"Reintegrating into society?"

Ms. Springle giggled again. "Sure, that's one way to put it."

"It's been… different," Ronnie said.

"It'll get better. These things just take time. I don't want this class to feel like class to you. Art should be an escape."

If only she knew where Ronnie's artistic expression had gotten him. "It doesn't feel like class," he assured her. "I enjoy being here. Malleck's been a good mentor."

"Wonderful. She's a very talented girl. Let me know if you need anything, okay?" With a warm smile, Ms. Springle migrated to another table.

Ronnie looked back at his canvas, eyeing lines of white paint that hadn't been there before. He leaned back in shock, nearly falling out of his seat. The lines connected into text that read:

MEET AT KNOLLWOOD PINES PARK AT NOON

With one blink, the white text was gone.

Knollwood Pines Park was two miles from the school, separated by a large intersection cutting through three lanes of traffic on each side. Ronnie figured he could walk two miles in forty minutes tops, factoring in the wait time at the crosswalk.

Chapter Twenty-Six

R onnie walked down the paved entrance of Knollwood Pines Park, past the parking lot, which was relatively empty at that time of day, and onto the pale sidewalk that separated the park into halves. On one half was a fenced-in dog park, a children's playground, and a basketball court. On the other half were two baseball fields and a sand volleyball pit. The grass on either side was a lush green so vibrant it looked artificial. Maybe, Ronnie thought, that was the point of parks. These so-called natural areas weren't meant to make us feel closer to nature, they were meant to give the illusion of nature. Truthfully, every square foot of Knollwood Pines Park was the result of intensive, and very expensive, planning and construction.

Ronnie slid his hood off the top of his head, inviting the warmth of sunshine onto his face. Whether the park was an illusion of nature or not, there was an undeniable ease to a space free from the clutter of metal and concrete that a town like Knollwood Pines couldn't avoid. Even though the October air was cold, it still carried the pleasant smell of grass, bark, and leaves.

His watch revealed that he was twenty minutes early. Two dogs played while their owners watched in the dog park. A jogger in a puffy vest and tights passed. Everything seemed completely normal as he scanned his surroundings...

Except for the man in a gray suit and gray fedora on a park bench at the side of the walkway, waving Ronnie over to him.

Davion sat with his legs crossed and his arms propped up against the back of the bench, smooth and casual.

Ronnie began to close the distance. The man's features became clearer in the daylight. The olive skin on his face was tight and wrinkled. His pale blue eyes were gentle and bright. His white dress shirt was unbuttoned at the top, giving way to a pad of gray chest hair.

"I knew you'd come," he said. "And I'm so glad you did."

"I didn't know whether I should," Ronnie replied. "But I figured if you got me out of that situation last night, you're a friend, not a foe."

"Not a foe at all," Davion said happily. "Would you like to sit?"

"Uh," Ronnie thought for a moment. "I'd prefer to stand actually."

"Right, right, very well." Davion's slight Southern drawl turned his i's into a's. "Well, I suppose we should get introductions out of the way, shouldn't we? How do I... I'm trying to find the words to express..." The man stammered. He pulled his suit jacket snug against his shoulders then took the same position, legs crossed, arm over the back of the bench. "This all must be so confusing for you, Ronnie." the man said.

Ronnie's stomach dropped at the sound of his name, disturbed that the stranger knew it.

"This may be difficult to hear, but..." Davion stopped for a moment and seemed to reconsider what he was about to say. "No... I think I'll wait on that, actually."

"Thank you for what you did for me," Ronnie said. "If you hadn't shown up... I don't know what would have happened to me."

Davion laughed. The laughter turned into a hacking cough. "You saw what happens when an old, sick man runs to your rescue. I thought the run was gonna make me drop dead, but the magic... Well, my magic ain't what it used to be. Quite the embarrassment, really."

"You threw that guy off his feet," Ronnie said. "How did you..." He wasn't sure what to ask.

"Here, you know what," Davion stood and smoothed out his suit jacket and pants. "This is a lot to take in, son. Why don't you have a seat? It's occurred to me that maybe you'd prefer to not share the bench with me, and that's fine, but it seems like you need to take a load off more than I do."

Ronnie remained standing. "You said you've been looking for me for a while. Why?"

"Well, you have to understand, Ronnie, I'm..." Davion took a deep breath and put his hands on his hips, brushing back either side of his suit jacket. He looked at the sky, then looked down at the boy before him. "I'm your father, Ronnie."

In the past few days, Ronnie had learned of murder, sacrifices, and extraordinary supernatural abilities, but this was by far the most surprising thing to fall at his feet that week. Were he not sitting, he would have fallen straight to the ground as the words turned his body into bricks.

For sixteen years of his life, Ronnie had only known small morsels of information about his father. He had heard that his father wasn't a good man, and that very shortly after Ronnie was born, his mom decided it best that she leave him and start fresh. Whereas so many other children had two parents, he only had one. He never knew the excitement of a father coming home after work. He only knew a rotating catalog of masculine faces that would pick his mom up for dates. They'd smile and wave and some would shake his hand, but very few of them stayed around longer than six months.

Davion Stivert, the man who claimed to be Ronnie's biological father, spoke quickly as Ronnie listened stone-faced.

"Let me ask you somethin', son," Davion said.

"Don't call me that," Ronnie said quickly, like a reflex. This wasn't a strange man simply calling him son the way a teacher or a coach or a doctor would—this was a man who believed it in context. That context was too much for Ronnie to process all at once.

"Okay, right. Baby steps," Davion corrected himself. "You've been getting hurt and healing almost immediately, right?"

Ronnie looked down and thought back to his shoulder that healed overnight—the bruises that lined his midsection like a quilt, then disappeared. He nodded his head in recognition. "Almost a year ago I fell off a water tower. All the doctors said it was a miracle I survived, much less came away without any sort of long-lasting injuries at all. The kids at school call me 'the indestructible kid'. But... how did you..." He didn't finish the question. He looked over at Davion who had his hand against the light scruff of his chin, nodding to himself.

"It's starting, just like they said it would. Everything's comin' together now," Davion said. He looked directly at Ronnie. "I always wondered why I couldn't feel you before. Believe me, I tried. The world seemed so massive, and my reach felt so insignificant, but about a year ago, I felt somethin'... Like a shockwave that slapped me in the face and pushed me to the ground. Somethin' I'd never felt before in my life. And I saw you. I stepped into the world you created, and for the briefest moment, I saw a boy I didn't know then was my son." He grinned and let out a small laugh, choking on it. "It took me a while to find you. My power's been dwindling for years. I'm glad I got to you before that sumbitch."

Ronnie's knees began to give. He fell against the bench, letting his weight sink against the wood. Davion took a seat next to him, resting his elbows on his knees. "Ronnie... You were born under... unusual circumstances. You may have felt your whole life that you're different from other kids. That you're some alien from a distant planet and have to walk and talk like these other earthlings amongst you, but it's just not you. Well... I can tell you you're not an alien, but... you're certainly different. Let me start at the beginning. I know your mind's probably spinnin' in circles right now, but trust me, the more you hear, the more things will start to make sense."

Cynthia was twenty-two and directionless when she met Davion Stivert. Having just dropped out of college for the second time, she scraped together any money she could to move from city to city, preferring a nomadic lifestyle to the career woman in a shoulder-padded blazer like many of her colleagues aspired to be. She preferred to meet interesting people and do interesting things in exciting places, but mostly she ended up getting waitressing jobs at bars in rural areas with low populations.

One day she swung open the saloon doors of a western-themed bar in Grace City, Idaho. She'd been attracted to the state because of its vast mountain ranges and natural areas, which she visited frequently in her van that moonlighted as a bedroom. Even with a roof between her and the sky, she'd never felt more free than she did sleeping under the stars. She was quickly waved out of the bar rather apathetically. The town had fewer than a thousand residents, so unless some population boom happened soon, there was no need for another helping hand.

Cynthia caught Davion's eye as she exited the bar. He had gone into town to fetch some supplies for his woodland-based community. They made the most out of the acre of land, living in bunks inside of sturdy homes built ten years prior. They mostly lived off the land, but came into town in the fall when the crops couldn't produce. Davion asked Cynthia for directions to the nearest grocery store, even though he knew the town well. She feigned a confident response, offering to walk him there herself. Thirty minutes later, they had nothing but a dirt road in front of them and civilization behind them. The entire walk, Davion knew she was leading him in the wrong direction, but he didn't much care.

They had an instant connection. Davion, ten years Cynthia's senior, kept up an earthy bohemian style, accentuated by long flowing hair, loose pants, and worn shoes that paired well with Cynthia's carefree aesthetic. They talked, laughed, and made eyes at each other. It wasn't long before he extended a very gentlemanly invitation to see the commune. She obliged.

Cynthia instantly fell in love with the commune. No technology, all smiles. Everyone had a role to play. Each member, forty-two in total, had purpose and drive. Davion, the leader of the group, worked as hard as anyone else, his only distinction between the other members being an individual room where he stayed. It was the side room of the largest structure, which functioned as a school for the six children they had and a rec center for indoor meetings. She parked her van just outside the entrance and it stayed put for months. She moved into one of the cabins and eventually moved in with Davion. As they became closer, Davion made the decision to reveal the true purpose of their community.

Their group harnessed incredible abilities, which they intended to use to create a new utopia. With their gifts, they could access each other's minds and create a true shared consciousness. There would be no shame or guilt, only empathy and understanding. They could enter an alternate plane of existence that allowed them to create beautiful landscapes, where they could design a better world and experience pure expression and joy.

They built the commune with the purest of intentions but no real guidance on how to spread their gift. Was it even possible to do this? It wasn't until they met Sebastian Kraek, a powerful and wise elderly man who found them while traveling the plane, that they were given true direction. He explained that they were given the power of the gods and so only gods could grant their power to others. The gods, Sebastian said, were angry at the state of the world, sickened by the purveyors of evil, and shunned humanity. The power Davion and his following possessed, therefore, was merely the result of lineage. Luck and nothing more.

Sebastian Kraek spoke of a prophecy. A child born of pure intention would one day have the ability to create an entity. The child wouldn't be a powerful sorcerer, but rather an architect. The child would be born to create the instructions that would lead to the conjuring of a new god, one of their own making. When all of the gods had left humanity behind, the child would create the ritual to make a new one.

When Cynthia became pregnant with Ronnie, Sebastian assisted Davion in performing daily rituals to ensure the prophecy came true. Cynthia spent each day at the center of a large circle of people, focusing all of their energy into Cynthia's womb as the fetus grew.

When Ronnie was born, Sebastian, Davion, and the rest of the commune had no way of verifying whether the prophecy had been fulfilled.

But a week before Ronnie's first birthday, Cynthia took him and vanished in the night.

Davion made it his life's mission to find Ronnie again so that they, together, could bestow the power of the gods onto the world.

Ronnie took this history in without saying a word. It was absurd and unbelievable but delivered with such unbroken confidence that it had to be true.

"You see, Ronnie," Davion said, "when you fell off that water tower, it must've set something off. That sudden jolt, that fight or flight response, it awakened what's been in you this whole time. You're connected to the entity, protected by its magic."

"What?" Ronnie said, trying to comprehend. "Protected by magic?"

Davion spoke. "He grants life to the righteous..."

Ronnie's stomach sank. How could Davion know that passage from Ronnie's book?

"And damns evil committed," Davion continued. "He gives power to the powerless... And banishes the wicked. Provide the severed offerings and roar into the night... For they who summon..." His mouth hung open, inviting Ronnie to speak.

"Karnalaxe," Ronnie whispered.

"For those who summon *the entity* control its very might," Davion corrected. "That's what we chanted night after night until you were born. We never named it. That was a responsibility given to you. It's your birthright."

It was all true—Ronnie sensed it in his gut and deep in his bones.

"You can't jump inside someone's mind like I can, and you might not be able to conjure images, but you're the most important thing our people have ever had... A way forward. You're our chance at salvation."

Ronnie sat with his brows furrowed and body limp against the cool bench. The Neverwells worshiped him as some kind of idol, following his written word like gospel. Davion's explanation, farfetched as it was... actually made sense.

"I know this is a lot to take in. I'm so sorry I haven't been there for you. I wish with every fiber of my being that I could have been in your life, but... Oh, I'm sure your mother's done a wonderful job raising you. I've forgiven her for how she left. If you want to walk away forever, I'll respect your decision. It's a decision you're old and mature enough to make for yourself. But if you want me to stick around, I promise you, we will figure this thing out together. I will help you get through this."

Ronnie took a few deep breaths. "Let's say I believe what you're saying. You talk about me creating a pathway to some being or entity or whatever you call it. The book I made is for a *demon*. It's... awful. It came from a very dark place during a very bad time. It's already resulted in two deaths."

"We poured so much energy into you. Day in and day out, transferring waves of magic into you so that you can do this very thing. You call it a demon. You could just as easily call it a god."

"It comes from the Underworld."

"It doesn't matter where it comes from. What matters is the power it wields. It can end all evil. It can give our power to the weak. It can make the world better. *That's* what we worked so hard to conjure. *That's* what *you* created, Ronnie. Sometimes revolution requires sacrifice, and I think you knew this when you created the book, maybe not consciously, but deep down. Down to your core, you knew the path forward to make the world better."

Every ounce of sanity left in Ronnie made him want to scream at Davion to stop. "This plan, I... I have to stop it from happening. You say I can make the blueprint, right? I'll just make another one. Something that doesn't involve sacrifice or demons or body parts. Something *good* that isn't just rattled out of my messed-up head on a whim. Something that doesn't put my friends in danger."

"Then let me help you," Davion said. "Son—uh, Ronnie—I'm growing weaker by the day, and so too is my power. Every time I use it, I can feel myself slippin'. What I'm sayin' is, my days are numbered. After all these years, I've found you. If getting that book back is the last thing I do for you—the one good thing I do for you—then I can die happy. Whatever you decide to do after that is up to you."

Ronnie took a long look at Davion. Years of pain, emotional and physical, were suddenly evident in his expression where they weren't before. The man was too thin, disappearing under a tailored suit from a bygone time, his wrists swallowed by the cuffs, his collar spaced generously around his neck.

Ronnie thought back to Malleck, the first person who revealed a world of magic and mystery to him, but every piece of information she gave was like a jagged piece of a puzzle that didn't fit the whole. She had refused to help. Davion made everything feel complete. Davion wanted to march into battle by Ronnie's side.

"So, what do you say? Are we gonna get these shitheads or what?" Davion asked.

Chapter Twenty-Seven

Ronnie left the park with a card in his pocket that had Davion's number on it. For a man who spent the last couple of decades in a cult, he went to great lengths to present himself professionally. As for Davion's offer, Ronnie gave no answer. A random stranger just confessed to being his father, and he didn't take that lightly. It was as if he'd awaken from a long sleep—the truth of his upbringing revealed to him.

But there was one other person he needed to speak with, the only one who could validate his very existence as a child born to a free-range cult.

He walked across the highway and right past the high school. He had no intention of going back. The guilt of lives lost and the solemn environment was too much for him. He'd be looking over his shoulder, expecting to be found out as the cause of all the dread. He needed to be alone with his thoughts. More than anything, he needed to be prepared to confront his mother and get answers, *real* answers, about his upbringing. His legs moved steadily for an hour until the joints in his hips ached and the bottoms of his feet yearned for relief.

The more Ronnie learned about himself, the more alone and confused he became. So he allowed himself to be alone and confused. He found the spare key under the mat on his front porch and went inside his home. He sat in relative silence with only the creak of a shifting house and his own thoughts to accompany him.

It was just after six when Cynthia arrived home. October nights began early in North Carolina and the sun was almost hidden completely from their neighborhood. She walked in with her suit jacket folded over her purse-holding arm and sneakers in place of her heels.

Ronnie was sitting in the corner chair of the family room, which gave a full view of the front lawn through two large window frames, but the drapes had been placed over the windows to further darken the room. Cynthia flicked on a light and jumped at the sight of him.

Holding her chest, Cynthia said, "Jesus, are you trying to scare me?"

"I need to talk to you," Ronnie said sternly. "And I need you to be straight with me."

Cynthia sat her purse down on the table that lined the wall. "Sure, okay... Would you like to help me with dinner? We could chat about whatever it is you—"

"I need to know about my father," Ronnie cut her off. "But I need to know more than 'he wasn't in the picture' or 'he wasn't a great guy'. I've gone my whole life knowing virtually nothing about where I come from. I'm a bastard and I need to know why."

"Don't you ever call yourself that," Cynthia said. She put her suit jacket on the arm of the living room couch and sat at an angle facing her son. "Never call yourself a bastard."

"Where was I born, Mom? Where was I raised? Where were we before all this?" Ronnie asked in rapid-fire succession.

"Why are you asking all of these questions now?" Cynthia asked.

"Because I'm sixteen, mom! And I'm messed up!" Ronnie slapped his head hard enough for it to hurt. "Can't you see that! I'm not right!"

"Stop it!"

"Either you tell me or I'll go out looking," Ronnie said, giving Cynthia a deathly look. It was as angry an expression as he'd ever directed at his mother, and it was clear to him that it frightened her.

That fright turned to sadness.

"The reason I don't talk about it," Cynthia said, pressing her back against the couch, "the reason I *never* talk about it... is because I'm ashamed. I was so stupid, Ronnie. I was young and I was dumb and I made every bad decision until I had you. All of a sudden I had this beautiful baby boy that I would do anything for. I'd do anything to protect you. It took me too long to realize that where I was and the people I was with... I wasn't protecting you at all."

"Why do you say that?" Ronnie let a long pause linger between them, daring her answer.

Cynthia clenched her teeth. "Your dad and I were in a... I guess you would call it a cult."

Ronnie's chest seized.

"There's no other way to say it," Cynthia continued. "It seemed so beautiful and peaceful. It was everything I ever wanted, but it was just a dumb fairy tale. There was no way I could raise a child in that place. The things they were doing there..." She paused. She took a quick side glance at her son.

Ronnie could tell she was thinking carefully about what to say next. "What kind of things were they doing, Mom?"

"Look... I've done drugs in my life. I know what it's like to have a good trip and a bad trip and feel like you're in another world, but what these people were doing—your father included—was trying to conjure up... gods. That's what they told me." She put her hands up to her face in frustration and breathed hard into them. "It was so stupid. *I* was so stupid. The whole thing was nonsense."

"Are you... sure it was all nonsense?" Ronnie asked. Surely, she had to have seen something out of the ordinary while she was with Davion.

Cynthia, her face red from rubbing it against her hands, gave Ronnie an *Are you kidding me?* kind of look. "We're talking about magic, Ronnie. Candles and spells and all that dumb shit. I don't remember a lot from that time. The whole time I was pregnant with you, everything was so... fuzzy. But sometimes..." She thought hard, recalling a moment in her mind. "I get the faintest memory of being surrounded by a circle of men. They're chanting. All these candles everywhere. And there's your father with his hands on my stomach... on *you*... And his hands are glowing... Glowing red."

Ronnie tried to suppress his shock. He remembered being on the trail, seeing Davion's white eyes. The man's hands were glowing red.

"It's bullshit, of course. I've been through enough therapy to know that it was just a coping mechanism to deal with the stress of pregnancy in isolation. Hands don't glow. Magic isn't real. And, depending on who you ask, there's only one god."

Ronnie studied her expression. She wasn't trying to make herself believe what she was saying. She believed every word.

"When I confronted your dad about wanting to leave, he... he got angry with me. He said you were important, not just to him, but everyone there. He forbade me from leaving. And that was when I knew it was time for us to go. He didn't hit me or anything. I just didn't feel good about being there any longer." Cynthia looked at Ronnie, indicating that she was finished.

"Wow." Ronnie imagined Cynthia's brain going in circles trying to find a proper way to fill everything in without making it crazy. "And where were we before moving here?"

"The mountains in Idaho," Cynthia said.

And that was it. Ronnie ran his fingers over his jeans pocket and the edges of Davion's card within it.

Suddenly, his phone buzzed. It cut the tension in the room between him and Cynthia.

"You go ahead and answer that," Cynthia said, wiping the moisture away from her eyes. "I'll go get dinner started. But listen, from now on, no more secrets. If you have questions, I'll answer them. You're not messed up. You're *my* son and I love you. Very, very much."

"I love you too, Mom," Ronnie said.

Cynthia smiled, looking relieved, then sniffled. She stood and walked out of the living room.

Ronnie took his phone out of his pocket and unlocked the screen. There was one unread text message in the group chat between Ronnie, Preston, and Leslie.

The text from Preston read:

Guys Jack says he's coming to my house now.
Thinks I had something to do with Gavin.
He's not in his right mind. I'm afraid of what he might do.

Ronnie thought for a moment, then texted back:

Meet at The Rambler in twenty minutes. Avoid Jack.
He's next.

Ronnie left a note on the kitchen counter telling his mother that he was out with friends and she shouldn't worry, though he knew that was an impossible thing to ask of her. He left the house and mounted his bike while Cynthia was changing in her room.

He took the business card out of his pocket and dialed Davion Stivert's number. The wind rushed into the phone as he took a right turn out of Surry Dale Street. His voice must have been horribly muffled on Davion's end, but as soon as Davion answered "Hello?" Ronnie told him he'd accepted his offer. In the fifteen minutes it took him to ride his bike, drifting between sidewalks and streets, they devised a plan with Jack Sutter smack dab at the center of it.

Chapter Twenty-Eight

Leslie walked into The Rambler and spotted Preston over the half-wall in the last booth down. The Rambler was lively with patrons drinking and laughing. A group of four waited idly for a way-too-intense pool match to finish up so they could finally snag the table.

Preston's face was smeared with shame or guilt or embarrassment, Leslie guessed. She couldn't tell which emotion it was specifically, but for such a conventionally handsome guy, Preston could morph into a scared puppy instantly. Leslie was even more drawn to him because of that. He wasn't one to fake his emotions. Just like Leslie's *screw you and screw the system* attitude, everything was in plain view.

Leslie rounded the half-wall and joined Preston on the other side of the booth. He had three waters sitting at the table. The glass in front of him was only a quarter of the way full. The glass to his left and the glass on the opposite side of the table were both full. She took the seat next to him.

"How you doin' there, champ?" she said.

Preston shrugged. "Oh, you know... Former best friend hates me, probably thinks I murdered his buddy that I've known since elementary school and now is out to get me."

Leslie chuckled, though knew immediately that it was in poor taste. *Shit*, this was an awkward situation. "If he actually thought you had anything to do with it, he'd be calling the police. Jack's a real jackass, but he hurts just like you and me. Probably worse, as a matter of fact. All that pent-up masculine energy just can't mix with genuine sadness. He's looking for someone to blame right now."

"Well, he has a reason to hate me. Whether he's in the wrong or not," Preston said.

"Oh," Leslie said. "Am I missing out on some tea?" She made a cup with her hand and stirred it with an invisible spoon.

Preston took a quick minute to tell her the history between him and Jack, from Ronnie's accident up until the present.

"What a frickin' baby," Leslie said after Preston finished.

"Hey, be nice. Two of his friends just died. I mean…" Preston rubbed his face hard enough that Leslie thought he'd pull his skin clean off. "Were brutally murdered and staged like mannequins."

This was really getting to Preston and Leslie wondered how much more any of them could take.

"Yeah," Leslie said, "even though he's a jackass, we should still have sympathy for him."

"And even though Gavin was a terrible guy…" Preston thought back to his experience inside Malleck's memory, that vivid recollection of Gavin trying to force himself on her and failing. "He didn't deserve what happened to him. Whatever Ronnie wrote up for Jack… He doesn't deserve it either."

They both sat in silence, allowing space for each other to breathe for one melancholic moment.

"I talked to my uncle about your band," Preston said, breaking the silence. "He said he can't pay you but he'd love to host you all."

Leslie perked up in her seat. "Really?" She tried to play off her excitement. "Doesn't he, like, want to hear a demo or something?"

"Nah, I told him you were in a punk band and told him the name and he was in. He said Acid Gum Drops was all he needed to hear," Preston smiled.

Leslie smiled back. "It's a working title... But it works for now. What do you think about 'Square Pegs'?"

"Doesn't have the same edge to it."

"You're probably right... So, when are we doing this thing?"

"In a couple weeks? I think we could use some music to, you know..." Preston paused, looking for the words.

But Leslie found them for him. "To thrash to." She made horns with her index and pinky fingers and stuck her tongue out.

Preston smiled again and gave her a few cool nods. The smile was goofy and dumb and tickled her stomach.

Chapter Twenty-Nine

A row of aged oak trees with long branches hung over the street that separated the Collinsworth home from a small park area with a soccer field. The homes were lined with pumpkins and skeletons and cobwebs. Orange and green light punched the fronts of houses and holograms of ghosts danced in the windows. A cool evening breeze kicked bundles of leaves down the road and sidewalk.

Ronnie pedaled up to Preston's house, a cozy two-story home that looked quaint in comparison to the goliath that was Gavin's home, and squeezed his hand brake lightly, coming to a smooth and quiet stop at the front of the driveway. He immediately noticed Jack's car parked outside the garage with its dark blue paint and leather interior.

Getting rid of the book meant securing the book first. The only chance Ronnie and Davion had of doing that was to find the Neverwells in the middle of their ritual. This meant allowing Jack to be captured and putting him at extreme risk, but Davion promised he wouldn't be hurt. He promised he'd do right by Ronnie if it was the last thing he ever did.

For Davion Stivert, he didn't have to tail someone by car in order to follow them. He could follow what he called the energy signature. Every person, he informed Ronnie, vibrates at a frequency and radiates energy that goes unnoticed to the standard human eye. Davion, however, could trace the energy signatures of any individual if given one of their possessions. He was like a bloodhound, but with a nose for magic. His task for Ronnie was to secure an object from Jack—an article of clothing, or a pencil, or a notebook, perhaps.

Ronnie slid the kickstand out on his bike and circled the exterior of the car, eyeing the rolled down window and the goofy-looking fuzzy dice hanging over his mirror. An item with his energy signature that could be tracked, perfect for the taking. He began to reach for it, but stopped. He looked up at the second story of the house, where he imagined Jack was waiting. Even if he stopped the bloodshed, it wouldn't end any vendetta Jack had with Preston or with him. He didn't even know if Jack would make it through the week. He owed Jack nothing but had this urge deep in his gut to make amends. The guilt of Therber and Gavin was too much for him to bear.

Ronnie walked to the front door, up the porch steps, and rang the doorbell. After about a minute of waiting and Ronnie pondering whether he should leave, a youthful-looking man in his forties answered the door in a tee shirt with a ring of sweat around the neck and gym shorts. He was panting heavily, but smiled through the short breaths.

"Hey there!" he said energetically.

"Hey, um... Mr. Collinsworth?" Ronnie asked with his finger pointed awkwardly, then immediately remembered Preston telling him about the cool stepdad.

"Nah, call me Fred," he said with a smile. "Are you here to see Preston? He's not home, but he should be back any minute. He's got another friend upstairs waiting on him too," the sweaty man wiped his face with his forearm. "Sorry I'm such a mess. I'm in the middle of a ride. Do you know Jack?"

"Yeah..." Ronnie said unconvincingly. "The three of us are working on a project together."

"Oh great. Well, come on in." Fred stood aside, opening the door wider for Ronnie.

Ronnie walked through and Fred closed the door behind him. Ronnie remembered that Preston's mother was looking to buy a house in another neighborhood, but he couldn't fathom anyone wanting to leave this place. The living room was beautifully decorated in dark green and gold accents. Such attention to theme that it could have been a page in a catalog. The living room branched out into the kitchen and the den, spaced apart in a way that was foreign to Ronnie, who had grown up in a much smaller, more compact home.

"Preston's room is upstairs, first room on the left. Hey..." the man lowered his voice. "Were you close with Therber and Gavin as well?"

The question punched Ronnie in the gut. He swallowed the small amount of saliva in his throat, resulting in an embarrassingly comical gulp. "No. We weren't close, but, uh..."

"It's hard losing a classmate," Fred's breathing had slowed to a more comfortable cadence. He put his sweaty hand on Ronnie's shoulder. "You tell me if you need anything, okay?"

Ronnie was touched by the blatant sincerity. *This is the environment that produces a kid like Preston*, he thought. He thanked Fred and walked up the stairs.

The door to Preston's room was cracked open and it was quiet on the other side. So quiet that the creaks of Ronnie's footsteps in the hallway seemed to echo. He stood at the front of the door and took a deep breath, then pushed it open.

Jack was sitting at the edge of Preston's bed, limp and hunched over. The ceiling-high bookcase between the bed and the closet offered Ronnie momentary comfort as he recognized it from his video call with Preston and Leslie. He wished he was with them now.

"What are you doing here, shit weasel?" Jack asked.

Shit weasel... Clever, Ronnie thought. "What are *you* doing here?"

Jack tilted his head left, then right, causing two loud cracks. He put on a phony sincere voice. "I'm just here to see my old pal Preston. You know, the guy who seems so fond of you." He then got deadly serious. "So, what, are you two, like, 'with' each other now or whatever? He seems to be really protective of you."

Ronnie didn't answer, not because it was a dumb question, but because he took it to be rhetorical. Jack, at his core, was an asshole.

Jack stood from the bed. "And you know what... My friends seem to be dying all around me. And Preston just... *happens* to be there right before shit goes down. I just thought I'd ask him what's up with that."

"Preston wouldn't hurt a fly," Ronnie said. "You've known him longer than I—"

"Hate to burst your bubble, kid, but he's not the sweet innocent guy you think he is. But since *you're* here now, and you seem to be so close with him, I'll ask you... What's up with that, *Ronnie*?" He said Ronnie's name with a mocking inflection.

Looking into Jack's crazed, depressed gaze, Ronnie had no idea what the high school senior would do and it terrified him. There was nothing he could say to make the situation better, so he said nothing.

But Jack continued, blowing warm, pungent breath into Ronnie's face. "Why do my friends keep dying, *Ronnie*?" His eyes began to water. Something clicked in his brain and he tilted his head. "Why are my friends dying... the same week we roughed you up in the woods?"

This is it, Ronnie thought. *He found me out.* The guilt was boiling inside Ronnie, ready to pour out of his mouth like vomit. "I'm really sorry about Gavin and Therber. I hope whoever killed them gets what they deserve."

"You don't mean that, shit weasel. You hated their goddamn guts. Don't even pretend like you care." Jack turned around, slowly and aimlessly walking the length of Preston's bedroom. "You know, I woke up this morning a little groggy. Another bad night's sleep. You ever lost someone you cared about, Hendrix?"

Ronnie didn't respond. He knew Jack wasn't a guy to exhibit high emotion. He was a leader. And leaders can't show weakness. All of the sadness that must have been radiating through his bones had to be dealt with alone.

"In the locker room, I've been rallying the team around this idea. Making them believe that Therber's spirit would lead us to victory. Just trying to find some silver lining in all this. It's all bullshit. Every time I close my eyes, all I see is a face without eyes staring at me.

"So I checked my phone this morning. See an unread text from the night before." Jack took out his phone and brought the screen to Ronnie's face.

On the screen, Gavin smiled at the bottom left corner of the frame, with Preston at the upper right corner, standing mid-motion in a failed attempt to hide his face. The caption from Gavin read: "Can you believe this asshole?"

"I just thought it was funny," Jack continued. "Probably just Preston putting on his big boy trousers and trying to intimidate his former buddy-turned-foe. But shit, the nerve of that guy to show up on Gavin's doorstep before Therber's body was in the ground. Then the texts started rolling in and I found out that Gavin…" He choked back tears. "You're a bastard, right Hendrix?"

"What?" Ronnie said.

"Everyone knows it." Jack took a seat on the bed, his exhaustion evident in the way he sunk down on the mattress. "Your mom begged all the other football moms to pitch in for your medical bills. Single mom who couldn't support her own kid in a coma. Pretty sad, really." Jack said it with so much apathy that Ronnie considered just leaving him to the Neverwells. Let whatever was going to happen happen.

"Funny thing is, though," Jack said. "You might be lucky. My dad... kinda sucks. It's dominance over everything with him. All that financial stuff he does, it just bores the shit out of me, but even at a young age he taught me that it wasn't about the substance of what people did for a living. All that mattered was the respect you can command... Dominance over everything, Hendrix."

Ronnie wasn't sure where this was going. Jack was spiraling in real time, convinced that words he was speaking would help make sense of his emotions.

Jack's veiny eyes met Ronnie's. He held that angry, devilish stare as he spoke. "When I was younger, my dad would take me boating. No motors, no luxury quarters with a bed underneath, even though he could have afforded all that. Just the two of us and the sea, guiding the boat by hand with nothing but sails and ropes. If we veered off the path and lost our way, my dad stayed composed, confident that we'd find our way back."

Crazed aggression radiated from Jack, causing the air to thicken in Ronnie's lungs. He wanted so badly to sprint down the stairs, but feared that Jack would strike. If Ronnie knew anything, it was that he was no match for Jack in a footrace. Jack would find him. Quickly.

"This one time when I was ten, we went out to the coast, ignoring these fat dark clouds that were rolling in. My dad had had a rough quarter and, dammit, he needed to find peace in the sea." Jack laughed. "The farther we went out, the thicker the waves got and the darker the clouds got. Until we were hanging on for our lives hoping the boat wouldn't capsize. It was the only time I'd shown fear in front of my father. He shielded me from the waves and I couldn't even tell whether I was crying or just wet. Everything was so slippery. He yelled at me to be strong, but I just cried and cried and cried. It was the most scared I'd ever been.

"He didn't take me boating for eight months after that. The day after I turned eleven, I asked him when we could go take the boat out again.

You know what he said?... He threw on his overcoat and picked up his briefcase and said, 'When you're strong enough', then walked out the door. That was it. I was a disappointment to him because I couldn't stay composed. Because I couldn't handle my shit. So that's what I intend to do."

Ronnie let the silence grow between them.

"What are you gonna do?" Ronnie asked. "You think using your fists is going to make everything alright?"

Jack let out a crazed laugh. "With Therber, it was easier, you know. I loved Therber like a brother, but, honestly... I kinda felt sorry for him. Every time I introduced Therber to a girl, it was like handing bug spray to a hornet's nest. Therber didn't get along with a lot of people and didn't really say much. He was just kind of... there. But Gavin... He was my boy. And it turns out he was found dead in a similar way to how Therber was. They were... carved up. As far as I can tell, there's one common link. Preston, who seemed to be standing in front of each of them the night before they died."

"Jack, I'm telling you... Preston had nothing to—"

"I know I can't prove shit. I could send that picture to the cops, but what's the fun in that? Nah, I'm handling my shit. That boy scout you think you know is no boy scout at all. It's a front for a little boy who feels bad about things he didn't tell anyone. Things that he was too prudish to take part in. Things that he would ask about, pretending like he didn't know what was goin' on."

"What are you talking about?"

Jack grinned. "I know something about Preston that you don't."

"Well, you might as well leave. He's not coming back as long as you're here."

"Yeah, because he's a coward." Jack stood and turned his back to Ronnie, pacing in a sleepless daze. "I'm not goin' anywhere."

The conversation was over. Ronnie needed to leave before Jack did something stupid.

He tiptoed down the hall, careful not to make a sound, and went down the stairwell. At the bottom of the stairs, he looked back up, paranoid that Jack was following him. But Jack was there for Preston. He cared about Ronnie as much as the dirt on his shoe.

Ronnie left the house and swiped the fuzzy dice out of Jack's car.

Chapter Thirty

Ronnie brought his bike to a stop in the parking lot next to Davion's Oldsmobile. Between the miles of walking and pedaling, soreness was starting to creep into his legs. The motel Davion was staying in sat next to a busy street that connected Knollwood Pines to Holly Springs, a rural town that had seen its share of development over the past decade. The area around the motel was junky and uninviting. It didn't feel particularly safe, but, for a man with Davion's abilities, Ronnie figured, safety standards were a bit more relaxed.

The door of a motel room opened and Davion waved at Ronnie from the other side of the frame with a full-toothed smile. Davion was down to his vest and suit pants with the sleeves of his dress shirt rolled to the elbows. His style of dress perplexed Ronnie, given Davion's off-the-grid background. With his fedora removed, Ronnie could see thinning silver hair atop his head.

Ronnie walked toward Davion, the fuzzy dice dangling from his hand.

"Fuzzy dice. Very... retro?" Davion said.

"It's like a post-ironic thing, I guess," Ronnie replied.

Davion chuckled. "Ah, this generation, I tell ya. Come on inside."

Ronnie walked into the motel room, eyeing the walls lined with beige paint. The carpet was coarse under Ronnie's shoes. The bed, made up neatly, faced the TV and a striped chair sat in the corner of the room with a side view of a large glass panel that displayed the unflattering view of the parking lot.

"I know, I know. It's no Ritz Carlton," Davion said while closing the door behind Ronnie.

"It looks... cozy," Ronnie replied.

Davion laughed again. "You're a sweet kid. I know it doesn't look like the best area, but, shoot, I've been homeless once or twice in my life and these are my people. Ain't no one gonna hurt you out here. Why don't you take a seat?"

The question hit Ronnie's legs like a reminder of what they'd been put through that day. He walked over to the striped chair and sank into it.

Davion inspected the fuzzy dice closely.

"So, what happens now?" Ronnie asked.

Davion lowered the dice and turned to Ronnie. "Oh, where are my manners? Can I offer you anything? I got some cold ones in the fridge. You like lite beer? I can't handle the regular stuff myself."

"I don't—I mean, I *can't*—drink," Ronnie said.

"What do you mean you *can't* drink? Course you can. Here." Davion marched over to the mini fridge at the corner of the room, opened it, and pulled out a brown glass container of beer. He twisted off the cap and walked over to Ronnie with his arm extended. "Go 'head. It ain't gonn' bite ya."

Ronnie took the drink and eyed it.

"Tell ya what..." Davion went back to the fridge and got himself a beer as well. "Take a few sips and see if ya like it. If ya don't, no worries. Definitely don't drink the whole thing though, because, if it's your first time... It *is* your first time, right?"

Ronnie nodded.

"Then it'll either make you sick or too drunk to function properly. And tonight... Well, it could be that we're gonna need to function properly." Davion twisted off his cap. He sat at the corner of the bed, which emitted a crunching sound like Ronnie imagined cheap motel mattresses would make. "Every boy should have their first drink with their dad. It's a rite of passage. Cheers to you, Ronnie, for believing in me." He reached his glass over to Ronnie, nearly falling off the edge of the bed.

Ronnie reached his beer out and clanked it against Davion's. He put the cold glass to his lips and tilted the bottle up, tasting the sour liquid against his tongue. As it sat in his mouth, he found himself wondering why people actually liked it. But he swallowed it down and looked back at Davion, who let out an audible "Aaahhh" like it was the most refreshing sip of beer any man had ever had. Here Ronnie was in a dingy motel room, having his first drink with Davion Stivert, his father, feeling more at home than he had in some time.

"You must have some questions, right?" Davion asked. "I'm an open book. Ask away."

"Um..." Ronnie couldn't figure out where to start. He let the thought linger long enough to make the moment awkward.

"Not a very decisive young man, are ya?" Davion took another sip. "I'll wait."

Ronnie took another sip as well, hoping it would change the taste, but the second was just as sour and bitter as the first. He scraped his tongue on the roof of his mouth. "How did you make that guy... fly, or whatever?"

Davion giggled. "Do you know what you are, Ronnie? No, I don't imagine you would. You were born of Manarian blood. The Manari go back centuries and centuries. There are so few left now... So few left." He wore a forlorn expression for a moment.

The silence gave Ronnie a moment to contemplate that word. *Manarian*. Davion confirmed what Malleck had already told him. He and Malleck were more alike than he had known. "So Manari are... magic people? Wizards and witches?"

Davion laughed. "We don't ride broomsticks and carry wands, if that's what you're thinkin'. Nah, Manarians are just born with certain abilities. It's random, but people find ways to hack it. Some people are more sensitive to magic than others. I was born with very little skill at all. And for that reason, I had to study magic hard—study the texts, what very few texts we had left. Through my studies—and I can do some good studyin'—I expanded my mind. Learned to channel my energy in ways that most wouldn't dare. There are many things I used to have the ability to do... before I got sick."

"Could I throw people with my mind?"

"Even if you studied like I did, kid, the prophecy doesn't work that way. You'll remain powerless from an external standpoint. All of the magic in your blood has one purpose... Creation." Davion smiled. "Besides, those texts are long gone, stolen by people who've been tryin' to wipe us out for decades."

"That Neverwell mentioned using the ancient texts. He said they didn't work."

"Then I wonder where in the hell he got 'em from. I hear they're locked in a vault in some remote location, along with our magic artifacts."

Ronnie's face twitched in curiosity.

Davion caught the expression. "Got ya hooked now, don't I? Son, let me tell you how you became... you." He leaned forward in his chair, taking another swig of beer. "Remember I told you about that old guy Kraek? Well, he brought with him the Leberoz stones and the Leberoz staff. Now, it was said that Leberoz was a god who could transfer power from one being to another. A common practice for preservin' a powerful bloodline. Remember how I said people could hack the strain? That's one way.

"When Leberoz became old and weary, he decided to gift his power to the Manari. He transferred his full energy into a set of eight stones and a staff. Whoever sits within the stones and follows his spell will transfer their power to whoever wields the staff. Our people channeled their power over to me so I could perform the ritual, but we had to do it just a little bit at a time so as not to drain them too much. Day by day—drain, replenish, drain, replenish."

People in a circle chanting, Ronnie thought. His mother's memory.

Davion leaned back in his chair. "Pretty wild stuff, right?"

After a long moment, Ronnie, wide-eyed and perplexed, said, "Yeah." With no other words to fill his mouth, he instead filled it with a sip of beer and nearly spat it out.

He sat the bottle down on the nightstand.

Davion sat his bottle next to Ronnie's. "Nobody likes their first drink."

Davion got to work reading the energy of the object Ronnie gave him. He swapped places with Ronnie and sat comfortably in the striped chair with the fuzzy dice held in his palm. Ronnie watched TV on the bed, which Davion swore wouldn't be a distraction. Every so often, Ronnie would look over at Davion and see rapid movement under his eyelids. Davion appeared to be sleeping or meditating, but under the serene appearance of his relaxed body, he was searching.

Ronnie took out his phone and sifted through the many missed calls, voicemails, and texts from his home screen. Most of them were from his mother and some were from Leslie and Preston.

"You can tell your friend that Jack has left his house," Davion said, startling Ronnie. His body was still, and his eyes were closed. "Sorry, man," he continued, "I should've told you that ten minutes ago."

"So you actually *can* track energy signatures? That's... insane," Ronnie said.

Davion grinned. "If you were skeptical, then why'd you go along with it?"

"I think I'm starting to find it easier to just accept the things I can't explain than question them," Ronnie said.

"There's a lot of mystery in the world, son," Davion said. "Lucky for you, I'm here to help you through it all... For as long as I'm around." With that, he went silent.

Ronnie texted Preston and Leslie first to let them know that Preston was in the clear and told them to lay low. He didn't want to be secretive with them, but he had no choice. This was something he had to do on his own.

He texted his mom back and assured her that he was okay. Knowing her, it would only be a matter of time before she panicked and called the police. He received a call back from her and ignored it. He'd deal with her wrath later. His body was tired and all he wanted to do was flip through channels to get his mind off of the dread that he might be facing tonight.

Cheers to you, Ronnie, for believing in me. Words from a man who, in a short amount of time, was beginning to feel less like a stranger.

Chapter Thirty-One

Malleck's vision came in and out, fuzzy and disoriented. Aunt Helga peered above her, jaws flapping, eyes wide, jerking her by the shoulders. Malleck's head bobbled clumsily above her neck as she propped herself up against her elbows.

Quickly, her hearing became more clear.

"We have to leave now!" her aunt yelled. "Malleck! You have to get your ass up and moving!"

Malleck shook her head, which seemed to scramble and blur her vision. Something wasn't right. "I can't," she said. "The Affliction."

"I gave you a tranquilizer," Helga said. She held up Malleck's unlaced combat boots so she could see them. "Now get on your feet!"

Malleck pulled the wool cover off of her body, forced herself upright against the stiff cot and mattress, slid her feet into boots, and laced them up as quickly as she could, every movement a slow drag. "What's going on?" Malleck asked as she laced the second boot.

"I'll explain when we're on the road," Helga said. "I know you're groggy, but we need to hustle."

Malleck stood to her feet, surrounded by an unwelcoming clay brick structure. It made her miss her room back home. The purpose of the wool blanket became evident as soon as a cool gust blew in from the bottom of her white nightgown. "Good to go."

"That's my girl," Helga said. She ran to the wooden door of the hut and looked back. "You didn't think I'd actually poison you, did you?" She opened the door to a dark world outside.

Malleck hobbled closely beside, finding her footing like a newborn deer. Helga grabbed an arm and propped it over her shoulders as they both walked out together. Malleck gazed upon the village lit in orange hues by torches with swaying fires. A chorus of agonizing wails filled the crisp air. Members held their stomachs while curled in the fetal position. One resident burst out of his hut and vomited a thick stream of bile, forming a puddle, then landed in it with his knees. It was as if the entire commune had become sick.

"What the hell?" said Malleck.

"This, Malleck, is the Affliction. I put it in the well."

They ran together with Malleck propped against Helga's side, into the forest and away from the shrieks.

"I'm good. I can run," Malleck said, stabilizing herself. She took a few quick steps on her own behind Helga, her thighs, calves, and feet showing signs of life. She spoke through panting breaths. "I thought the Affliction took away your abilities?"

"It does, but it also makes you sick as hell," Helga responded.

The light from the commune faded from their vision quickly. Helga lit their path with a flashlight and they ran and ran and ran—for too long, Malleck thought—before making it to Helga's pickup truck.

A quick view from the flashlight's beam made Malleck come to a sudden stop. She pointed her finger above the truck. "Aunt Helga, what..."

Helga, holding the handle of the driver's side door, looked behind her and waved the flashlight above her head. A pane of what appeared to be translucent film was fading upward like a wet spot on a car drying in the sun. She waved her light left and right, revealing that it was fading in a curve around them.

It was a dome.

Helga turned back to Malleck. "Yeah, whatever. I'll explain that too. Get in the truck."

Malleck did as she was told. She flung the passenger's side door open, hopped in the seat, and slammed the door shut. Helga started the truck and took off down the dirt path.

"That's the way the Manari stay hidden," Helga said. "With their combined magic, they can keep that dome over their commune perpetually. It helps them live in secret. Without magic, there's no dome."

"So the Affliction ceremony," Malleck said. "You put me to sleep, but afflicted everyone else?"

"What they tell you is that you're prohibited from interfering against threats to the natural world. What they don't tell you is that they'll fight tooth and nail to *keep* you from interfering, all in the name of peace. They'd rather poison you than investigate what's going on in Knollwood Pines."

"Won't they be coming after us?"

Helga shook her head. "It'll take weeks for the Affliction to wear off. Maybe months for some of them. They'll be scattered wondering how to rebuild the dome. That'll give us some cushion to find the book and end the Neverwells. You're too important to stay locked up."

"Why? What makes me so important?"

"Whether that book can actually summon a demon or not, *they* think it can. The only way they can do that is with dark magic. If they can conjure dark magic... We'll need to fight them with dark magic."

Malleck's hands glowing red flashed in her memory, a violent thunderstorm erupting in her hands.

She laughed drunkenly, causing Helga to glance at her in confusion.

"What's so funny?" Helga asked.

"Oh, Helga... or should I call you Nu?"

Helga gave her a knowing look. The secret was out.

"I should be pissed at you for using me as bait," Malleck told her.

"You should. But I didn't see another way. You're better than they are. We need to find the book and kill it."

"Since we're laying our cards on the table now... I have something to tell you."

"Yeah, what's that?"

Malleck watched the dirt road wind ahead, a cluster of dirt and trees bobbing in the headlights, and prepared herself for the long trip ahead. "I know who wrote the book."

Chapter Thirty-Two

"They've taken him," Davion said, jolting Ronnie awake after he had nodded off to an old sitcom.

"Are you sure?" Ronnie asked.

"It's not my first rodeo, kid," Davion said. "We need to skedaddle. One sec." He stood from the chair and walked quickly to the bathroom, closing the door behind him.

Three garbled heaves came from the other side of the door, followed by a flush. *Every time he uses his power*, Ronnie thought.

After a few spits and the sound of running water, Davion stepped out of the bathroom grimacing.

"Everything okay?" Ronnie asked, immediately regretting it. Everything was most certainly not okay. The man was dying.

"We're together," Davion said. "That's all that matters." He walked to the closet and took his suit jacket off the hanger.

Ronnie checked his watch—10:34.

His mom was going to be so pissed.

Ronnie had practiced driving in empty parking lots with his mom. The idea of driving a car seemed so simple when someone else was doing it, but once he got behind the wheel himself, he was overwhelmed by the breadth of sheer *stuff* that he had to pay attention to. Rear view and side mirrors, levers on each side of the wheel that each did different things. Which one had the turn signal? Which one worked the wiper blades?

He drove the Oldsmobile slowly and cautiously, minding every stop sign and red light, even panicking at the yellow lights. They seemed short and long at the same time. Davion sat in the passenger's seat, eyes closed, holding the fuzzy dice in his palm as if it were an actual pair of dice that he was preparing to toss on a craps table. He'd utter the occasional "turn left", "turn right", and "stay straight", and sometimes "you're doing great" for added reassurance. Ronnie supposed it was a night of firsts, as this was his first actual drive in the wild. The forced concentration on the road kept his mind off the looming threat they were quickly barreling toward.

The Oldsmobile rumbled on until the Knollwood Pines city limits became New Hill. The Neverwells must have gone far off the beaten path for this kill. Ronnie imagined them traveling by way of shadow, slipping from one pillar of shade to the next as fluid as a quarry stream. But, of course, they were people composed of flesh and blood just like him and so they must have traveled by vehicle. Perhaps one large, dark, rusted van with the bulk of them sitting on steel benches SWAT-team-style in the back. Perhaps in a convoy of SUVs. However they did it, they seemed to slip in and out of locations undetected. It had to do with their mind manipulation abilities, Ronnie thought. When you could control the field of view, you could make yourself invisible and inaudible, like an artist painting over a mistake. That's what the Neverwells were: a mistake, and one that needed to be corrected.

"Stop here," Davion said, his eyes finally open.

Ronnie lightly tapped the brake and looked at the rural area surrounding him. Nothing but the winding road ahead in a jagged rectangle of high beam light, with trees and leaves at either side of it.

"There's nowhere to stop," Ronnie said.

"Sure there is," Davion replied. "Pull onto the grass. We're gonna have to slip through these here woods." He held his finger up to the driver's side window, pointing at the trees as if Ronnie couldn't see them. "If we keep goin' we'll get closer to where *they* parked. We can't tip 'em off that we're here."

Ronnie slowed the vehicle down and pulled off to the left side of the road.

"We're gonna have to use our eyesight and the good ol' moonglow to guide us. They see a flashlight and it might as well be a flare to let 'em know we're comin'." Davion readjusted himself, straightening his posture.

"Can't they, like... *feel* your energy?" Ronnie asked.

"Not if you're skilled enough to conceal it," Davion said. "Which I am. We'll be practically invisible... You know you don't have to come if you're scared."

Ronnie's heart was pounding in his chest. He *was* scared. But he couldn't turn back now. "What the hell else am I gonna do?" he said.

Davion grinned. "Thataboy."

Ronnie took his phone. No reception. If things went south, he wouldn't be able to call for help. Even if he could, what would he say? He stuffed the phone in his pocket and looked back up at Davion.

"Is Jack okay?" Ronnie asked.

"For now he is," Davion replied. "Last I could see, he was being led out the back of a rather rickety van all naked and whatnot."

"Before we go," Ronnie said, "there's something I gotta tell you." He took a few deep breaths and continued. "The Neverwells have killed two kids so far. Kids whose names I put in the book. I constructed the deaths of four people in total. If they kill Jack... They move on to the fourth." His heartbeat picked up. His breath became scattered. Saying it out loud would make it real. "They can't kill him," he said finally.

"Who is it, son?" Davion asked.

Ronnie shook his head, incredibly aware that he was wasting precious seconds on a pointless confession. "There were four people there that day I fell off the water tower. And somehow one of them has become my friend."

Davion put his hand on Ronnie's shoulder. "A strong friendship is a hard thing to come by, but when you have it, it's worth protecting."

They held a long stare. Ronnie nodded and Davion nodded back. Then Davion's chin shot back towards his neck, his throat seizing. He wrestled to keep a cough contained in his throat. He pulled a handkerchief out of his pocket and put it against his mouth. A series of deep, violent, liquid coughs followed.

The coughing fit subsided. He folded the handkerchief and placed it back in his pocket.

"What are you sick with?" Ronnie asked.

"Don't you worry about me, kiddo," Davion replied with a wink. His eyes turned white. "Let's go shock these punks." He opened the passenger door quickly and stepped out.

Deep breath... Slowly push out the one.

Deep breath... Slowly push out the two.

Each number vanished into the darkness of Ronnie's closed eyes.

After the tenth breath, he got out.

He and Davion gazed out toward the endless row of trees and the small amount of moonlight that lit them in a pale shade of blue.

"We're close," Davion said as his foot pressed against another small pile of leaves and twigs. The entirety of the woods was surrounded by fall debris—flimsy, crunchy, loud.

Ronnie stopped and listened intently, trying and failing to take in anything but silence. "How can you tell?" Ronnie asked.

"I can feel them," Davion said, lowering his voice. He scanned the surrounding area and continued talking. "Think of a wave in the ocean. When you're on the shore letting the wake tickle your feet, it's gentle. It's still movin', but it's calm. You walk further into the ocean, you start to feel this pushin' and pullin'. Then, when you get right up to the peak of the wave, you feel it break and it's like a weight against you, throbbin' over and over again."

"Why can't I feel it?" Ronnie asked.

"You're an architect," Davion said. "You're the visionary. You create so that others, like me, can execute your vision."

"Uh, okay..." *Sure, why not?* Ronnie thought. "So, we're at the break in the wave now?"

"Yeah," Davion said, still scanning. "We're just about there... Swimmin' in the ocean. Stay behind me, now."

Davion crept cautiously through the trees and Ronnie followed closely behind. A twist of fire came into view fifty yards ahead of them, creating a small orange halo around the wooded area. Davion scrambled behind the base of a tree and Ronnie did the same.

Davion peaked out around the edge while Ronnie stayed still, too afraid to look himself.

"It's hard to tell," Davion whispered, "but it looks like there's seven in total."

Suddenly, a shriek shot through the air. "Untie me, you bitches!" It was Jack.

"And it looks like the boy's awake now," Davion said.

A series of threats wove through the trees, angry and venomous. Any other teenager would be begging for this life, but Jack Sutter didn't beg. Jack Sutter demanded he be released. He asked if they knew who his father was and if they knew what kind of resources he had. "You're screwed already," he said, "but if you harm a single inch of this body, you'll wish you were dead."

Here was Jack Sutter, threatening a death cult.

"Let's move in closer," Davion said.

They paced from tree to tree, their footsteps muffled by the cover of Jack's threats and screams. "I'll get out of this," he yelled. "Bet your ass I will. And when I do, you better run. I woke up feelin' dangerous this morning, fellas." So bold and so incredibly, deeply stupid. Ronnie caught glimpses of Jack's predicament and pieced them together half a second at a time. It was the first instance of him actually seeing his writing and his illustration being followed. This was one passage he was particularly not proud of.

A tall torch was planted in the ground, separating a naked Jack from the Neverwells. Jack was flailing upside down on a wooden beam—something the Neverwells must have planted beforehand—his legs were bound with leather at the shin and thighs, tight enough for Jack's skin to bulge from underneath them. His arms were splayed at each side and bound at the wrists against an intersecting wooden beam. A sphere of briar thorns lay below his head like a pillow preparing to absorb his fall. Ronnie wondered how it got there and from where. It must have been extremely painful to carry this bundle of thorns through the woods.

A machete gleamed like crystal beside the fire as a Neverwell held it to the sky and circled Jack, who continued to rattle off insults. The beam was thick enough to take the impact of the machete, and if Ronnie and Davion didn't act soon, Jack's feet would be cut clean off at the ankles. More realistically, it would take several whacks to cut through the tendons, flesh, and bone, and Jack's insults would become desperate pleas as he realized he couldn't be saved. The blood would spurt and trickle from his ankles to his head and then to the thorns below. A negative crucifixion for Jack Sutter, who fancied himself a god, but would die for his sins alone, his feet no longer belonging to him and instead becoming a gift to Karnalaxe.

Ronnie remembered every emotion that had surfaced while he wrote the passage, the pain and frustration coming back to him. The yearning for revenge, for a sick personal brand of justice. It was intoxicating then, like he was channeling his anger into something dark and therapeutic. But knowing that he was guided by a power instilled in him at birth triggered by a traumatizing event, it was no longer his revenge fantasy. The best way he could get back at Jack Sutter was by rescuing him from certain death. How much of an ego hit would that be?

They were twenty yards away.

Fifteen yards.

Ten yards.

A Neverwell removed the leatherbound book from his robe and held it above his head. The Neverwell with the machete continued to circle Jack like a predator stalking prey while the others put their hands to the sky in worship. It was his first time Ronnie had seen the book in what seemed like an eternity, and he observed an inexplicable darkness emanating from it.

Ronnie joined Davion behind a tree. They were getting eerily close to the Neverwells' radius of light. "Do you see it?" he whispered.

"I see it," Davion whispered back.

The Neverwells began uttering a passage in unison. It was too low for Ronnie to hear, but he knew the sequence. There would be sixteen lines in cadence as they pledged their loyalty to Karnalaxe, followed by the cutting of the feet.

"They're starting," Ronnie said. "We have to do something."

"You sure you're still up for this?" Davion asked.

"You provide the distraction," Ronnie said, "I'll get Jack and the book. Just make sure you scare the absolute shit out of them."

Davion chuckled. "Boy... I'm about to send these dopes on the trip of their lives."

Ronnie absorbed Davion's confidence. As Davion grinned, the white in his eyes rolled like the funnel of a tornado. "Now, listen," Davion said, "just keep an eye on them. You'll know when the time is right." Davion turned his head and leaned out from behind the tree. He focused his gaze on the Neverwells.

Ronnie ran diagonally toward another tree and found cover behind it. The chanting became louder and more ominous. Truthfully, Ronnie couldn't remember what exactly he'd written for them to chant, but the surrealness of these murderers reciting it like churchgoers in a pew chilled him to his core. Davion muttered something, but Ronnie couldn't quite make it out.

It came to him a few seconds later.

Fire ants.

The Neverwells stopped chanting and started patting themselves, brushing their robes. Some jumped. Some stomped. They all yelped like regular people reacting to an ambush of fire ants. But there was nothing there.

One Neverwell threw off his robe, revealing casual clothing underneath—jeans and a sweatshirt. Ronnie questioned what he had expected under the robes. Something more akin to medieval wardrobe? But one thing that gave him pause when the robeless Neverwell pivoted in a frenzy was the twin daggers sheathed on his lower back. He had to assume they were all armed with this type of weaponry. It only made sense that beings who possessed extraordinary gifts would reject modern weapons and instead indulge in more old-fashioned forms of violence. Either that or they were punks cosplaying as sixteenth-century thugs.

The one with the machete began swinging it right, left, and down, like he was sparring with the air. Did Davion make the ants fly? He then dropped the machete with a soft thud against the dirt and joined the rest of the Neverwells in swiping their clothing frantically.

The one with the book dropped it at an angle, causing the covers to widen against the dirt and the pages to curl in below the spine.

"What is that?!" a Neverwell yelled out with a finger pointed high above him.

Ronnie looked over at Davion, who smiled with dead white eyes in a way that was frightening and also childlike. The rest of the Neverwells stared up at whatever was being pointed at. They all cowered and took slow steps backward. Ronnie remembered how silly Preston looked fighting off an invisible dog in the front seat of his car, afraid for his life over something imagined. The Neverwells, whom he'd feared before, now looked like an improv troupe receiving prompts randomly from the crowd. Ronnie was no longer afraid.

"What the hell are you assholes looking at?" Jack said.

The Neverwells scattered, running in different directions away from the scene they created, ingested by the surrounding woods and gone from the torchlight. Ronnie made the most of his opportunity, running as fast as he could, his feet crashing against leaves and dirt, his jean jacket flapping like a cape under his armpits.

"Hey!" Jack yelled, spotting Ronnie. "Don't come over here! I'm warning you!"

Ronnie would have loved to challenge him on what exactly that threat entailed, but he was too busy rescuing the insufferable piece of shit.

Ronnie clasped the machete on the ground so swiftly that he barely lost speed, then stopped in front of Jack's upside-down body. The bed of thorns was half the size of a twin bed and sat awfully close to Jack's head.

"Who the..." Jack tilted his neck to each side, attempting to get an upright view of Ronnie. A look of recognition came over his face. "Hendrix? You're behind this, you little shit weasel?"

Ronnie gripped the handle of the blade so hard his knuckles turned white. Jack, the primary source of his pain, was before him, helpless. Did he have this whole thing wrong? Jack was *bad* and Ronnie was *good*, right? This whole time he'd been running from his destiny, maybe he should have been considering the net positive. Purging the world of bad people and making the good ones better, just like Davion said.

His first interaction with Preston flashed into his mind. He remembered the himbo tank top, the shorts that were embarrassingly high, and the kind look on Preston's face, too genuine to fake. He thought of what Preston had done and endured for him this week. He thought of Preston's attempt to visit him in the hospital and how Preston had come clean to the police, even at the risk of losing his own social status. He realized that Preston was looking out for him since before they even knew each other. Preston's life was worth saving Jack's.

Jack was too rich and privileged not to fail. He'd follow in his dad's footsteps and work his way up to the highest floors of the tallest buildings, forming flimsy relationships with similarly wealthy people. He'd vacation even harder than he worked. He'd never see his family and would think of them as a burden. He'd probably die of heart failure due to chronic stress and then argue with the grim reaper that, no, actually, it's not his time and he'd like to propose a different plan, thank you. Jack Sutter would live a long life he didn't deserve. He'd die someday.

But not today.

Ronnie stabbed the thorn bed surrounding the wooden pillar and put both palms against the grip. He walked backward, dragging the bundle with him.

"What are you doing?" Jack asked.

"I'm saving you, you moron," Ronnie said through gritted teeth. "I'm sorry, would you rather land on this when I cut you down? If those people come back, they will kill you."

"Yeah, how do you know?" Jack asked.

"I don't have time for your aggressive shittiness right now, Jack. You can stay here and die, or you can come with me."

"Yeah, like I'm supposed to trust you," Jack said. "Why would *you* save *me*?"

Ronnie sawed through one of the leather straps holding Jack's wrists, freeing it. "Because I'm not aggressively shitty." Then he sawed through the other one.

Jack pressed his newly-freed hands to the dirt, bracing for his imminent fall. "Who are these people?" he said with what sounded like a degree of trust. "I think they gave me a bad edible or something, because I've been seein' some messed up stuff."

Ronnie cut the strap around Jack's thighs, causing Jack to sink quickly, then cut the strap around his ankles. Jack flopped to the ground head-first and landed sideways in a fast series of motions that was delightful to Ronnie.

"Shit, are you okay?" Ronnie asked, not sure whether he cared about the answer.

Jack got to his feet and rubbed his neck while grimacing. "Happy to not have all the blood in my body rushing to my head. What now, genius?"

Ronnie stepped over to the unattended notebook and picked it up, closing the splayed edges. "I can get us out of here. Come on," Ronnie said with a wave of the machete, instructing Jack to follow him.

He led the way for Jack, cupping the book against his chest like a running back protecting a football.

He made it to his previous spot where he had stood directly next to Davion.

But Davion was gone.

"Davion?" Ronnie whispered. "Davion!" He said in a combination of a whisper and a yell.

Jack scampered behind him. "Gimme that thing." He ripped the machete out of Ronnie's grasp. "We both know it's better off with me."

Ronnie let the grip slide out of his hand easily, his mind occupied by the sudden disappearance of Davion.

"Did you bring any clothes?" Jack asked. "My nuts are freezing."

Ronnie realized that the yelling had stopped. With Davion gone…

There was no one to distract the Neverwells.

"Hey!" an angry voice called out from behind him.

Ronnie spun around, confronted by the Neverwell without a robe charging toward them, flailing his thin arms crazily.

"Oh, shit!" Ronnie yelled. He lowered himself, ready to take off.

Jack let out a battle cry, machete raised, and darted forward.

The Neverwell stopped, his shoes skidding across the ground, and threw his arm behind him for balance. For the moment, Ronnie was glad to have Jack on his side.

"Yeah, that's right," Jack said with a cocky grunt, followed by a spit.

The Neverwell reached both arms behind his back, and in one swift movement raised them, elbows extended, displaying a dagger in each hand.

"Yeah, nuh-uh." Jack turned and ran, slapping his bare feet against the ground right past Ronnie.

Ronnie ran close behind as the darkness closed in around him. Soon it would only be the moonlight making shapes in his vision. Soon he would lose Jack in the forest and he wouldn't know how to get back to the car.

Where was Davion?

Ronnie pumped his legs, still clinging to the book, following Jack's bare ass as it zigged and zagged through the trees. The machete swayed in the air with the movement of his arm. One slip-up and Jack would fall right on top of it. What a depressing end to the night that would be.

Ronnie looked over his shoulder. The outline of the man with daggers was closing in. When he turned back, Jack was snatched off the path by a pair of long arms.

Jack yelled furiously as his legs bucked in the air. He fell to the ground hard, then whipped around and swung the blade blindly, nearly swiping Ronnie in the process. For a brief moment, Ronnie caught a glimpse of Jack's eyes in the moonlight.

Fear.

Jack belly-flopped on the ground as his legs were pulled out from underneath him. He flipped over to his back and tried to swing at whatever was holding his ankles, but just as soon as he folded his body, he was dragged away and out of sight.

"No!" Ronnie cried out as Jack disappeared from his view against the fading sound of rustling leaves.

The Neverwell behind Ronnie grabbed him by his collar and spun him around, pinning Ronnie's neck with one blade behind it and one blade in front. The Neverwell gasped. When he spoke, Ronnie noticed the roughed, rugged voice underneath the mask.

"Ronnie Hendrix," the Neverwell said. "We meet again."

"Anson," Ronnie responded, careful not to move his neck.

"Where's your guardian now?"

Ronnie stared into Anson's eyes through the twig mask as they began to swirl into clouds of white.

"It appears you have something that belongs to me," Anson said.

Ronnie repositioned the book with the spine facing out. "Here you go." He shoved the spine into Anson's throat with enough force to make a soft crunch. Anson stumbled backward, pulling the dagger behind Ronnie's neck with him and making a shallow cut through Ronnie's skin.

The open air stung Ronnie's newly exposed flesh. He prepared to run again, hoping that the blow to Anson's throat was enough to slow him down.

Anson grunted, then removed a hand from his throat and growled through gritted teeth. He seethed behind the mask. "If you are not with us," Anson croaked through a damaged windpipe, "then you are against—"

A body slammed against Anson with incredible speed and power, sending the Neverwell off his feet and into a tree. Anson's head made a hard knock and he lost consciousness instantly, his legs buckling under his own dead weight.

Jack, panting wildly, stood above Anson defiantly. Ronnie was never more happy to be in his presence. Jack put his hands on his knees, catching his breath.

"Shit... Thank you," Ronnie said in disbelief.

"Don't mention it," Jack said between short breaths.

"You good?" Ronnie asked.

"I got cuts all up and down my ass," Jack replied. "But so far so good. I lost that big knife back there. Nicked it on a tree and almost stabbed my damn self." Jack stood up, his eyes hovering over Ronnie's head, a strange, confused look forming on his face. "Do you see that?"

The darkness revealed nothing to Ronnie. Whatever Jack saw, it was adjacent to the path Ronnie and Davion came.

"There's nothing there," Ronnie said.

"Are you blind? It's a lighthouse. Let's go. There'll be people there who can help us." Jack took off. "Keep up, Hendrix!" he yelled back to Ronnie.

Ronnie tried to match Jack's pace, but could barely manage to track him in the darkness. Where was he going? "Jack, stop!" he yelled. "Their messing with your h—" Ronnie's foot caught a branch and his entire world tilted fast. He landed on his elbow and spilled the book on the ground.

He got on his hands and knees and crawled to the book. Any sight of Jack was lost within the woods.

Trust in me. Ronnie remembered Davion's words. Yet here he was—abandoned. Ronnie was crouched in the dark woods alone, his only ally having vanished, surrounded by enemies, fearing that he'd made a mistake. He thought quickly, opening the book against the ground and flipping through the pages, straining his eyes.

Chapter Thirty-Three

With the notebook tucked under his armpit, Ronnie crouched outside a clearing in the woods encircling a man-made fire pit. Jagged stones surrounded a stacked bundle of twigs that were burning with fresh orange flames, flapping against two figures. One was a man in a gray suit, with his face lit under the brim of his fedora, eyes white.

Davion.

The figure next to Davion was Jack, on his knees and spouting tears in a way Ronnie never thought he'd see. A myriad of red streaks lined the skin of Jack's back, arms, and face.

Ronnie approached the scene timidly, having no other option but to stay close to Davion.

"Where were you?" Ronnie said.

"I had to run. They would have found my position and I'm too weak to fight," Davion said.

"Bullshit. You left me out there. We were supposed to stay together."

"We got 'im, Ronnie. We got Jack." Davion was incredibly relaxed—too relaxed for the situation at hand.

"And I have the book," Ronnie said. "So let's go." As soon as he said it, Ronnie knew something wasn't right. The fire flickered high in the air and Ronnie caught the gleam of a machete next to Davion's foot.

"*We* have the book," Davion said, correcting Ronnie. "Now we control our destinies." Davion bent down and grabbed the handle of the machete, then stood back up.

"What are you doing?" Ronnie said.

"I'm so proud of you, son," Davion said. "You truly are a blessing. This thing you created will give us unimaginable power. The power of the gods. You and I can make the world pure again. Free of disease and struggle and turmoil. Free of evil—"

"Free of disease?" Ronnie cut in. "For everyone? Or just for you?"

"For... everyone, son," Davion said.

They shared a long, tense stare. The bigger picture became clearer. A sick man disappearing into his own bones, knowing his only chance at restoring his life was a genie in a bottle. Something he could control, with the power to take life and also grant it. A demon with the power of the gods. A being conjured by magic, made flesh.

How long had this plan been in motion? How long had Davion been sick? All this time Davion was searching for Ronnie...

It was only to help himself.

Ronnie may have been the architect to summon Karnalaxe, but as each second passed, as his mind twisted to rationalize his own existence, the more he adapted to his new reality. His life was only a construct meant to serve someone else.

He imagined glowing hands touching his mother's stomach, reaching down for him, shaping him into something beyond human. An instrument. A weapon.

A lifeline.

"Shit," Ronnie said in disbelief, his muscles relaxing in surrender. "This was never about helping me, was it? This is about you not dying. So that instead of wasting away in a hospital bed, you can create some hippie utopia and cross out whoever you consider evil." He waited for Davion's confirmation, hoping it wasn't true.

"We must vanquish those who oppose us," Davion said.

"So you just get to decide who's evil now?" Ronnie said.

Davion took a deep breath. "Son, I'm asking you to come with me on this journey. You're capable of remarkable things. I made it so. You can continue forging the path to prosperity for our people. You must realize that prosperity for the many requires sacrifice for the few."

"You sound ridiculous," Ronnie said, noticing that Davion's Southern accent had seemingly slipped away. "And don't call me son."

"Alright then," Davion said.

He then raised the machete stumbling in a woozy way that Ronnie hadn't noticed before. Davion truly was a weak man feigning power. "It's the feet, right?" He leveled the blade above Jack's ankles. "Give me the book."

There were no options that led to Jack's safe return. Ronnie thought briefly about appealing to Davion's humanity, but it was clear that the human side of him was a veil. The Southern gentleman with a fun twang was a projection meant to blind Ronnie from his true nature.

"Bluff called," Davion said, dropping the blade. "I can't stand the sight of blood. I can, however, drop you into a perpetual nightmare. Forced to live in that space indefinitely. Would you like to see what's in Jack's mind now?"

"No..." Ronnie didn't want to slip. He couldn't hand his mind over to Davion. Not now when he finally had the book.

But he was no longer in control. The ground grew dense with fog as a vision came to Ronnie of a memory that wasn't his. Davion and Jack were replaced by a rocky shore with violent waves. A lighthouse sprung from the ground, the black stripe swirling from bottom to top. A long wooden dock sprouted from the shore into the ocean ahead.

A thought formed in Ronnie's head uncontrollably, telling him that whoever was inside the lighthouse would let him in, but then a long boat with two large sails that streaked over a story tall appeared at the end of the dock, bobbing up and down against the unsteady water. Was it there a second ago? How did he not see it before? A hand waved to him from inside the boat. The man inside, wearing poncho, was obscured by the movement of the boat and the haze.

The man motioned for him to come hither as the rope connecting the boat to the dock tightened with the pull of the ocean. Ronnie's legs moved, forcing him to run down the sloping shore and onto the boardwalk, his feet unstable against the warped wood. The splash of waves punched his skin as he took heavy steps and long strides. The man in the poncho was slick with seawater and smiling—the smile of a man relishing adventure, ready to take on the sea.

Ronnie leapt from the dock to the boat, his feet sliding against the hull, catching himself clumsily against the main sail. The man's sturdy hands clutched his hips, steadying his landing. Ronnie turned to face him, crouching as the boat rocked in every direction.

The rope attaching the boat to the dock snapped and the sails rounded toward the ocean, catching an intense surge of wind. The dock moved farther and farther away, obscured each second by the side of the boat rising and falling. It was all happening so fast. *Too* fast. Ronnie flung his body to the mast and held it between his arms. One slip-up and he'd be over the edge. He remembered being ten years old under a storm cloud, his father covering him against the railing. He looked up at the man, who seemed unphased. He was simply sitting, almost as if he was enjoying the turbulent ride. He wasn't scared.

"Be strong!" the man yelled.

The side of the boat dipped far enough to catch water. A thick wave reached from the sea and snatched the man out of the boat.

There one moment.

Gone the next.

"Dad!" Ronnie screamed, releasing his hands from the mast and sliding toward the edge of the boat. He grabbed hold of the railing and looked out toward the sea, trying to steady his vision amidst the rapid, unpredictable movement of the boat. There was no sign of the man. The ocean had swallowed him whole.

"Thank you for the book, boy," Davion echoed.

And suddenly Ronnie was back in the clearing, staring at Davion and Jack.

The book was no longer in his hands.

Boy. Not son. A pawn and nothing more.

Ronnie's legs shook as he adjusted to the firm ground, realizing he'd been given a nightmarish glimpse into Jack's current state of mind. "Did you make Jack see his father... die?"

"Fear is a powerful thing," Davion said coldly, holding up the book. "It has the ability to leave people paralyzed. You of all people should know that." He tucked the book under his arm, letting out a warm breath, victorious.

Paralyzed, Ronnie thought. He of all people *did* know that. From the moment he froze on that water tower, his fear had become an entity itself, following him. Taunting him. It was that fear that led him to this moment, the fear of being revealed to the world as a freak.

"Neverwells! Come out!" Davion's booming voice shot through the woods.

Ronnie stood frozen as one masked Neverwell after the other stepped out of the woods and into the clearing, having found their way to the book. Davion raised the book in the air.

"Hear me!" Davion yelled to them. "You all are coordinated and bound together by a common goal, but your powers are infantile, and your scope is small. This book will guide us to prosperity, and I will be your guide. Trust in me, and I will not lead you astray. I, Davion Stivert, will summon Karnalaxe."

A small rumble of chatter surrounded Ronnie as the Neverwells looked between each other. Davion Stivert was a name they recognized.

"He can perform the ritual," a hoarse voice sauntered through the woods. Anson, standing taller than the rest, walked into the clearing, struggling to speak through a damaged windpipe. All heads turned his way and followed his slow walk to Davion. "I have witnessed firsthand his power. This man conjures magic from the forbidden texts. He can bend the laws of nature. He harnesses dark magic." Anson nodded. "You have my allegiance."

Davion nodded back. He pointed at Ronnie. "This here is my son. He is the reason we are here, and though he has not decided to carry on in our pursuit, he is not to be harmed."

Ronnie caught a side-eye from Anson, who had tried to kill him twice.

"If you will follow me henceforth," Davion said. "Then kneel."

A tense moment passed.

Anson was the first to kneel. The rest of the Neverwells began kneeling until all were down on one knee.

Only Ronnie remained standing.

Davion walked toward Ronnie slowly, stepping over Jack's limp body, and put a hand on Ronnie's shoulder.

"I am sorry I deceived you, son," Davion said. "I hoped in time you would see just how special you are and follow the vision *you* created. You'll see that we're the same."

Ronnie's eyes darted between the psychos in masks kneeling, the high school football player who would be dead before the night was over, and the white orbs above Davion's sickly lips. "This isn't my vision. And I'm nothing like you."

"You have a piece of me within you, Ronnie. Maybe you can't see it here on this plane, but you can see it reflected in the outer realm that you've traveled. Your Gray World, as you call it. Your creation, your environment, was so bright, son. It drew me toward it. And when I saw the deepest depths of the Underworld in the sky, I knew it was you. You see... the inversion spell was taught to me by Sebastian Kraek. I'm the only one who can do it. It's the final piece of the prophecy. Father and son reunited."

Ronnie thought *he* had invented the inversion spell. He believed the deepest, darkest parts of his mind constructed it in a fever dream, but it was another lie. The spell was imprinted. A piece of Davion's magic given to him. Ronnie was simply a delivery mechanism. "I don't have a father," Ronnie said. "Whatever piece of you I have in me is the worst part."

Davion removed his hand from Ronnie's shoulder and shook his head in disappointment. "You shouldn't disrespect your father like that." He took a breath. "One day you'll learn to travel the outer realms on your own. It's when you burn brightest. When you do, I'll find you there. As for this boy here, I'll do as I said. I'll make it painless. I owe you that at least. I'll do the same for your friend, Preston Collinsworth."

No! Ronnie's brain throbbed in misery. He imagined Preston surrounded by robed men in his dark bedroom, wondering why he was being taken. How long would it have taken to click for Preston that Ronnie had targeted him as well? That several months ago, Ronnie considered him the same kind of bullying scum as Jack, Therber, and Gavin? Ronnie imagined how hurt Preston would be after he'd done so much to make amends. This entire week, Preston had assumed he needed to earn Ronnie's friendship because he didn't deserve it, but now Ronnie realized that he didn't deserve Preston.

"Yeah," Davion said. "I jumped inside your head when you were sleeping. I saw how fond of the kid you are. He seems like a real good guy. He'll serve his purpose."

"You mean he'll serve yours. I hope your purpose dies with you."

Davion's expression became grim. "Now… I'm going to do something it's clear your mother never did. You need to be disciplined. I know you'll heal from this."

The last thing Ronnie remembered was Davion's fist rising above his shoulder and a stab of pain against his cheek. He lost his vision as his knees gave out.

Chapter Thirty-Four

Leslie cut the headlights off of her Corolla as she pulled into the driveway of the Collinsworth house, stopping behind Preston's car. It was a little past eight and Preston didn't want to blast his neighbors with their lights, which was confusing to Leslie considering the abundance of Halloween lights and decor. The only way anyone would fall asleep facing the street was by blacking out the windows. But that was Preston, nice and considerate to an annoying degree.

She'd insisted on escorting Preston home because, while Preston could definitely handle himself, no one was a match for Leslie's special brand of crazy. And if Jack popped up, she'd unleash that crazy all up and down on his ass, partially for Preston and partially because she hated Jack.

They were concerned that Ronnie was so off-grid that night. Was he freezing them out for some reason? Leslie and Preston, though in over their heads with all this magic stuff for sure, had a deep desire to see this through. Leslie loved Ronnie like a brother and would do anything for him, even if it meant stepping up to some idiot wizard in a robe.

Leslie got out of her car and trotted to Preston energetically as he exited his vehicle.

Preston closed his door. "Well… Thanks for seeing me home. See?" He waved his arm from one side of the lawn to the other. "No sign of Jack. I think we're in the clear."

"He could still be inside," Leslie said, looking up at him. She pursed her lips and squinted, mimicking a serious face. "I think we'd better check, don't you?"

"Oh, you wanna…" A nervous moment caught Preston's tongue. "You wanna come inside?"

He was *so* not smooth. "Yeah, man," Leslie replied. "For your safety, of course."

Preston smiled awkwardly, "Yeah, of course. For my safety. Thank you for being so considerate."

No one was in the living room when Preston slowly opened the door, looking like a spy on a stealth mission. He whispered to Leslie, "Okay, I'll meet you upstairs, my room is the first one on the left. And *be quiet.*"

Leslie giggled. "What, are you not allowed to have girls over?"

"Yes, I'm *allowed* to have girls over," Preston said.

"Wait. So you've *never* had a girl over?"

"Shhh. Yes, I have."

"Preston, is that you?!" A voice called from another room.

Preston opened the door wide and straightened up. "Yeah, it's me, Fred! I have a friend with me! We're going upstairs!"

"Jack's not up there anymore! He left!" Fred yelled.

"Yeah, I know. Just a… miscommunication!"

Leslie grabbed Preston's shoulder and pulled him toward her. She whispered, "Tell him you have a girl with you." She giggled.

Preston sighed. "Hey, Fred! The friend I have with me is a girl! And we're going upstairs!"

After a brief pause, Fred yelled back, "Thanks for the heads-up! Let me know if you need anything!"

"I'm good, sir, but thanks!" Leslie yelled giddily. She added, "I'm Leslie by the way!"

"Pleasure having you with us, Leslie! And call me Fred!"

Preston looked down at Leslie. "There. You happy?" His cheeks were flushed and he looked annoyed.

"Very," Leslie said. "Your stepdad seems cool."

"He is," Preston said.

They walked up the stairs. Preston led Leslie to the first door on the left. Leslie pushed the door open cautiously and flicked on the light switch.

"Well, look what we have here," Leslie said, for no particular reason. The room itself was bland and boyish, but she figured the affectation would make him sweat. She walked around the edges of the room, brushing her fingers against his desk, his laptop, his dresser.

"It doesn't look like he destroyed anything," Preston said, standing under the doorway. "Everything looks like it's in the right..." His eye caught a thick white envelope resting at the bottom of his pillow. "What's that?"

"It's your room, genius." She walked over to the bed and picked up the envelope, then sat at the edge. It wasn't a letter—the contents were thick and bulging against the thin paper. She eyed the back of the envelope, which read, "Mr. Boy Scout".

"What is it?" Preston asked.

Leslie turned the envelope over and unsealed the flap, then removed the material within. A collection of Polaroid photographs. She began flipping, placing pictures from front to back, her reaction becoming increasingly horrified.

Young girls lay on couches and chairs, unconscious and in various states of undress. As she flipped through the images, Leslie pieced together portions of the house and realized that they were all taken in the same place. Wood paneling, pink drapes, stained carpet. These were trophy pictures. So many trophies. So many girls.

A burning sensation flooded Leslie's skin, pissed as hell that anyone would think to do this. That so many girls lost their dignity in this house. The photos were documents of several awful moments in time. These girls would live on and grow and mature, establish their careers, maybe even start families, but in these photos, they would always be this age, in this state, kept under the eyes of someone with a unique kind of evil.

She stood up and handed Preston the stack of photos, staring daggers into him. "What do you have to say about this?"

Preston took the stack of photos and looked. He flinched at the sight of the top photo. "Oh my god."

"Look at them," Leslie said. "Jack put them here for a reason."

Preston forced himself to look picture after picture, his hands beginning to tremble. Leslie saw him give a slight heave and thought he might vomit. *Good.* That was an appropriate reaction.

"Why'd he leave these photos here, Preston?" Leslie asked. It came out like a mumble as she clenched her jaw tightly.

Preston put the stack of photos back in the envelope and placed it face down on his desk with the "Mr. Boy Scout" address visible. "I didn't have anything to do with this."

"Then I ask again," Leslie said, raising her voice. "Why did he leave those photos here?"

Preston's breath quickened as he searched for the best way to answer. "There was this place Jack used to call the shack. It was his grandparents' old house or something. Sometimes we'd just hang out and watch TV or play video games, but... sometimes they'd take girls there to... hang out."

"To *hang out*?" Leslie repeated.

"I didn't ask what they did in there. They'd just tell me to leave and so I left."

"So you just had no idea?"

"I mean, they would tell stories, but I thought it was just guys talking themselves up. I didn't think they were doing anything bad."

"Didn't think or didn't *want* to think?" Leslie asked. "These girls are barely conscious. They look drugged. Did you know they were drugging these girls?"

"No. I just... I knew there were pictures, okay?" Preston said nervously, his voice shaking. "They talked about it, but I never looked at them. Yes, okay? Yes, I thought there was something going on. How'd they get all these girls to take their clothes off for them? It just didn't make sense." Preston put his hands on his head and shook it as if trying to rattle out the memories. "I just didn't speak up." He sniffled. "They were my friends. I didn't want to lose them."

Leslie pointed her finger at the envelope. "Do you have any idea what those girls lost, Preston?"

"I messed up." A tear rolled down Preston's cheek and he didn't bother to wipe it. "I really messed up."

"Some company you keep," Leslie said. "Maybe they deserve to be dead."

Preston didn't argue. They shared a somber silent moment with each other.

"Later." Leslie walked past Preston and out the door.

Chapter Thirty-Five

R onnie woke up on his back with the thick stench of smoke heavy under his nose. As his eyes began to focus, the strangely familiar view of a blood-red sky appeared above him, with arms reaching downward and their owners screaming in pain. He pressed himself up against his elbows. A heatwave hit his face.

He was still in the forest, but it wasn't how he remembered it when he blacked out. The woods were on fire, every tree twisting up in a blaze toward the sky. The resulting smoke wrapped around every free inch of the woods and rolled around Ronnie. He hacked and covered his face. Embers from the burned forest fell like flaming confetti.

Ronnie brought himself to his feet. He kept inhaling the smoke, his lungs begging for air, but only got something dirty and wretched with every breath. He reminded himself that *he* created this. *He* could stop it. He just didn't know how. Between the screaming sky and roaring fire, he couldn't hear himself think, much less muster the brain power to determine how he'd get himself out of this hellscape. If he died in the Gray World, did he die in real life?

The smoke became thicker, wisping wildly, the red of the flames painting the smoke clouds like hellish clumps of fog. The smoke rose around Ronnie, first breaking along his ankles, then traveling up his legs.

A stomp echoed through the forest, the impact hard enough to shake the earth beneath Ronnie's feet. Then another, rumbling like an explosion. The sounds followed each other in sequence. Footsteps from something big. Very big.

"Karnalaxe," Ronnie said to himself between coughs.

The footsteps became louder, and the small earthquakes vibrated harder until Ronnie could see a set of twisting ram's horns cut through the smoke high in the sky—five stories up, if Ronnie had to guess. The rising smoke collapsed around the giant demon's snout and washed over its glowing red eyes, which stared down at Ronnie. Ronnie's creation in the flesh, mostly concealed behind a wall of smoke.

Karnalaxe's head lowered from view. His hand emerged from the smoke, with tight skin bleeding from the palms and long, jagged fingernails, reaching down toward Ronnie. Veins branched along its bulging, muscular forearm, pronounced enough for Ronnie to climb them. Ronnie was strangely calm as the hand reached for him, mesmerized by his creation and somehow knowing he was safe.

The hand cupped around Ronnie and he fell backward into it, the warm blood wet against his head and clothes. The hand lifted him up slowly, but with a velocity that he didn't expect, like going up a slope on a roller coaster. The smoke brushed past him as he went higher, higher, higher, until he was directly under Karnalaxe's nose. The head of a ram stared down at him, the air hot from its nostrils, its red, glowing eyes curious. He kept Ronnie there, high above the smoke and flames.

Ronnie breathed in the cool air, harnessed in the rough texture of Karalaxe's palm, close enough to his head to smell the smoky fur that had soaked in the harsh stench of burning woods. Ronnie was safe.

"Ronnie!" a familiar voice screamed out in a distant echo. "Ronnie, come back!"

A splash of black filled his vision like an inkblot, wiping out his view of the demon.

A second later he was greeted by Malleck, her black hair outlined by the morning sun. He blinked, blinked, blinked, reorienting himself in the present, having been pulled from the grip of Karnlalaxe, the glow of the ram's eyes still blotched in his retinas.

"He's protecting me," Ronnie said.

"What?" Malleck asked. "Ronnie, what happened?"

Ronnie turned to his side, pressing his palm against the ground. "Karnalaxe. I saw him in the Gray World." Ronnie pushed himself up, shuffling his knees under his body, and stood slowly. "How did you find me?"

"Same way I have been. Your Gray World energy."

Davion was right. His energy output in the gray world was like a signal.

Behind Malleck stood a short, stout woman in a tattered sweater. "Who's that?" Ronnie asked.

"My Aunt Helga. She's... well... magic. Like me," Malleck said.

Helga gave an unexpressive nod and a wave. "That's me. Magic," Helga said.

"What are you doing out here?" Malleck asked Ronnie.

"I... I really screwed up, Malleck," Ronnie said. "I trusted someone I shouldn't have. Someone who's like you, and..." He pointed at Helga. "Like you too, I guess, but..." Ronnie put a hand over his mouth and paced, recalling the impact of Davion's skeletal fist against his jaw.

The indestructible kid survives another concussion.

"He must have gone back and finished the ritual," Ronnie said. "Killed him."

"Who was it?" Malleck asked.

"Jack Sutter. Somewhere in these woods he's hanging upside down." He pressed his palms against his eyes, pressing back tears of anger, frustration, sadness. "Without feet... He was free. I freed him, Malleck."

He had to know for sure.

Ronnie bolted, tracing his steps back into the sea of trees, batting away stray branches, the same ones that had scraped his arms and face a few hours prior.

He stopped at the spot where Jack had tackled Anson, recalling the only nice thing Jack had ever done for him—a glimpse of the type of guy Jack could have been, and maybe his last good deed.

Not too far from that spot was Jack's body, which hung lifelessly at the spot Ronnie had rescued him from, having been placed back on the pillar upside down. Ronnie kept running, in denial at the scene before him. Lines of dried blood ran from Jack's ankles down to his pale head, which hovered above the bed of thorns, now drizzled red. His eyes were open wide and staring directly at Ronnie, stuck in a perpetual state of surprise. Perhaps a look of acknowledgment that this was really the end and no one was coming to save him.

Ronnie slowed his pace, then collapsed to his knees a body's length away from Jack.

"Oh my god," Malleck said, panting behind him. A second set of footsteps followed behind her as Helga caught up, panting louder.

"Davion, he... He tricked me," Ronnie said. "I can't believe I let him trick me."

"Davion?" Helga repeated from behind Ronnie, panting heavily. "Did you say Davion?"

"Davion Stivert," Ronnie said. "He's... my biological father."

"Well shit," Helga said. "We're not dealing with fools playing dress-up anymore. Does he have the book?"

Ronnie turned to Malleck and Helga. "I have to warn Preston."

Ronnie sat in the bed of the red pickup truck, his tailbone rattling awkwardly against the plastic grooves, waiting for signs of reception to appear on his phone. His back was pressed against the glass of a sliding window, separating him from Malleck and Helga. The trees of New Hill floated past the ends of his vision, replacing each other endlessly. The woods seemed so vast from where he sat, and he wondered how long it would take for anyone to find Jack Sutter's body.

Police sirens twirled in sharp repetition, giving him his answer.

He lay flat against the truck bed as the sirens faded in— closer... closer—and shot past him. Three cars in total.

Maybe this was their game. They perform the ritual then call in an anonymous tip the next day. Either they wanted the public to fear them, or they wanted to recruit new members. This wasn't a warning of things to come. It was a promise of a revolution.

Ronnie sat up in the truck bed once the sirens had gotten far enough out of earshot. Suddenly, the lock screen on his phone populated a series of texts. Some were from his mom, but one from Leslie caught his eye:

Where ru?? Preston's not at home.
No one knows where tf he is!!

"No," Ronnie said, barely able to hear himself over the rip of the wind. "Nonononono." Of course. Davion had taken Preston that night. Why wait to complete the ritual?

Ronnie yelled into the screaming wind.

The truck slowed, then pulled over to the side of the road. The back window slid open.

"You alright back there?" Helga asked from the driver's seat.

Ronnie curled his knees up to his chest, placed his forearms against them and held his head in his hands.

"Ronnie, what is it?" Malleck asked.

Ronnie repositioned his body to face Malleck and Helga. "They have him now. Davion took him while I was unconscious."

"That means he can complete the ritual," Malleck said.

After a few frustrated breaths, Ronnie replied, "Not quite." He reached into the bottom left pocket of his jean jacket. "There have been so many things out of my control that have happened this week. But since I created the blueprint, I thought... maybe I can break it too." Ronnie pulled out a folded wad of pages, torn at one side. "He may have Preston, but he won't have the ritual."

"Is that..." Malleck began to ask.

"Yeah. It's Preston's passage. I tore it out."

"Well aren't you full of surprises," Helga said.

"He'll be coming for me—for these pages. And he has a small army now." Ronnie put the papers back in his jacket pocket.

Helga's eyes faded to white. "He won't find us."

"What do we do now, Aunt Helga?" Malleck asked.

Helga put her white eyes back on the road and thrust the stick shift hard into first gear. "We have a small army as well."

Chapter Thirty-Six

They'd been driving for an hour and change and the terrain had gone from rural to highway and back to rural. Ronnie's face was still plastered with the tears he didn't bother to wipe, which stuck to his skin like glue, and his eyes had gone dry. Halfway through their drive, he'd gone numb and surrendered to the noise vacuum of the rustling air around him and the occasional silence and screech of brakes.

The flat land gave way to lush green fields that appeared immaculately kept. It was a far cry from the regular terrain of any given rural town in North Carolina.

Pinehill Manor was revealed to Ronnie in reverse from the back of the truck. The green fields and tall trees gave way to an open steel gate. The ends of the gate were attached to stone walls, which appeared to stretch for miles in either direction. The electronic gates closed behind the truck shifted against a gravel road.

Never in his life had Ronnie seen a mansion like Pinehill. It appeared more like a castle, with bricks in shades of gray stacked four stories high and containing large windowpanes that could fit a school bus through them, topped with a roof of high green pyramids. The gravel road opened into a wide circle in front of the manor, which functioned as a parking lot containing shiny luxury vehicles. The parking lot branched off into lines of tall square bushes that wrapped around the sides of the manor.

With his palms against the top of the truck, Ronnie stared in awe at the structure. He was struck with confusion as to why Helga had taken him to this massive estate. He had expected low-key, and this was so not low-key.

Helga found a spot in the gravel parkway, her rusted pickup truck sticking out amidst the wealthy car collector's paradise.

One of these things is not like the other, Ronnie thought.

She killed the engine, and she and Malleck got out of the truck, their doors squeaking on rusted hinges.

"Welcome to Pinehill Manor," Helga said.

"It's not very incognito, is it?" Malleck asked.

"Niece, you should know by now that when you got what we got, people see what you want them to see," Helga said boastfully.

Ronnie threw his legs over the side of the truck and landed on the gravel. "What is this, like a... school or something?"

Helga started walking. Ronnie and Malleck followed at each side of her.

"It's a bed and breakfast," Helga said. "Extremely expensive. People come for the peace and quiet. There's a gym, a spa, outdoor activities, gourmet breakfast, lunch, and dinner. Everything the mega-rich need to feel like they've earned something."

"Why are we here, though?" Malleck asked.

"Nine months ago," Helga continued, "there was this massive wave of dark energy radiating from somewhere near the center of North Carolina, around where you, my dear niece, resided. I'd been in communication with a small group for quite some time, the same group you know as Nu. The group needed an outpost to monitor the land, so they decided to hide in plain sight."

"How big is this group?" Malleck asked.

"Let's go have a look, shall we?" She looked over at Ronnie. "And you, harbinger of the apocalypse—"

"Be nice," Malleck said.

Helga went on. "Yesterday, I was ready to kill you. This girl here is what kept you alive. You created something very bad, but I hope she's right about you."

"Can you separate the art from the artist?" Malleck asked.

"Eh, usually it's the artist that's a piece of shit and the art that's actually good."

At least she doesn't think I'm a piece of shit, Ronnie thought. "Thanks... for not killing me, I guess."

"You're welcome," Helga replied.

A stone staircase led to ten-foot-tall double doors. Two young women opened a door on each side, wearing silver vests, white button-down shirts, and black dress pants. A thick green rug streaked through the marble flooring of the lobby. Two women stood behind the counter in their silver vests, smiles on their faces. To the right was a rounded staircase with a polished wooden railing and an elevator was stationed straight ahead. Engraved signs with arrows were positioned to the side of the elevator, guiding visitors to the "Dining Hall" to the left, "Spa" and "Pool" to the right, "Gymnasium" on the third floor, and so on. The sign that read "Banquet Hall—2nd Floor" was accompanied by a sign next to it that read "Under Construction".

Helga nodded to the women behind the lobby counter. They nodded back in unison with smiles on their faces. It was clear to Ronnie that Helga was a bit of a big shot here. The type that could walk into a prestigious bed and breakfast and not say a word. Ronnie waved to the women at the counter, which seemed like the right thing to do. Without breaking her smile, one of them said, "Welcome to Pinehill, sir. I see you keep good company."

They walked to the other end of the lobby and Helga pressed the button to call the elevator down. The three of them stood in silence as they waited, listening to the grinding sounds of gears lowering the elevator down to them.

"It seems like you're enjoying this," Malleck said to Helga.

"Maybe a little," Helga replied.

The elevator dinged and the doors opened. They all walked in and turned, waiting for the doors to close. Helga pressed the 2 button as the doors folded their view of the lobby.

"This place is pretty dope," said Malleck.

"Bit of an understatement," Ronnie cut in as the elevator began to rise. "How can anyone afford to make this a hideout?"

"The girls all work here and they train in the meantime," Helga replied.

"It's all girls?" Ronnie asked.

"Yep," Helga replied. "Manari culture is far behind the times. Women need special permission to practice magic, regardless of the power they're born with. The elders believe it interferes with their motherly duties."

"But some of the elders were women," Malleck said.

"Any hierarchy requires a certain level of complicity," Helga said. "It's why many of the young ladies here abandoned their communes."

The elevator stopped and the doors opened, leading to a hallway. Helga stepped out first, followed by Malleck, then Ronnie. "When you can do what we do, you make people see what they want to see. It makes it easier to hide in plain sight. As for getting us all into one location and on the same bankroll, well... That just takes a little influence."

"Mind manipulation," Ronnie said.

The ceiling of the hallway was almost comically tall. Several glass panes and doorways on the left side separated the hallway from a stone balcony with steel tables, chairs, and umbrellas. To the right was a wall of large frames, all empty.

"A little manipulation for the good of the people," Helga said.

"Why don't you, like... manipulate the mega-rich into giving their wealth to poor people?" Ronnie asked.

Malleck responded before Helga had a chance to. "Because it's a brush stroke on an infinite canvas. You can influence a few people, but you can't eliminate greed. Change has to be genuine."

"Otherwise, we'd spend all of our days mind-controlling the most important people in the world. There are simply too many." Helga stopped at two doors that met on the wall midway down the hall. A sign beside the doors read "Banquet Hall", accompanied by an "Under Construction" sign. Helga took a set of keys out of her pocket and looked left, right, behind. She inserted the key and twisted the lock.

"You've seen the way the Manari people live, Malleck. Well, some choose not to uphold their oath of peace and passivity. Several years ago, a group of Manari people seceded and branched off from the tribe. They trained to fight the battles their brothers, sisters, mothers, and fathers refused to fight." Helga turned the handle on the door and pulled it back. "I give you the Manari Nu."

The double doors gave way to a massive room, so big that Ronnie struggled to understand how it fit inside the second floor of the manor. The left wall was lined with metal cages six inches high, which housed medieval weapons—axes, swords, arrows, and other pointy things. Two dark wooden tables with accompanying wooden chairs lined the center of the room. The tables appeared to seat two dozen in total, but at the moment seated only one young woman, no older than twenty, eating a sandwich off a white plate.

The right side of the room consisted of loosely-constructed frames with soft sheets in pale greens, pinks, and yellows hung over them, creating room spaces between the frames. Each space had an assortment of plush pillows and comfy chairs. Ronnie counted two teenage girls sitting cross-legged opposite each other with their eyes closed, seemingly in a trance.

The far side of the room was matted with blue tape running across the mats, creating a cell grid. Three stations total. In the middle station, two women in their twenties bounced light-footed in a circle with sparring helmets, shin guards, and boxing gloves, arms raised. They were both average size and build. One had a butterfly tattoo on her shoulder and long braids tied back, which whipped around with every bounce and bob of her head. The other woman had short hair dyed red, with the right side of her head shaved from temple to ear.

Red gave a short series of jabs with her lead arm, not forceful, looking for an opening. She dove for Butterfly's legs and grappled with the backs of her knees.

Ronnie had seen a wrestling match at Knollwood Pines and anticipated Butterfly's movement. She'd kick her legs back and sprawl out, straightening her body and pinning Red against the ground.

Instead, she sprang into a shallow side flip, skimming Red's spine with hers, then landed with her feet facing her opponent. She had Red in a headlock instantly. She let up and they both moved to the ends of the cell, breathing heavily. They caught Helga in their view and waved.

"Damn," Malleck said.

Helga walked forward. "This is our safe space to train. Here we create within the Gray World and, of course, train for combat."

Ronnie stared at the wall of weapons. "Are those for decoration?"

Helga laughed. "No, of course not. Those are the weapons we train with. We reject modern weaponry."

"Why?" Ronnie asked.

"It doesn't take much skill to shoot a bullet, does it?" Helga asked. "Plus, it's extremely damn loud. The battles we fight need to stay hidden from the world."

"The Neverwells. I saw them using daggers and machetes," Ronnie said.

"Even bad guys have a code, I guess," Malleck said.

They passed by the tables. The sparring women had raised their fists again, beginning another round. Helga walked around them.

"Let's do an early lunch first," Helga said. "Then we'll figure out how the hell we're going to stop this monster from being unleashed."

Helga sat on one side of a wooden table in the banquet hall opposite Ronnie and Malleck as two young women walked off with empty plates. They'd eaten in relative silence. Ronnie and Malleck traded glances at each other when they weren't staring at every inch of the room.

Helga looked at the two of them and grinned. "I know. It's a whole new world."

"Why didn't you ever tell me about this place?" asked Malleck.

"I was always going to tell you when you were ready," Helga said. "No time like the present. Even when factions secede, the Manari have a way of... interfering."

Malleck noticed the puzzled look on Ronnie's face. "It's kinda complicated."

Ronnie looked at Helga. "My father, Davion. You seemed like you knew him."

Helga slid her chair out and stood. She put her arms to the sky and stretched her pine, then let out a deep exhale. "Knew of him, sure. I know he's bad news. Yes, Davion Stivert was a Manari, just like Malleck and I. The Manari culture is peaceful and quiet. That peace, the lack of challenge... That boredom can lead a man to seek out alternative forms of entertainment. For Davion, it was dark magic, so I've heard. He was interested in using his gifts to conjure entities."

"Power of the gods," Ronnie said. "That's what he called it."

"Not gods, Ronnie. Demons."

Ronnie took a deep breath. "He's dying. He seems to think that by completing the ritual he'll be able to restore his health."

"Yeah, I figure he'd be sick. His punishment for practicing dark magic was a long spell of the Affliction," Helga said.

"The what?" Ronnie cut in.

"It's like a sickness potion," Malleck said. "It's how you're punished for violating the Manari doctrine. It strips your power and makes you weak."

Helga continued. "His power had grown so strong that the Affliction couldn't suppress it. He was able to overpower the elders and leave the Manari even in his sickened state. The thing about the Affliction is that it has to be monitored closely. If it goes without the proper care and treatment, it causes irreparable harm to the body."

"So he's dying from the Affliction," Malleck said.

"Yes. He lived for decades with it. Initially it wouldn't have shown signs of physical damage, but it's been slowly rotting his insides. It's said that he who conjures a demon can make it do his bidding. Whether it means he can use the powers of the demon to heal himself, I have no idea."

"He said I was born to fulfill a prophecy," Ronnie said. "To create the blueprint for bringing the gods to Earth."

"It was rumored that he used countless dark magic spells leading up to the conception of his child," Helga said. "His plan seemed far-fetched, but... here you are. You're that son. And it seems that a lot of people believe in the prophecy."

"So... I could actually make Karnalaxe real?" Ronnie asked.

"Karnalaxe?" Helga repeated. "Is that what you named him?"

"It just came to me in a dream," Ronnie said.

"In the Gray World," Malleck said. "It was the first time he traveled. That's how we found each other."

"Cute," Helga said dryly. "*You* cannot make the demon flesh and blood. You write the text—the scripture, if you will—and someone else has to execute it. If the prophecy is correct, that's the only way it works. You might be of Manari blood, but you don't have all the gifts."

"To Davion Stivert, you *are* the gift," Malleck said.

Just then, the double doors opened. Ronnie, Malleck, and Helga turned their heads in unison toward the sound of the doors gently sliding along their hinges. A woman in a white, silver, and black uniform stepped into the room and pulled the doors behind her. She turned with a bewildered look on her face.

"Helga," the woman said. "There's a young girl in the lobby saying that she's looking for a... Ronnie?"

Ronnie straightened in his seat.

"She's saying that she knows he's here and if she doesn't see him soon she'll call the police." The woman delivered the message in a confusing mix of question and statement.

Ronnie remembered back to Monday morning—*What day is it now?*—when Leslie took his phone from him and tinkered with it gleefully. He didn't know what she was doing with it then, but it became clear now. She could track his phone.

The woman continued. "She says her name is—"

"Leslie Masood," Ronnie said before she could finish. He then looked at Malleck, who then looked at Helga.

"Leslie knows a lot already, Aunt Helga," Malleck said. "She's okay."

Helga gave a begrudging shake of her head. She turned to the woman at the door. "It looks like I'll have to do the tour all over again."

When the elevator doors opened, Leslie was standing under the high chandelier, which fractured the natural sunlight in colorful streaks. True to form, she wore distressed denim jeans, a Misfits t-shirt with a peeling screen print, and her biker jacket. The leather slapped against Ronnie's chest as her tiny arms engulfed him. She held him tight, settling her head against his shoulder. This was a Leslie he wasn't used to. Ronnie had always known her to be confident and fully in charge of every situation, but the long embrace carried vulnerability and sadness.

"I thought I'd lost you too," Leslie said, her voice muffled against Ronnie's jean jacket. She let go of Ronnie, making some space between them, then gave him an open-handed punch to the chest. "What the hell have you been doing? I thought we were a team! Your mom's been calling me nonstop asking where you are and I've been covering for you this whole time, only to find out you're in a goddamn mansion?! Preston's gone, Ronnie!"

With Leslie's outburst finished, a sharp silence fell into the lobby. Ronnie eyed the staff, who each quickly diverted their attention away from them.

"There's a lot I have to tell you," Ronnie said. "Why don't we take a walk?"

Leslie walked with Ronnie past the archery targets on bundled hay behind Pinehill Manor. The back area was more of a ranch than a traditional backyard, with a horse stable, a fenced-in riding area, and a skeet-shooting station.

"So your bio-dad, who's some magical mind-wizard, saved you from the Neverwells, then used you to *find* the Neverwells, then became the leader of the Neverwells all in the span of, like, half-a-day?"

"Uh, yeah... Pretty much," Ronnie replied.

"I knew your family situation was screwed up, but I didn't know it was *that* screwed up."

"Don't rub it in."

"Shit, I'm sorry."

"I'm sorry too. I should have told you about Preston. I just never thought it would get this far."

I should have told you about Preston. It repeated in Leslie's mind. All she could think about was the last time she saw him. The heatwave of anger that scorched her skin and made her nearly belligerent. The look on Preston's face—shock, terror, emotional anguish. He'd known about horrible things and made a choice to do nothing, and that was inexcusable. But if that was the last time Leslie ever saw Preston, she'd never forgive herself for how she stormed off.

She decided not to tell Ronnie about the Polaroids. It wasn't her secret to tell.

"Do we have any chance at getting him back?" Leslie asked.

"That's why we're here. I tore Preston's pages out of the book before Davion had a chance to take them from me. All we need now is a plan."

Leslie imagined this Davion guy flipping excitedly through the leatherbound notebook, sliding pages right to left, searching for the passage, only to see scars of torn paper in the binding.

PART III.

Chapter Thirty-Seven

"I can round up a group in an hour's time," Helga said to Ronnie and Malleck in the banquet hall. "As long as Stivert and the Neverwells are out there, they're a threat to the natural world. We can use Ronnie to lure him out."

"Using kids as bait again?" Malleck said. "I'm starting to think you're a bad strategist."

Ronnie appreciated Malleck's concern, but he'd already considered this. If they had any chance of launching a counterattack at Davion, the plan would have to revolve around him. Davion had been inside his mind, had seen the fear coursing through Ronnie's weak, fragile mind. It was the only thing Ronnie had to use against him. An edge that Davion wouldn't expect.

A rattle of metal shifted Ronnie's attention to Leslie as she tugged on the caged entry door that secured the wall of weapons.

Helga puffed out a frustrated sigh and said, "There will be no weapons training for you today, but I admire the enthusiasm." She turned back to Ronnie. "Are we expecting any other 'normal' children at our secret headquarters today or can we carry on?"

Ronnie gave Leslie a "behave yourself" look. She released her grip from the cage and joined their circle.

"With Davion sick," Helga continued, "We might have a fighting chance."

"Do you think it's possible?" Ronnie asked. "To summon Karnalaxe?"

"Davion's been studying dark magic his whole life," Helga replied. "If anyone can do it, it's him."

"I'm not asking if it's possible for Davion to do it. I'm asking if *we* can."

"You can't be serious." Helga scowled.

"He's deadass," Leslie said.

"Karnalaxe was created by the darkest parts of me, but... I feel like he could be a force for good. Davion told me that by summoning the power of the gods, we could vanquish all evil in the world. Well... Isn't evil just subjective to whoever has the power to fight it?"

"Are you saying we should use Karnalaxe to kill the Neverwells and... your father?" Malleck asked.

Ronnie furrowed his eyebrows, lost in deep concentration within his own mind. After a moment, he spoke. "As far as I'm concerned, I'm the same bastard kid I was a week ago. Davion's desperate. He won't stop. We actually have a way to end this. And I intend to."

"And how do you plan on doing that?" Helga asked skeptically.

"I write a new passage," Ronnie said. "One that doesn't involve Preston. We fulfill the ritual."

"No," Helga said. "Absolutely not."

"I can do it, Helga," Malleck said. "You know I can."

"Your dark magic up to now has consisted of low-level telekinesis, and even *that* you have a hard time controlling," Helga said. "To summon a demon, you need to rip open a hole between worlds. People spend their whole lives studying dark magic to get to a point where they can do it and they still die trying."

"But I won't," Malleck said, "because I haven't had to spend my whole life studying it. I was born to summon dark magic, Helga. You know it and I know it. It's time I do something with it."

Leslie's face twisted into a grin. She nodded her head. "Let's summon a freaking demon."

The other members of the circle turned their heads to Leslie. Ronnie returned a smile, knowing that Helga and Malleck wouldn't.

"What?" Leslie said. "I wanna help."

"I need to go to the Gray World," Ronnie said to Malleck. "I need to speak with Davion."

Ronnie had only entered the Gray World a total of three times, and each time it was under strenuous circumstances. An element of fear sparked his travels. Now that he was safe in this enclosed space with people he could trust, he had no clue how to access it on his own, short of having someone put a gun to his head.

He lowered to a prayer's pose inside one of the meditation booths closed in by thin, pink cotton sheets that distorted the light, causing a pastel glow on the pillows that surrounded him. Malleck kneeled down at the front of the station. Helga stood behind with her arms crossed next to Leslie, who also had her arms crossed and her back arched too far back in an attempt to mimic and mock Helga. Ronnie saw Helga catch Leslie in her periphery, then roll her eyes and pivot away from the small girl.

"Get in any position you feel comfortable," said Malleck, kneeling on the ground. Several thin pieces of metal shimmied on her wrists as she pulled her long hair back and tied it into a ponytail.

Ronnie unfolded his legs out from under him and laid back, repositioning a pillow against his neck and head. "I should probably lay down for this, right?"

"If that's how you feel comfortable," Malleck replied.

Malleck rose and repositioned herself near the top of his head, then lowered to a cross-legged position. Ronnie could smell the rubber of her boots hovering just above his head. The tips of her fingers lightly touched his temples and he loosened his muscles, lying still on the floor.

"Wait... Won't I be giving away this location?" asked Ronnie.

"Your mind only knows how to reference your location at any given time. Don't worry. I'll displace you. You'll go back to where it all started," Malleck replied.

"With the giant axe?"

"Yeah, with the giant axe. I could travel with you, you know. If you go alone and something goes wrong, I won't know when to get you out."

"I have to go alone," Ronnie replied. "Give me five minutes. He looked for me for sixteen years. He'll know how to find me."

Malleck sighed. "Okay. Here we go."

Ronnie closed his eyes and waited as bright splotches pooled around his vision.

A sudden darkness pulled the splotches away and the floor dropped beneath him. Instead of sinking down, he hung in the air, dangling in a dark void, so dark that he no longer knew whether his eyes were closed or open. He willed his body to tilt into an upright position, his feet slowly pressing against a hard surface. A distant static grew in intensity.

No, not static.

Shrill cries of pain, sharp as razors in Ronnie's ears. The screams came from high above, drowning Ronnie in a hail of awful percussive agony.

In an instant, the scene around him came into view. A street lined with abandoned cars, buildings charred and releasing smoke into the air, a blood-red sky with a million hands swaying, reaching down. Ronnie swatted embers floating in front of his face, obscuring the object sticking out of the pavement twenty yards ahead of him.

The double-bitted axe was surrounded by a circle of yellow flames, stuck at an angle with its leather handle and twisting vine of barbed wire aimed high toward the sky. It stood twice as tall as the highest of the surrounding brick buildings. It was exactly how Ronnie remembered it nine months ago.

The clock was ticking in Ronnie's head. No time to waste. He walked toward the axe, the heat of the flames pushing against his body as he got closer. "Davion!" he yelled. "Davion!" He was as close as he could be to the flames without them reaching out to burn him. He stopped and looked around.

Tick tock. Tick tock.

"Would it kill you to call me Dad?" Davion's voice projected over the hum of fire.

Ronnie walked around the flaming perimeter, searching for Davion through red streaks. "Coming from a man who would sucker-punch his own son in the face," he said.

The gray fedora floated just above the fire, then Davion's olive skin came into view as he rounded the perimeter from the opposite direction. "You survived a fall from a water tower. I knew a sock in the jaw wouldn't phase you." He stopped inches away from Ronnie, the flames at their side. "Besides, I did you a favor. You wouldn't have wanted to see what happened to Jack, even though, well... You *did* put his death to paper." Davion chuckled to himself. "Okay, I admit it. I was disappointed that you refused to join me. That is until I opened the book this morning.

It was a clever move, but I don't know what you expect to do next. You know I need those pages."

"Where's Preston?"

"He's safe. For now. I'm sorry, Ronnie. You can't stop him from dying. You gotta know that."

Ronnie looked away, his face burning—not from the fire, but from the swell of anger.

"Listen, Ronnie. You're my son," Davion said, softening his voice. "I love you—"

"You don't know a thing about me!" Ronnie yelled.

Davion clenched his jaw. "When we start the new beginning, you'll be by my side. You'll see how beautiful the world can be. And all the people you love, we can take them with us. Or... I can turn them over to the Neverwells. And they can hurt them... One by one until you give me the damn pages."

Ronnie's eyes widened in fear. Even in this dimension, a plane beyond his known reality, his hands dampened and shook.

Davion turned away from Ronnie. The smiling, charming gentleman was gone, replaced by this deadly serious, weary man, heavy with the weight of his own slow demise. "You must think I'm some kind of monster. I promise you I'm not. But I need you to understand the consequences of defying your father. I've seen the world through your eyes, kid. I've walked through that cute little house and smelled your momma's skin." He closed his eyes and sniffed in through his nostrils. "Mmmmm. She smelled as sweet as I remember." He opened his eyes. "How about that little girl who likes rock music? What if her mommy and daddy just happened to... I don't know... walk into a lake with their coats full of rocks? You think she'd forgive you, knowing you could've done something to stop it?"

"You hurt them and you'll never—"

"You really wanna play this game? I'm dying. What else do you think I have to lose, son?"

Ronnie let out an animalistic howl from deep inside his gut, bursting through his exposed teeth. "Stop calling me son!"

A louder roar followed from above, with a bass that rattled the ground beneath them. Ronnie looked towards the sky, the jagged rows of limbs swaying downward, as the roar continued, then faded.

"Sounds like something up there heard you," Davion said. "Here's what's going to happen. You're going to bring me the pages at midnight... At the Knollwood Pines water tower."

Of course it would be the water tower. Ronnie tried to mask his fright, but Davion caught it and smiled cruelly.

"Don't think me a murderer, son. I don't kill unless it's the absolute last resort. This wasn't how I imagined things playing out. I can't be too disappointed, though, considering you've been raised by a woman who abandoned our cause. She may have very well robbed you of your true purpose, had I not come into your life."

Ronnie wanted to scream from deep in his chest, to defend his mother, to threaten him to never mention her ever again. He wanted Davion to know that ripping him away from that cult—from Davion's cause—was the best thing his mom could have ever done for him.

But he kept the anger still inside his chest, knowing that he had a role to play. All he had to do was appear weak, which, it turns out, was something he was intimately—if not exclusively—familiar with.

"The truth is, this sickness feels like a weight dragging me down, getting heavier by the day. Every ounce of energy I expend is energy I can't get back.

"When you fell asleep in the motel, I took the chance to dive inside your mind. The trip through your unconscious was burdensome and painful, like trying to stay awake behind the wheel of a car while being stabbed in all directions, but I reveled in the presence of your thoughts.

All your memories creating a tapestry of a boy wandering through life, slowly becoming a man. So much confusion. You couldn't even form an image of yourself to present to others, and so you resorted to isolation, finding solace in written words and artwork. And you were good at it—*are* good. Very good.

"As for your mother, well... for a brief period in time, I hated her. Having my child ripped from the home I built, a child that was so special—not just to me but to my entire race—was devastating. But I realized soon after that the hate I felt was self-hatred. I had felt Cynthia slipping away from me long before she left and decided to keep her mind in a stupor rather than trying to help her reconcile her new reality. I had been so focused on *my* world that I disregarded hers, instead resorting to mind manipulation akin to a sedative. How long could we have continued that way? My attempt to render Cynthia barely sentient turned against me. It made me complacent. I didn't realize the strength of mind she had."

Thoughts of his mother, blank-faced, dazed in a state of mind control, were inescapable. They made Ronnie hate his father even more. In the Gray World, Ronnie had seen an axe, and now all he could picture was the axe coming down on Davion's head.

"I know you share the same strength Cynthia did, nerves and all. It's true that dark magic protects you. To what extent, the world has yet to see. I can't wait to see your vision made whole." Davion breathed deeply. "I'll make it quick for Preston, I promise you that. He won't suffer. You have my word. Your mom and little Leslie will stay safe... And that'll be the end of it."

The end of the world as we know it, Ronnie thought as he fought back against his nerves. Davion didn't deserve the power he asserted over Ronnie.

But *that* was the power Ronnie had over Davion. In Davion's mind, Ronnie was helpless, with his back against the wall and without a single card to play. Ronnie's knuckles cracked as he clenched his fists, imagining how good it would feel to knock in his father's awful bleached teeth.

"I'll give you the pages, just… Please don't hurt them." The words coming out of his mouth sounded pathetic. Exactly what they needed to be.

"No games this time, Ronnie." Davion walked closer and pressed his palms against Ronnie's shoulders, giving him two light pats and staring into his eyes. "I can't wait to see the future we build together. I know it may not be clear now given the circumstances, but… I am so incredibly proud of—"

In a disorienting flash across Ronnie's vision, Davion's face was replaced with Malleck's, hovering over him. Her ponytail had fallen from behind her and the thick sensation of a heat wave against his cheek was replaced with the tickle of several strands of hair delicately stabbing the side of his face.

Malleck removed her hands from his temples. "How'd it go?"

Ronnie clinched his eyes, adjusting to the light in the room, and slowly worked his way up to stand. He turned his view from Malleck to Leslie and Helga, who all waited for his next words. "I need something to write with."

"Done," said Helga.

"Davion wants the pages at midnight," Ronnie said. "We're gonna give him what he wants."

Chapter Thirty-Eight

R onnie wrote at a desk in a private room with his head as clear as it had ever been, the words pouring out of him and falling onto the pages. He was compelled by a new understanding of his purpose. His entire life, he'd been a passive participant, helpless to combat any challenge that life threw at him. He was born to do something unique and awful, gifted a power that he didn't understand. Something that was inevitable and unstoppable. Once again, he was helpless.

Until now.

The pathway to Karnalaxe was clear. The final ritual required eyes, a tongue, feet, hands, and lungs. Those sacrifices would make Karnalaxe whole. The only portion that was missing was a set of lungs. Ronnie tried his best to block out the image of Preston's lifeless, sagging body, bent over with gaping gashes torn through his back outlined with thick, dripping circles of blood pooling beneath him, two concave holes drilled through the back of his ribcage leading to the missing lungs.

Karnalaxe needed lungs, that part was clear, but the owner of the lungs could be changed. Ronnie had no powers of mind control or illusions. He couldn't track someone's energy simply by touching their belongings. He couldn't speak telepathically. But he *could* do this. He alone could change the trajectory of the night.

Ronnie finished the final line with a stab of his pen. He set the pen on the desk and collected the sheets, squaring them together. He left the room and found his way to the banquet hall, planning to speak with Malleck and Helga first.

"She's a spirited one," Helga said, referencing Leslie. She placed her hands on the ledge of the stone balcony that overlooked the entryway. Pristine grass stretched for miles in all directions, striking the stone wall that lined the property.

Ronnie approached the ledge and stood next to her.

"She loves you, you know," Helga said. "Like a... platonic love. She'd do anything for you is what I'm trying to say. We could use her spark, but there's no way we're putting her in harm's way."

"What if we made her disappear?" asked Ronnie.

"What? How do you mean?" Helga replied.

"If there's one thing I know about the Manari, it's that you can control what other people see. Davion's only expecting me."

Malleck's voice cut in, quick and angry. "Are you out of your mind?" Ronnie's pages rattled in her hand. She held them high over her head and marched her way over to him. "*This* is your new plan?"

"You asked me to trust you once. I need *you* to trust *me* now. This is the only way. I can't let anyone else get hurt." Ronnie's voice was controlled and his head was clear. He looked at Helga. "Are the Manari Nu prepared to fight?"

"Yes," Helga said without hesitation.

Ronnie addressed them both. "I have a plan. It's going to be danger-ous... Probably reckless... And in case anything goes wrong, we're gonna need something loud and obnoxious."

Ronnie followed Helga into the banquet hall with Malleck at his side. At the far end of the room, Leslie tiptoed in one of the sparring squares with gloved hands raised to her chin. The woman with the butterfly tattoo danced around her with padded hands raised, calling out combinations. "One, two," the woman said, smiling. Leslie gave two quick jabs—left, right. "One, one, four." Left jab, left jab, right hook. "Yeah, you're gettin' it."

"Can you give Ronnie and me a moment, Malleck?" Helga asked.

Malleck nodded and walked over to the sparring square to spectate, leaving a cold and silent Helga alone with Ronnie. She waited a few seconds before speaking, making sure Malleck was out of earshot.

"You really think this'll work?" Helga asked. "I know you're the architect, but... it seems like you're putting the ceiling on a house that isn't finished yet."

"I'm pretty sure that's exactly how you build a house," Ronnie said. "Otherwise, if it rains—"

"Okay, I'm not one for metaphors. What I'm saying is it seems like you're breaking your own sequence."

"The inversion spell is just a delivery mechanism," Ronnie said. "It's separate from the final ritual. Once the offerings are together, the final ritual can start."

"You have to understand what you're asking them to do," Helga said. "Me? I'm damn-near fifty. I've been looking for a fight like this my whole life, but those two girls there..." She pointed out to the other side of the room, where Malleck stood with her arms crossed, hollering atta-girls at Leslie. "They're not soldiers. You're asking me to put my niece and your best friend in harm's way. I'm the most powerful Manari here and you're asking me to keep up an incredibly difficult illusion for... as long as it takes."

"You *can* keep up the illusion, right?" Ronnie asked.

"Goddamn right I can," Helga replied. "But if anything goes wrong, I won't be able to protect them."

"Davion has no reason to hurt either of them as long as thinks he's gotten what he wants."

Helga put her head down and scratched at the carpet with the tip of her shoe. "I hope you're right."

"Thank you. Really," Ronnie said. It was sincere and gentle and the only thing that needed to be said.

Ronnie left Helga's side and made his way to the sparring square, where Leslie finally dropped her arms and brushed the hair from in front of her face, panting.

"Shit. I gotta do more cardio," Leslie said.

Ronnie gave her a smile. "Can I chat with you for a minute?"

Leslie huffed. "Why don't you come in the ring and talk with your fists?" She turned to Butterfly Tattoo. "Hey, you want to teach me how to do that jumping twist-flip thing?" Butterfly Tattoo gave a belly laugh.

Ronnie led Leslie out of the banquet hall to the stone patio. Leslie's breathing calmed as she flapped the bottom of her shirt against her stomach, circulating the cool fall air.

"So, what's up?" Leslie said. "We jailbreakin' Preston or what?"

"Yes," Ronnie replied. "I did what you told me to do. I wrote a new ritual that doesn't involve Preston."

"Someone else is getting chopped? Please tell me it's your psycho father."

"I have to keep that to myself. Just know that whatever happens, I have a plan and I know what I'm doing... I think."

"You haven't known what you're doing since elementary school, Hendrix. But, oh, yeah, I forgot. You have this like 'destiny' or whatever." Leslie's arms swam mockingly in the air to overemphasize the sarcasm.

"I survived a drop from the water tower without so much as a scratch. I have the power of a demon in my veins. I think I might actually be indestructible."

"Ronnie..."

He changed the subject quickly. "We need your electric guitar. Do you have access to an amp and a generator?" he asked.

"I'm sure I could pull some strings with my old bandmates," she said with a confused look on her face.

"With Davion's mind magic, the only way I see this working is if we have something—"

"Loud and frickin' obnoxious," Leslie said, realization settling on her face. "Ronnie, my friend... Are you asking me to carry my guitar into battle to save the human race from destruction at the hands of a crazy wizard?"

Ronnie thought for a moment, then shook his head. "Yes, actually, that's exactly what I'm asking you to do."

Leslie folded her arms across her body, her palms landing on her shoulders. She stood there ponderously, taking the request in so sternly that Ronnie thought she might decline. Instead, she released her arms and threw them around Ronnie. "This is the best day of my life," she whispered. "I won't let you down. And you..." Leslie took a hard look at Ronnie. "Don't do anything stupid. I thought I'd lost you once. I will reverse-haunt your ass if I lose you again."

They stood together with the beautiful scenery of the manor at their side until Leslie released Ronnie from her grip and trotted off as determined as Ronnie had ever seen her.

"You text me where and when to meet and I'll be there with Sasha in tow," Leslie said, facing away from Ronnie. She threw open the glass door leading to the hallway and headed toward the elevator.

Sasha? Ronnie thought.

Oh yeah... It was the name of her guitar.

The sun fell and masked the serene exterior of Pinehill in darkness, triggering the nighttime lights aimed upward at the manor's first story and surrounding bushes. Ronnie couldn't shake the terrible churning in his gut that came with the complete absence of the sun. It meant that time was winding down, and the most important moment of his life would become a reality in mere hours.

The moon was nearly full above the second-story balcony. He remembered being a child and noticing a face, two pits for eyes and a wide mouth, unable to grasp the distance between him and the enormous rock. The closer he got to it, his mother told him, the less visible the face would become, and if he were to stand right on top of it, he'd see nothing but dirt, rough edges, and craters.

As he grew older, he realized that from the perspective of the moon, he wasn't even a face. Not the pit of an eye nor the gape of a mouth. He wasn't even a speck. He was wholly insignificant and at the whims of the universe. If nothing mattered, then what was the point of carrying on? He always hoped desperately that purpose would be given to him, that someone would give him direction. What was he meant for? That question had been answered for him. But though he was meant for terrible things, he understood now that it was not his purpose. Purpose, he decided, was chosen, not given.

"Helga's calling everyone together," Malleck said from behind Ronnie in a quiet, tender tone.

Ronnie took a few deep breaths, willing the knot in his gut to unravel.

"Ronnie," Malleck said, "I don't know if I can—"

"Please," Ronnie said. "Please let me do this. I'm scared. More scared than I've ever been in my entire life, but I just have this feeling that everything's going to work out."

Malleck was riddled with uncertainty. Her entire face sagged like it was falling to the ground. "How can you be so sure?"

"Because the bullies don't win. Not this time. Not if we fight back."

They walked together through the glass door, across the hallway, and into the banquet hall. Helga stood, hands behind her back, before a row of a dozen Manari Nu soldiers like a general commanding her troops. The women were all youthful, some still with acne on their cheeks, and were covered in smooth, padded, black body armor. The pads were thin and separated by a tight, sleek material, and the uniforms appeared to be built for a combination of stealth, power, and protection. Ronnie scanned the weapons they wielded—spears, hatchets, daggers. He recognized Red and Butterfly, who both carried swords sheathed behind them with thick handles angled toward the ceiling.

Helga gave her niece and Ronnie a nod, then addressed her soldiers. "Manari Nu," she said. "You're some of the greatest and bravest women I've had the good fortune of knowing. You've prepared tirelessly for a threat we all knew was looming over Knollwood Pines. Tonight, we have a chance to end that threat once and for all. You are here because you've rejected a fairy tale that peace, tranquility, and kindness will one day reign supreme and overpower the evil forces that would do harm to our fellow people. Instead, you live in the reality of knowing that some of those who are given power abuse that power. And that peace, tranquility, and kindness allow such abuse to go unchecked." She pointed to Ronnie and Malleck. "Tonight, you will protect these two at all costs. One holds the key to ending this mess, and the other..." She gave Malleck a loving look. "She's a once-in-a-generation anomaly. She was born with the ability to summon dark magic. Even at a young age, I knew she'd be more powerful than even me. She's more powerful than all of us."

Helga looked down and paced. "Tonight, we'll fight in secret. I will keep you hidden from the natural world. No one will know what you've done tonight... But I wouldn't have it any other way. True heroes don't fight for glory. They fight for virtue. You, my sisters... and I guess Ronnie... are truly virtuous."

"I'll take it," Ronnie said under his breath.

Chapter Thirty-Nine

The air was cold and bitter as the Knollwood Pines downtown clock tower neared midnight, urging Leslie to seek the comfort and warmth of her bed. But to hell with that. Leslie drove with the windows down, welcoming the chill against her leather sleeves, her knuckles going numb against the steering wheel. It must've been under forty degrees, but gloves weren't an option. She needed her fingers, frozen or not, to strum the tight strings of Sasha, which lay diagonally from floor to ceiling in the backseat like a silent passenger. The body of the guitar was thin and pink with a waxy gloss that reflected streetlights onto the ceiling of the Corolla. Next to Sasha was an amp, old and rusted. The red metal that housed the important parts was caked in dried, rustic dirt.

The trunk contained a microphone stand, cables, and a speaker box. The combined weight of the trunk and backseat caused the back of the car to sag. Every time Leslie went over a speed bump, her suspension grunted against the weight.

This time of night, barely a single soul was out on the town, save for the packs of kids who ran from bush to bush in suburban neighborhoods smashing eggs against windows or passing around a carton of cigarettes, trying desperately to love the stomach-churning stench of tobacco.

The top of the water tower came into view at the corner of her windshield, high above a line of bushes that separated it from the sidewalk. It was at the center of town, which meant that, prior to tonight, Leslie couldn't avoid it if she tried. It was always there, hanging stagnant in the sky, reminding her of the time she thought she lost her best friend.

She couldn't see through the darkened bushes what was at the base of the water tower. What did she expect? A group of robed men surrounding a bound and gagged Preston as he screamed for his life? Even in the seclusion of midnight, the spot was visible from the intersection, and any driver would have seen it.

She took a left into the community center entrance. Her headlights shot through the empty parking lot and landed on Malleck, who was standing in front of the bright building, blowing out icy puffs of breath that caught the light. Malleck waved a hand, her face straight and serious. She walked to the car and opened the passenger's side door.

"Right on time," Malleck said.

"Isn't it a little risky to meet this close to the water tower? Can't you people, like, sense each other?" Leslie said.

"My aunt's running interference," Malleck said as she got in the car and closed the door.

"Like blocking a signal?"

"Exactly. Now, you're going to cut the lights and drive slowly. There's a high spot at the north side of the hill we can use. You *have* to be quiet. I can clear you from their vision, but I can't mask sound, I can only muffle it. And don't do anything unless Ronnie or myself goes under. Do you understand?" Malleck delivered the words with genuine care in a jittery in, caffeine-fueled rush.

"I understand," Leslie said. "No shredding unless you and Ronnie are eating it."

Malleck took a long, somber look at Leslie, then lowered her eyes and sat in silence. The words didn't come, so Leslie decided to fill them in for her.

"You're a square peg."

Malleck thought for a second. "What?"

"When I was driving Ronnie to school—the first day he came back after his accident—he said he felt like a square peg trying to fit in a round hole. I think all of us—you, me, Ronnie, Preston—we're all square pegs, you know?" Leslie gave Malleck a smile. "It's kinda weird to say, but... I'm really glad we all found each other."

Malleck contemplated Leslie's words, then began to nod. "Yeah," she said, then chuckled. "I'm a square peg."

"Now let's shove that square peg right up Davion Stivert's—"

"Leslie, I love you, but don't be gross."

"Okay, fine... Down his throat."

Malleck's eyes went cloudy as she sat upright in her seat, facing forward. She was statuesque, with a slight downward tilt of her chin, in deep concentration. Leslie drove slowly, the back of the car hobbling uneasily, guided by the light of lampposts. As she drove past the row of bushes lining the side of the field, Leslie craned her neck toward base of the water tower, which showed no signs of life around it. "Where are they?" Leslie asked herself.

"They're hiding themselves," Malleck said, causing Leslie to jump. Malleck's body was motionless, save for the movement of her lips. "It's magic. I can't feel them, but... they're over there."

They took a right turn at the intersection and edged down the road that faced the north side of the water tower. Leslie pulled off the road and onto a dirt curb that ended at a collection of trees that fed into the forest and wrapped around the field. She'd parked there before, having gone with groups of friends to explore the woods in the nighttime with nothing but flashlights and jackets zipped against their chests to comfort them. Since the town was so quiet at night, every small sound of the woods was amplified, which made it perfect for telling spooky stories. After this experience, she would never tell nor willingly listen to another spooky story again.

Leslie killed the engine, then looked past Malleck through the passenger's side window, seeing only the water tower. The dirt area below them was just wide enough for the vehicle and fell into a gradual eight-foot slope on the side.

"Do you know if Preston's out there?" Leslie asked.

"I'm sure he is," Malleck answered.

Under the cover of Malleck's magic, Leslie unpacked the contents of her car, first dragging out the generator sitting atop a smooshed cloth seat. It came down hard on the dirt, causing Leslie to wince and take a quick look around. She continued to the trunk, where she ripped out the cables as fast as she could, then pulled out the amp, microphone, and stand, and placed them at the side of the car a healthy distance from the slope of the hill. She took glances at the water tower as she plugged in the various cables with precision, her mind doing jumping jacks to convince her that what she was seeing was real while knowing that just beyond the field Preston was in danger.

Finally, she gently removed Sasha, glowing pink and beautiful, from the back seat and held her with reverence, remembering that the last time she'd played had been to raise money for Ronnie's medical bills. Here she was at the water tower again. She'd be playing for Ronnie, for Preston, for Malleck, and, by extension, the entire human race.

She put her right arm through the guitar strap, letting it hang tightly against her body as the weight of the electric guitar sunk into her palms. She stepped over the snaking cables and eyed the orange cord handle on the generator. Her hand jittered at the thought of ripping it. He looked over at Malleck in the passenger's seat of the car. "Ready," Leslie said. She then gazed out into the not-so-empty field, where her audience of robed men in masks and armed warriors would drown in the sporadic rhythm of her guitar. If they were lucky.

"I'll wake up this entire town if I have to," Leslie whispered to herself, ready for battle with the weapon of choice in her hands.

Chapter Forty

The ground was hard against Ronnie's feet as he trekked through the woods on his way to the water tower. A flashlight carved his path and warm puffs of breath formed clouds in front of him as he walked, vanishing as soon as they appeared. Inside the lower left pocket of his jean jacket, he fumbled over sharp edges of paper. The pages weren't going anywhere, and he knew this, but he kept checking his inside pocket every few steps, paranoid that they would disappear.

His pulsating heart sent shockwaves through his limbs. So powerful was his heartbeat that he could nearly hear it. He couldn't discern whether it was fear for his life or fear of revisiting the place that set off this entire chain of events. To Ronnie, his life was less important now than the lives of the people he cared about.

Deep breath... Push out the one. He was now living for Leslie.

Deep breath... Push out the two. For Preston.

Deep breath.... Push out the three. For Malleck.

Deep breath... Push out the four. For Mom.

The spherical top of the water tower came into view, divided by the last row of trees that stood before Ronnie. He stopped. The red lights surrounding the metal edges of the wraparound walkway highlighted giant letters. All he could see from his vantage point was "KNO" and "NES". Ronnie scanned the water tower from top to bottom, tracking his fall with his eyes, imagining those scrawny limbs flailing as he plummeted to the ground. Curiously, there was nothing and no one in front of or around the water tower. The field past the trees was eerie and quiet, lit only by the streetlights that converged at an intersection and surrounded one half of the field at a ninety-degree angle.

That familiar anxiousness in Ronnie's palms returned, hot and moist. The friction of his thumbs and fingers anxiously rubbing together could have sparked a fire. He had willed himself to approach the water tower once and he knew he could do it again. *One step*, Ronnie thought, Leslie's words from earlier that week returning to him. *The first step's the hardest. It gets easier after that.*

He took the first step.

The distance between the trees widened in his vision, until the water tower was unobstructed and in plain view. He emerged from the woods, releasing one last crunch of the leaves behind him and stepping onto the grass.

As if a switch had flipped before his eyes, a small crowd appeared at the foot of the water tower. Neverwells flanked Davion—ten strong on each side, twenty total. Davion's glowing white eyes hung like lanterns above Preston as the kid kneeled with his bare knees against the grass, his head bowed and arms raised, palms to the sky, lit in jittered flashes of light by the torches surrounding him. Preston's arms were shaking in a way that made Ronnie wonder how long he'd been made to stay in that position.

As he stood far away, Ronnie couldn't see the look on Davion's face. He had seen multiple sides of the man, and now imagined a twist of Davion's cheek, that grin he had given Ronnie to signal a father's approval, now a grin of satisfaction that he could overpower his son with sheer influence. The satisfaction of being in control. It was easier to view him as comically evil than a soft-spoken, seemingly reasonable man with a grand plan.

The image of Preston with gaping, red holes in his back returned to Ronnie's mind, and he shook it free. *One step.*

And every step he took, Ronnie grew angrier, wearing his rage like warpaint. It was the darkness inside of him that created a monster, and the darkness inside of him would unleash it tonight. But as he moved closer, that grin he imagined on Davion's face was erased by a melancholic expression. Davion's eyes, cheeks, and chin hung low at the sight of his son. The trembling of Preston's arms became more pronounced, and his breathing shook his entire body, leaving a continuous fog of vapor.

Davion's pupils hadn't disappeared. He now had the Neverwells to do his bidding.

Ronnie stopped at the edge of the circle, which divided him from Davion and the Neverwells. The other sacrifices lined the edges—eyes, tongue, feet, hands—lying severed and bloody against the grass, with an empty spot at the top of the circle for a set of lungs, right at Davion's feet. For a tense few seconds, the only sound between them was Preston's hurried breathing. Davion coughed in a pathetic way, covering his mouth like a helpless old man. "Have you brought what I asked for?" he asked.

Ronnie browsed through the line of Neverwells, spotting Anson, the tallest one, who had nearly killed him.

Ronnie addressed his father. "Would you release Preston from... whatever hold you have on him right now?"

Davion considered the request, then nodded to Anson.

Preston's arms fell to the ground and he flopped to his side, his tired body soaking in the relief of relaxation.

"Ronnie?" Preston said.

"I'm... I'm sorry, Preston—"

"The pages," Davion demanded. He snapped his fingers. The Neverwell to his left reached behind his back and grabbed a metal stand, fixed to elbow height, and stood it in front of Davion. The Neverwell to his right pulled the notebook out from inside his robe and sat it on the stand, then flopped over the first two-thirds of pages in one fell swoop. "You remember our bargain, don't you?"

"Yeah, you threatening to kill everyone I love."

Davion's throat expanded, preparing for a frustrated outburst, but he collected himself. "I'm asking you to come to me and hand me the pages. Willingly... Do you even have them?"

Desperation didn't suit Davion. Ronnie reached inside his jacket pocket and slowly pulled out the pages, smooth and stacked, held together by his thumb and fingers. The look on Davion's face was pure, subdued elation. Davion waved him to come closer. Ronnie stood his ground with the papers held tightly in his hand.

"Are we really going to do this again, Ronnie?" Davion said. "I've been inside that scared little anxious head of yours. Felt the sweat stabbing your armpits in the cold. I know your fear. I've seen it. Standing here in front of this water tower, I only wish to imagine the restlessness inside you now. I have no desire to experience it. I will not control you. Give... me... the pages, boy!"

Davion waited as Ronnie walked around the perimeter of the circle, his focus trained on Preston. An abundance of words clung to Ronnie's lips. The boy wanted to say so much to his friend, so many variations of an apology, but they all stayed put behind his teeth. What could you really say to prepare a friend for sacrifice? The poor kid was devastated, but the mourning would be worth it for the future he would help create.

Ronnie took his eye off Preston and stood in front of Davion's steel podium. He reluctantly raised the papers and placed them atop the book. Davion thought the boy would cry and a tinge of sadness touched his chest. This wasn't what he wanted from their reunion. But he remembered being young, his mind clouded with stubborn idealism, so sure of what was good and true with no reinforcement of lived experience. Davion would make him see the truth.

Davion took control of Preston's mind once again, forcing the helpless young man back to his knees. This came so effortlessly to Davion in years past, but what was once as easy as lifting a pebble was now like lifting a boulder. He embraced the struggle, letting his knees rattle. The dome was too much, but it would have to stay until the final summoning—no outside interference before then. It wouldn't be much longer now.

Preston bowed his head and stretched his arms out with his palms pointed upward, emitting this pitiful wheeze. The young man had pretended to be strong in the hours prior, but beyond the muscle of his exterior frame, his mind had proven to be quite fragile. A sense of self-loathing was carving him from the inside, making Davion wonder if every goddamn teenager in this idyllic town was consumed by some negative emotion. Ronnie reacted by turning and kneeling at Preston's side, wrapping an arm around his back in comfort.

"Don't touch him," Davion said. "We can't risk interrupting the ritual."

With this, Ronnie stood and backed away, exiting the circle. Davion's ear caught a whimper from Ronnie's face as he turned away.

"Ronnie," Davion said. "Ronnie, look at me."

Ronnie turned, breathing angrily through tears.

Davion softened. "You don't have to watch. I can't tell you it won't be painless for the boy. After all, you wrote these rituals to necessitate dread and agony. It only works if there's fear." Davion placed the pages in the opening of the book, touching the tears in the binding to the rough edges of the missing papers. "I could put your mind somewhere else." The thought of inhabiting two minds at once seemed unbearable, but it might have been a small concession to keep any hope of having a relationship with his son.

"Just do it," Ronnie said shakily. "I have to watch. It's what I deserve."

The boy's soul and mind were broken to a degree that made Davion unsure of whether there was anything left to inhabit. He lifted the book off the stand, holding the loose pages against the right side of the opening to ensure a spontaneous gust of wind wouldn't take them away as he approached Preston. He read from the first page. "Read these words and follow them precisely, as this passage contains the proper sequence of imbuing the fourth and final offering with divine purpose. The sacrifice of Preston Collinsworth, whose soul is corrupted by evil intent, will hereby be purified and join the underworld in service of our..."

Davion stopped. Something was off.

The weight of the book perhaps. It was lighter than he remembered. The pages were a bit too smooth. It didn't have that rough scratch of paper on his fingertips. Or maybe it was that he was emitting so much energy he hadn't realized the slight decrease of energy Ronnie was producing. It was a small change, like the temperature lowering by a degree, barely distinguishable, but as he looked at Ronnie, his body registered a small decrease in the output of Ronnie's energy since he'd been standing before him.

Ronnie hadn't been standing before him. He'd been walking away.

Chapter Forty-One

"Give... me... the pages, boy!" Davion exclaimed.

The voice of Helga echoed in Ronnie's mind. "I have control now. Do what you need to do fast. Keeping up this illusion is like propelling the Titanic with a single oar."

Davion's attention drifted from Ronnie, tracking something that wasn't there. The notebook rose slowly from the podium and Butterfly's hand materialized with it, the rest of her body gradually appearing as well. She took small, quiet steps backward as another Manari Nu appeared out of thin air next to Preston's limp body. She pressed an index finger to her lips, signaling Preston to remain quiet.

Invisibility, Ronnie thought. *Way to go, Helga.*

Ronnie stepped back as well, hearing a mash of cold grass with each step. At the opposite end of the field, Malleck walked steadily out of the woods, her combat boots retracing Ronnie's steps. She was clad in Manari Nu armor, with a sword sheathed at her hip, her hair pulled back into one long braid.

The remaining soldiers followed behind her, freed from the cover of trees, their black armor glossed under moonglow, weapons ready. They represented the opposing battlefront, closing in on a small, masked army completely unaware of their presence.

Ronnie quickened his footsteps, hearing Davion behind him uttering something into the wind. The words stung Ronnie's ears, afraid that any minute the ruse would be discovered and the battlelines would clash. The Manari Nu were prepared for this, of course, but Ronnie and Malleck needed just a few minutes to complete the amended ritual.

Ronnie and Malleck closed the distance between each other and Ronnie handed her the pages. Quietly, Malleck spoke to Ronnie. "You better be right about this."

Ronnie responded, "No time to think. We need to do this now." Then he added, "It'll be okay, Malleck."

Ronnie raised his right palm to Malleck and held it there. Seeing her hesitation, he nodded and whispered, "It'll be okay."

Malleck unsheathed her sword slowly to muffle the metallic grind, looking over Ronnie's shoulder to study Davion and his masked gang, currently living in their own world. She pressed the blade into Ronnie's palm and sliced, forming a red line at the center of his hand. Ronnie winced and held his fist tight, breathing through the pain as quietly as he possibly could. He then held his palm close to the ground, walking with a hunch, pressing the blood out of his palm and forming a circle. The exposed flesh caused an intense stab of pain, but he knew it was nothing compared to what was coming next.

"Read it," Ronnie whispered. He threw off his jacket, then lowered himself to his knees with his head down. He spotted Preston, struggling to stay upright as Butterfly held his arm over her shoulders, guiding him away from the field and toward the foot of the slope, where Helga and Leslie stood side-by-side, Helga with white eyes in deep concentration and Leslie with her guitar held diagonally across her body. Leslie shook her head, unprepared for what she was seeing.

Ronnie prepared himself as Davion recited the passage, staring into his palm while holding an invisible book. Malleck, with the handle of her sword in one hand, moved the first page from the front to the back of the small stack. "Got the preliminary stuff out of the way." She read quickly. "Read these words and follow them precisely, as this passage contains the proper sequence of imbuing the fourth and final offering with divine purpose. The sacrifice of..." She stopped and swallowed her words down. "The sacrifice of Ronnie Hendrix, whose soul is corrupted by evil intent, will henceforth be purified by this ritual." She let out a shaky breath. "Short and sweet." Ronnie had written it to be simple. No elaborate display, just incisions through flesh and bone.

Malleck turned to the third page, displaying Ronnie's illustration of a young boy with his shins on the ground and chest folded down to his knees with dark red pits at each side of his back. "Dammit," she said.

She rustled the pages back in her pouch, then ran the blade between Ronnie's shirt and his spine. With one quick pull of the handle, his shirt split in half, revealing his bare back. Malleck placed the point of the sword just below his shoulder blade and prepared to add pressure.

"Fascinating," Davion said in the distance, louder this time.

The sound of his voice halted Malleck as she and Ronnie both turned their attention toward him.

"And what if I just..." Davion separated his hands and looked down. "Wow," he said. "The gravity of this illusion is incredibly convincing. Whoever your friend is, Ronnie, they're able to even mask *their* energy output while keeping yours intact. Very, very impressive."

Ronnie looked over at Helga, who remained statuesque. Was there anything she could do?

"The energy you're pouring out must be tremendous," Davion said to a captive and cautious audience. "I reckon, though, if you're a good witch, you must value the secrecy of our gifts. We only kept ourselves from plain view so that passersby wouldn't interfere, but you, my gifted friend... You have interfered."

Davion raised his hand, signaling the Neverwells behind him. "Neverwells, end the illusion."

Leslie stood from the top of the slope, guitar ready, listening to Helga's steady, controlled breathing. The field appeared calm and quiet, with not a single soul on it.

"Shit," Helga said. "He's ending the illusion."

In an instant, the Neverwells were revealed to Leslie, wearing their hideous signature hay masks and robes. Davion wore a blood-stained gray suit—*Please don't be Preston's blood*—and stood in front of Preston. A circle of six torches surrounded Preston, the glow of flames splashing against his physique as he sat on his knees with his hands to the sky, wearing only boxer briefs. Even in his compressed, folded state, he looked monstrous compared to Davion's frail and sunken figure. Behind the man's power was delicacy. He looked like he could fall and shatter at any minute.

Helga stretched out her arms and gritted her teeth.

Davion, Preston, and the Neverwells disappeared.

"It's too much energy," Davion yelled in the distance. "You'll have to let go of something or it'll break you."

"Do it now," Ronnie said in a hurried voice to Malleck. He tucked his chin to his chest, teeth clenched.

Malleck stuck the end of her blade below Ronnie's shoulder blade and ripped through his skin with a long cut to the bottom of his rib cage. Ronnie wheezed in agony, trying in vain to hold in the rush of nerves exploding in his back. Nothing could have prepared him for the jolt of his skin behind ripped open, the surging sting of oxygen grabbing the meat underneath. It begged him to scream, but Ronnie held it in his throat.

"I can't do this," Malleck said.

"Do it!" Ronnie yelled through his teeth.

Malleck made an incision on the other side of Ronnie's back. Every inch was devastating.

"You know, Ronnie..." Davion's voice grew louder and more aggravated. "When I first felt your energy output all those months ago, I knew it was something special. Your creation in the Outer Realm pulled me right in. I saw that magnificent red sky with all of those lost souls."

Malleck's fingertips forced their way into the gash on the right side of Ronnie's back. His skin slid across his flesh as she ripped the ends apart. The pain was so acute and massive that he was sure he'd pass out. His vision was beginning to blur at the edges, closing in around Davion.

"I was so proud when I read the end of the book. You actually described a perfect inversion spell. You wrote it for me. Of course you did. You were born of dark magic. It's a part of you."

The skin on the left side of Ronnie's back ripped apart. Everything was on fire.

Davion raised his hands to chest level. They began to glow and produce dark clouds, rolling and shapeless.

The image of Davion was so strange that Ronnie thought he might be hallucinating from the pain. Davion's white eyes developed bloody circles around the edges. His nose began to bleed as well. The blood snaked down his lips and onto his chin.

The mystical black clouds surrounding Davion's hands grew larger. Bright red sparks flickered within them like synapses firing, casting flashes of red through the black. He let out a fierce growl and the edges of his hands burst into thick red clouds. He dropped to his knees. "Let the sorrow of the underworld rain down upon us. For we are... all of us... unworthy of the wretched kingdom."

Davion spread his fingers. With a final shout to the sky, he came down hard, shooting his glowing red hands into the earth in a movement that seemed to recruit his entire upper body. A shockwave blossomed quickly, causing everyone to stumble. Preston fell, dragging the Manari Nu entangled in his weight.

Davion propped one leg up, then the other, holding a deep squat, then bared all of his teeth in immense struggle. He interlocked his elbows and rotated his torso, moving his hands like the arm of a clock.

The moon shifted slightly at first, a small enough movement to pass as a trick of the mind. But then it began to move more steadily, sweeping slowly across the sky, seemingly locked with the motion of Davion's arms. A red sky rose up from beyond the trees, at first looking like a distant fire, and with it a chorus of high-pitched shrieks. It lifted high above the forest, revealing arms—thousands of arms—flailing through the red mass, moving overhead, directed by Davion's violently shaking hands.

The inversion spell, Ronnie thought as the remaining night sky became red. *Replacing the heavens with the Underworld.*

A stillness came over the field. All parties, bathed in a red glow, gazed in shock at the sky, equal parts horrendous and ridiculous.

The sky shifted above Leslie—black replaced with squirming red. "What the hell is happening, Helga?" she muttered in bewilderment.

Helga screamed. "I have to let go!" Her arms dropped as she released her spell, revealing the scene to Leslie for the first time.

Leslie's eyes sprung open with horror as she witnessed the mutilation of her friend, Davion's nasty glowing hands, and Preston being led her way.

Helga's words trickled out in rapid breaths. "He's trying to draw my attention away from the illusion." She let out another harsh grunt. "We counted on him noticing the illusion, but—" *Grunt.* "—not this soon."

Leslie looked at Ronnie, bent over like he was hurling, his face wrinkled with agony, blood falling from the side visible to her. Ronnie mouthed, "Do it." The shock of the image faded and she finally allowed herself to understand Ronnie's plan.

He was the final ritual.

Helga held her hands to the sky and spread them apart quickly. A translucent dome spread around her and expanded rapidly.

Leslie clenched as the dome slid around her, spreading past the trees, past the intersection, into the sky of the Underworld.

"We fight our battles in the dark, you prick," Helga said.

With the inversion complete, Davion collapsed to his knees. He laughed, then vomited thick purple bile, covering the grass in front of him.

Untethered from the witch's illusion, the Manari Nu appeared before him, forming a line in front of Malleck and Ronnie.

Davion scanned the battle line in front of him and smirked, catching the motion of Preston hobbling to his feet with an armor-clad woman at his side. "Get my sacrifice!"

Behind him, the Neverwells spread their robes and revealed their weapons in unison—machetes, axes, swords, daggers.

A Neverwell tossed a throwing axe in Preston's direction.

"Preston, get down!" Leslie yelled.

Fortunately for Preston, falling was one of the few things he was capable of in his condition. He and the accompanying Manari Nu hit the ground and the axe sailed over their heads, losing velocity and sticking in the ground a few feet from Leslie. The Manari Nu sprung to her feet, cat-like, covering Preston.

Leslie flung the guitar strap off her shoulder and above her head, setting Sasha down on the grass. "I got him, sis!" she yelled with her sights on Preston.

"Get back here!" Helga yelled to Leslie.

And as Leslie charged...

So too did everyone else.

Black robes flew high in the wind, revealing leather hilts and metal sheaths.

The Manari Nu sprinted as a unified front, nearly synchronous in their movements, with Butterfly and Red leading from the center of the line, swords drawn. Their steps were quiet against the grass in juxtaposition to the clunky stomping of the Neverwells.

The lines clashed with harsh screams of metal against metal, rips of skins, and the accompanying cries of pain. The two groups became tangled in pairs, fighting viciously. The Neverwells, outmatched in skill, were unmatched in numbers. As soon as one dropped from a blow, another took their place.

Leslie struggled to pull Preston's limp weight higher. "I can't do all of the work here! Get your ass up!" she yelled, straining every muscle in her body.

Preston struggled to push himself up off the grass. Leslie dipped down and shot her shoulder into his chest, forcing him to his feet.

The Manari Nu guarding them drew a dagger and waited for an incoming Neverwell attack. Her opponent's robe drifted behind him like a cape, his machete swiping in the air as he ran.

"Wait!" Davion yelled from his safe position a good distance away from the battle.

The Neverwell slowed and stopped in his pursuit of the Manari Nu while the clanks and grunts rang loudly on the battlefield.

"Ronnie, what have you done?!" Davion stared through the skirmish beyond the whips of loose robe fabric, the agile arms of the Manari Nu and their accompanying blades, finally catching Malleck in his gaze, her sword raised high above her head, winding up for a powerful blow. Ronnie sat on his knees hunched over, blood seeping from his back. "He changed it!" Davion yelled to his minions. "He changed the ritual!"

Malleck brought the sword down hard on the right side of Ronnie's back.

Crunch!

The water tower shone in red under the hellish sky of Ronnie's creation in the Gray World. The sounds of battle were now absent and the screams of tortured souls above poured downward and echoed through the night. Ronnie was no longer in pain, though in the natural world his skeletal structure was being split open.

He was dead.

Loud, slow stomping rumbled through the woods that surrounded two sides of the field. Ronnie allowed his body to set downward, letting his heels sink into the souls of his shoes and press into the ground. His body shook as the stomping grew louder—something was coming closer. This time, he walked toward the sound.

The red glow of the sky outlined the top of a figure in the woods, knocking down trees clumsily. An unstoppable force smashing everything in its path. The twisted horns of Karnalaxe formed a rounded edge over the trees. The steel of his axe was visible to the side of his head as he rested the shaft against his shoulder.

Karnalaxe knocked down a pair of trees, which hovered in the air as they came down unnaturally slow, as he stepped onto the field. There was no smoke and no fire. The giant demon was in plain view before Ronnie. Red, glowing eyes, a snout that grunted and blew chunks of snot. His arms, bulky and lined with a network of veins, jutted out from a tight leather vest, exactly how Ronnie had drawn it on the page. His lower body was that of a ram. White fur covered his legs and shook with every movement. The joints of his legs were set backward, leading down to hooved feet.

Karnalaxe lowered his body, folding his legs, and removed the axe from his shoulder. He brought the head of the axe gently to the ground in front of Ronnie, forming a walkway up the shaft and to his palm. Blood trickled downward, running from his hand split by the piercing barbed wire and twisted around the shaft.

Ronnie walked up the axe with little effort, stepping over the metal barbs as he made his way up to Karnalaxe's hand. Karnalaxe dropped the axe and brought Ronnie close to his face.

"Hey, big guy," Ronnie said. "Ready to go to work?"

Chapter Forty-Two

The right side of Ronnie's ribcage cracked open on the third blow. His body had gone limp with his cheek against the grass, stuck in the position of a toddler sleeping. Malleck's eyes drew tears as she focused her next strike on the left side of his back.

Twenty yards away and on the other side of a jagged line of swiping blades, thrown fists, and bloodshed, Davion Stivert's eyes were stuck between their natural state and cloudy white. He wiped the blood from his cheeks and chin, causing it to smear and paint the lower portion of his face in crimson, mixing with the purple vomit around his mouth. He struggled with every last breath of his life to enter Malleck's mind, but he knew he had to preserve his energy. He was slipping, the edges of his vision going black.

"Anson!" Davion yelled.

The tallest member in his army sprung out of the fight with a kick to his opponent's stomach. He ran toward Davion, panting under his mask. "Yes, Davion?"

"Take that girl's mind," Davion raised his finger. "Trap her in a terrible memory."

Anson followed Davion's finger and found Malleck. His eyes turned white.

Malleck was no longer on the battlefield, but rather in the backseat of a car. She waved her hands wildly, but realized she had lost her ability to speak when the screams she intended didn't leave her throat. Her line of sight was lower than usual as she eyed the heads of two adults sitting higher than her. When the woman in the passenger's seat turned around, she recognized her mother, looking over a decade younger. This was several years before she'd allowed herself to go gray, as her hair was blond and straightened. She mouthed, "What's wrong, honey?" The words came out distorted and muffled.

Malleck studied the arms she'd waved in front of her. They were thin and short. She was younger now and sitting on the cloth seats of the old SUV her parents used to drive. A brown stain was on the left seat beside her just as she remembered. She had spilled a soda in her lap on a road trip the year before and they were never able to get it out.

Vehicles surrounded the exterior of the car, barely moving with the sluggish flow of traffic. Atlanta traffic, to be exact. The kind of stop-and-go movement that was irritatingly slow and added an unnecessary amount of time to their trips. Malleck knew this memory well, though the faces of her parents had been blurred with the passage of time. She mostly remembered the significance of the event, and now she was helpless to relive whatever cruel version Davion had implanted in her mind.

Malleck peered up through her window as a line of birds soared through the air. Her eight-year-old and seventeen-year-old brains battled as her younger version wondered how free it must feel to be in the air, untethered from metal and glass. She thought of how joyful it would be to have her parents with her high above, looking downward at the line of cars against pavement like ants marching in the dirt. It was an innocent thought.

She imagined being airborne with her parents, staring ahead at the flying row of birds, soaring with their arms splayed out straight. She could feel the touch of a hand in each of hers as her parents flew with her on each side, their clothes rattling against the wind.

That daydream ended when her parents let out a simultaneous scream, muffled again. They waved their hands in front of their faces in an attempt to correct their sight. Malleck's father slammed his foot against the gas pedal, causing their SUV to ram into the sedan in front of them. Tires screeched from the back of the SUV as he kept his foot on the pedal, blowing a cloud of smoke behind them and forcing the smell of burnt rubber into the air.

Her father clung to anything his hands could claim as real, which so happened at the moment to be the steering wheel. His mind told him he was in the clouds and his hands told him to hang on tight. He zipped the wheel to the right, grinding the front bumper against the car in front of him and veering off the shoulder of the highway, rumbling uncontrollably to the surrounding woods.

Malleck screamed for her father to stop the car, to snap out of it. This wasn't her memory. She knew this wasn't how it happened. She knew they only saw her vision for a few seconds, nothing more. It wasn't until she spoke with Helga about the incident that she realized how horribly things could have gone if she hadn't stopped. Her parents could have been hurt. She could have been hurt.

Could have been.

Malleck stared through the front windshield as the SUV shook against the grassy terrain, barreling closer and closer toward the treeline and picking up speed. There was nothing she could do. She closed her eyes.

The front of the SUV crumbled against the base of a tree, causing Malleck and her parents to jerk forward. Malleck's weight shifted suddenly in the vehicle, the strap of her seatbelt nearly piercing through her clothes and skin. She slid back into her seat. The crash was so loud it left a vacuum of noise. It wasn't until her body registered the stillness of the car that Malleck realized she'd been crying.

She hadn't heard the airbags deploy. Shouldn't they have gone off with a big *poof*?

Her parents' bodies lay hunched over the dash, their arms folded above their heads, twisted at crude angles, facing each other. The blood made their features nearly indistinguishable. They weren't breathing.

She tried to open her door but couldn't. It was locked.

She was trapped inside the car, sitting in the vacuum of sound, her younger mind panicked and her older mind slipping, forgetting it wasn't real.

Davion stumbled as he walked, losing energy with every step, his eyes outlined in red. The Neverwells forced their skirmishes away from him, parting a pathway. Their numbers were too great. As soon as a Manari Nu broke free of battle, a fresh Neverwell appeared and blocked her path to their leader.

Leslie led Preston up the slope, resorting to motivational verbiage she thought he'd understand. "Fourth quarter! We're behind and we gotta dig deep if we're gonna win this one!"

"What's... What's going on?" Preston asked through deep breaths.

"Ronnie's sacrificing himself, you big oaf. He swapped places with you so you didn't die." The words came out fast, detached from emotion. "Also, I'm pretty sure Ronnie's dad turned the sky into Hell." Ronnie's voice rang in her head. *Just know that whatever happens, I have a plan and I know what I'm doing... I think.*

Helga's voice boomed from Leslie's periphery. "We could use your help now, Leslie! Play it now!"

Shit, Leslie thought as she surveyed the field. Too many things were happening at once: Preston hooked onto her shoulder, Malleck swaying in a daze, clashes of metal, Davion walking shakily toward Ronnie.

She thought she'd be prepared for this.

She froze...

But only for a second.

She dropped Preston, letting his body fall harder than she'd intended. He rolled down the hill and stopped face up. Leslie gave him a hard slap on the cheek, then recoiled, regretting the intensity of it. "Wake up, meathead! Ronnie needs us!"

Leslie took long strides up the hill and toward the generator. She grabbed the pull cord and yanked it. The generator refused to come alive. She reset the cord and yanked it again. Nothing. She looked out onto the field. Just a couple more steps and Davion would be a touch away from Ronnie. "Come on, you clunky sack of shit!" Leslie yelled.

She ripped the cord and reset...

Ripped the cord and reset...

Davion stopped in front of Ronnie's collapsed and unconscious body, paying little attention to Malleck, who stood stiff as her mind wandered elsewhere. "Dammit, son," he said. "What the hell did you do?"

He wobbled as he bent down to pick up the sword lying next to Ronnie, every movement an immense effort. For a brief moment, he looked as if he might reconsider. He gazed at his son's torn back, considering whether the power Ronnie was born with would allow him to come back from this. Davion couldn't be sure. But he also didn't have time to waste. "Damn you for making me do this."

Davion raised the sword and slammed it against Ronnie's back, one blow after the next, trying with whatever strength remained to sever each side of Ronnie's rib cage. Chunks of flesh flew in the air with the movement of the blade, catching Davion's face, neck, and chest. He grunted, the tiredness and sadness coalescing, and when he dropped the blade and reached inside of Ronnie's flesh to twist and pull the bones in his back apart, he realized that the mass below him was now just a shell of his son.

Leslie had stopped momentarily, shaken by the assault on Ronnie's body and the unconscionable image of Davion digging into his back, a wave of fresh blood running from his hands to his face. Her friend was no longer there. She had to see the man in the bloody suit dead. She forced back tears and pulled the cord again.

Davion inserted the sword into either side of Ronnie's back, attempting to make an outline around the lungs, careless of how he preserved them. The passage said Karnalaxe needed lungs as a sacrifice. It didn't say they needed to be fully operational.

With a few tugs, he pulled out the left lung and let it fall to the grass. Then he pulled out the right. He cupped purple bloody masses together and held them to his chest to ensure they wouldn't slip away. With one last look at the body of his son, he turned and began his clumsy walk back.

The generator started.

"Yes!" Leslie yelled. She ran to her guitar and threw the strap around her shoulder. She rummaged through the bed of cords and found the one belonging to the amp. She plugged it into her guitar, then cranked the volume as high as possible. She pulled a pick out of her pocket.

She put her mouth to the microphone, the metal grid cold against her lips, and screamed into it, "Hello, Knollwood Pines!"

Leslie strummed the guitar hard and fast, creating a riotous symphony of grungy whines and howls, channeling the rage of her fingers toward Davion as he took heavy steps. Her heavy metal ode to Halloween was more fitting than she could've imagined, as witches, masks, and blood flooded the crowd before her. She screamed the words angrily into the microphone, her eyes wide and teeth out, growling through the strangest performance of her life.

Preston thought the sky was another hallucination. A waking nightmare spawned from the deepest corners of his mind. He tried to blink it away, but every time he widened his eyes, it remained. It was loud, furious, but didn't crack like thunder. It spiked and stabbed and moaned like a torture chamber spread across the atmosphere. The arms of distant beings, stuck in place, reached down toward him, clawing at nothing, begging for escape.

The chords of an electric guitar, swirling and whipping, overpowered the screams. Leslie's song was so loud and amplified it rattled Preston's brain, shaking him awake.

Preston finally got up on his own. The strength was coming back to him. His muscles tensed with each movement as his body got lighter. His ears cracked from the impact of Leslie's amplifier, but the uncontrollable pump of his heart and the surge of cortisol gave him an added boost. He turned to the sound of the music. Leslie, under the eerie glow of a red sky, stood above him, pumping her arm and wiggling her fingers, striking the microphone with vigor and venom.

She really is everything, he thought.

Let's shred.

The red-tinted battlefield came into view. Malleck hovered in a frozen state over a bloody corpse. Davion stumbled through the clashing factions of steel-clad soldiers. There was so much blood on Davion, as if someone had splashed a bucket and covered his entire front side. What was he holding against his chest?

Oh no.

Preston knew in an instant that the lump of meat under Malleck was Ronnie.

He recruited all of the power in his body to stand upright, setting his feet underneath him. He spotted the throwing axe stuck in the ground, not too far away. The memory of tossing darts with Leslie at the Rambler came back to him.

He had pretty good aim.

Malleck slapped her tiny hands against the window of the car. At her normal size, she was certain she could break through the glass. She kept telling herself it wasn't real, but the emotions of her eight-year-old self overpowered her in a way that was impossible to shake. It took her a minute in her confused state of panic to realize that there were sounds beyond her cries for help.

They weren't outside the walls of the metal cage she was confined to. There was no muffling of the sound. It was distinct and sharp, as if someone had put a speaker directly next to her ear. A wild throbbing noise, like a soundwave peaking over and over and over, and an angry voice straining through vocal cords that were close to bursting.

Is that... metal?

The hold on Malleck's mind slipped away. Her knees weakened as she bobbed, regaining control of her body. The chaotic sounds of battle flooded her ears. The crude lump of flesh that had once been Ronnie snapped her back into the present, his back torn apart in gruesome red pits with her own bloody sword next to him. Blood had filled the parts missing from Ronnie's back and surrounded jagged peaks of bone sticking out. Ronnie's blood was on her as well, spattered like a splash painting.

Farther on the battlefield, Davion was making a straight path to the sacrificial circle surrounded by torches.

Malleck raised the sword and bent her free arm, sliding the blade between her bicep and forearm, trying in vain to wipe the blood from it.

The Manari Nu soldiers took glances at her between their preoccupied movements. Whereas before they had been forced out by an overwhelming horde to make way for Davion, they now had to keep their attackers away from Malleck.

Keep the path clear, she said to all of them telepathically.

Malleck sprinted forward.

Davion took another pitiful step toward the circle. He could drop at any moment. maybe he didn't have anything left to fulfill the final summoning. That awful, wretched music scraped at his eardrums. There was no use in stopping. He had already won. Just a few more steps and he could let his arms go limp. Let the lungs fall.

Suddenly, a shot of pain stabbed his thigh just below the hip, so immediate and sharp that he dropped the lungs helplessly, yelping from deep in his gut. The blade of a throwing axe sat wedged in the meat of his leg, with the handle pointing toward the muscular boy in boxer briefs as he lowered his right arm, winding down from a tossing motion. "You little shit!" Davion belted through his teeth, wondering where he would take the boy's mind next. Someplace awful. Someplace that would break him indefinitely.

But *damn the gods*, he was so weak.

Davion's hamstring separated with a horizontal slice, causing him to collapse and shriek. Everything was so heavy. Everything burned. And now his damn leg was useless.

He was so close. Salvation for his people. Salvation for himself. The Underworld hung above him, ready to offer a new god.

He reached out for the lungs in front of him, then a blade touched his throat.

The music stopped.

Malleck circled Davion, her sword to his neck. "Davion Stivert... You don't look well." She raised her sword and sheathed it, then her hands on her hips. "That inversion spell was pretty impressive. It requires an amount of energy that could kill any normal individual of the Manari strain. Honestly, I didn't expect you to have much juice left over, but you sure did send me on a trip. Luckily, I have something you don't have." Malleck gave Leslie a salute.

Leslie took a hand off her guitar and made horns in return.

"And you actually ripped organs out of your own son," Malleck continued. "What kind of man does that? Ronnie sacrificed himself to make sure you and your kind could never complete his plan."

Davion's eyes sparked with flashes of white. Flicking... Flicking... Flicking like a dead lighter. The blood on his face, his son's and his own, pooled in every wrinkle, every crevice.

"You can keep trying," Malleck said, "but I think you're spent. I can't feel a lot of energy on you. If I were to close my eyes, I wouldn't even know you're here." She walked to the fallen set of lungs. "What I'm trying to say, Davion, is..." She scooped them off the grass. "Thank you for your contribution. I wouldn't have been able to do the inversion. Now I just have to reverse it. But, before we cross that bridge... I have a demon to summon."

"Neverwells!" Davion gave a long, desperate yell, as Malleck walked toward the circle.

What was left of the Neverwells turned their attention to Davion. Lumps of bodies lay on the ground surrounding them. Half of their horde had perished, and with the lapse in attention, another fell by the sword of a Manari Nu. They saw their helpless leader struggling to stand, reaching desperately for Malleck as she entered the circle. They dropped their weapons to the ground, surrendering.

Malleck placed Ronnie's lungs in the circle, joining the perimeter of eyes, tongue, feet, and hands. She stood in the center, showered by the screams of souls above her. The pupils and irises in her eyes faded into a rolling cloud of white. She raised her arms at her side, palms down, fingers extended. Streams of red energy, thin and translucent, rose from the severed body parts, twisting upward, forming smokey rings around her hands. She grimaced as she drew more energy. A burst of wind shot upward.

"Karnalaxe!" Malleck yelled. "With these sacraments, I summon thee!" She threw her hands to the sky. The sea of bodies above her began to part, forming a red hole that grew wider and wider. Malleck focused all of her energy into ripping that hole open, creating the gateway between worlds.

Ronnie sat perched on Karnalaxe's shoulder, gazing out into the version of Knollwood Pines presented in the Gray World. Karnalaxe stood still, staring at the town with him, chest expanding with each heave of his snout.

He was up higher than the water tower. The distance was great, but he wasn't afraid. With his tailbone against the hard top of the demon's shoulder, one palm against the leather vest, he felt safer than ever, even knowing that at this point his body was dead.

Karnalaxe craned his neck suddenly.

"Is it time?" Ronnie asked.

Karnalaxe grunted in return. He gripped the handle of his ax and raised it. Ronnie's reflection appeared on the head of the axe and swore that Karnalaxe was looking at the reflection as well.

"Whatever happens, thanks for taking care of me," Ronnie said.

With one last grunt, Karnlaxe disappeared. One second there, the next not. Ronnie was falling, willing gravity to force him down. He didn't know how to exit the Gray World, but he knew how he got there in the first place. He relaxed his body as the red sky moved farther away.

The dark red pits in Ronnie's back drained as blood seeped back into his body. Lungs sprouted. The bones of his rib cage connected. His loose skin converged and sealed itself together.

Within his body, the lungs expanded with oxygen. With one deep breath, Ronnie was alive.

The indestructible kid.

He awakened to the smell of blood and grass tickling his nose. *Holy shit*, he thought. Screams hung in the air as a rush of wind pushed him forward.

"Ronnie!" Leslie sprinted toward him with Preston limping slowly behind.

Leslie helped him to his feet. Even though he was covered head-to-toe in blood, she clung to him like a magnet.

"You little narcissist!" Leslie yelled over the wind. "Of course you'd let yourself die to save the world! What do you want, a trophy?!"

Preston's gorilla arms wrapped around them both. The three of them stayed embraced in the vortex of wind as it rushed toward Malleck, her glowing red hands reaching to the sky.

Malleck forced the hole in the sky wider, straining to move her hands apart. She howled viciously, fighting with all her strength.

"You can't hold it, girl!" Davion's yell was barely audible. "You can't complete this spell!"

With an angry screech, a burst of red energy widened from Malleck's hands and surrounded her entire body, like steam shooting from every pore in her skin. The hole in the sky ripped farther apart. An animalistic growl punched through the hole and shook the ground. An object fell from the red gash, spinning end over end, until it smashed against the ground mere feet away from Malleck, sending clods of dirt skyward. A giant, thick chunk of steel reflected Davion's pitiful appearance back to him, that of a frail man at his end, his once-beautiful three-piece suit destroyed. The leather handle of the massive axe reached upward, with barbed wire twisting around it.

A funnel formed around the hole in a twisting cyclone of red clouds, lengthening and reaching down toward the field. A giant, muscular arm emerged from the funnel. Its long black fingernails scraped against the top of the water tower as the creature gripped its wide hand against it and pulled. A shoulder gave way to the head of a ram with glowing red eyes and a snout that pumped out hard breaths. It looked fierce, deranged. Chaos incarnate.

Karnalaxe reached his other arm through the funnel and slammed his hand against the water tower. He reached lower with each arm alternating, pulling himself lower down the water tower, climbing it like a ladder upside down. His leather-clad torso escaped through the funnel, followed by the top of his bushy, furry legs. His legs fell, twisting his body into an upright position, landing hard on his hooves and shaking the earth. The demon, standing taller than the water tower, peered down at the being below him.

Every mouth on the field hung agape.

Davion was awestruck. The energy wave from Malleck was throbbing and heavy like nothing he'd ever witnessed before. It was a surge of power he once possessed, but he was powerless to stop it now.

And the demon... Dear gods, the demon was magnificent. At once beautiful and grotesque. A pure manifestation of infinite power. Endless possibilities. Surely this girl couldn't control it. But Davion could take control of her. He *had* to take control. He had to find his way back into her fragile mind.

One...

More...

Push...

A hand touched Davion's shoulder. "Remember what you said when we had our first drink together?"

He repositioned himself uneasily to face his son.

"Cheers to you, Dad..." Ronnie said. "For believing in me."

Davion, withered and slipping away, managed a smirk on his red-smeared face. With his entire life's mission crumbling around him, all desperation fled from his chest like a heavy weight removed.

Leslie, her jacket wet with Ronnie's blood, ran to the top of the slope and swung the guitar strap around her shoulder.

Preston, following in a sprint behind her, yelled, "What are you doing?!"

She positioned her fingers on the strings of the guitar. "Why the hell not?!"

She yanked the microphone to her mouth. "We summon demons, jackass! Not you!"

In the distance, Malleck yelled, "Evil souls be damned for eternity! I hereby remove you from the earth! For Karnalaxe vanquishes the wicked!"

Leslie gasped. "That is one badass bitch." Then she ripped into a crazed, thunderous guitar solo.

Davion held a proud grin as Ronnie backed away slowly. Ronnie wasn't everything he'd hoped for—he was more. He wasn't a follower for a cause he never chose—he was a leader for a cause he believed in. He saw the good in those who would harm him and risked his life to save them. Because Ronnie was good.

Everything Davion could have been, everything he failed to be, would carry on in his son. A boy he waited for over a decade to find. A boy he thought he could control. A boy he took for granted.

Ronnie was the future of their kind. Not Davion.

The whine of an electric guitar split his ears. *Not that god-awful music again.*

The remaining Neverwells, Davion's once-useful pawns, burst in an explosion of fire behind Ronnie, flames ripping at their flesh and turning them to ash.

Karnalaxe gripped the handle of his weapon, barbed wire and all, and ripped it from the ground. He threw his head back and roared to the souls in the sky, tensing the muscles in his arm. He truly was the king of the Underworld.

Davion turned to face the demon and with his last remaining breaths...

He laughed.

Karnalaxe raised his axe, then swung it down on Davion, smashing the man like a mallet, sending bits of flesh in every direction. All that remained was thick, bloody lumps surrounding each side of the axe.

The giant pulled the axe out of the ground again. The fleshy viscera caught fire, charring the meat and making a pungent smell. The flames subsided as quickly as they erupted, leaving no trace of Davion Stivert.

Karnalaxe turned to Malleck, flipping the axe upside down, and knelt with his head bowed and both hands on the grip.

"That'll be all," Malleck said. She had been holding the gate open for too long and was starting to lose her grip.

Karnalaxe stood and gave a glance to Ronnie. They locked eyes and made no gesture. They didn't need to. They were connected. The demon and the indestructible kid. Karnalaxe took a high leap up the water tower and propelled himself upward, falling into the inverted gravity of the sky, and slipped through the funnel.

Malleck lowered her hands and dropped to a knee. The funnel sank back into the sky and the arms converged to fill the hole quickly.

"And for my next trick," said Malleck. She pressed her hands to the ground and tensed as she grabbed hold of the axis of the world. She raised her arms together, forming a half circle in the air. The night sky followed with her, rising from the distant edges of the streets and blanketing the sky in black, slowly, and with great effort, replacing the red sea of souls. The moon moved sluggishly through the sky and finally stopped.

Malleck lowered her arms. She tried to walk, but stumbled, then collapsed.

Chapter Forty-Three

The sterile walls of the Knollwood Pines hospital offered some amount of comfort to Ronnie. After all, he'd spent several months there in recovery. Generic famed portraits hung on the walls of the lobby with colorful shapes and lines colliding with each other. Ronnie sat in a waiting chair with Leslie's head against his shoulder in a clean-enough state. He'd emptied a water bottle on his head and wiped the blood off with an old rag from Leslie's trunk. He wore his jean jacket, buttoned up and rough against his bare skin, breathing in the calmness of the lobby as Preston received an IV in a room tucked deep in the hospital.

Once Karnalaxe jumped back through the portal, Leslie had insisted on getting Malleck to her car as well, but Helga refused to let Malleck leave her sight. She promised that Malleck would be okay, though it was clear that she, herself, was in need of significant rest and relaxation as well. Holding an illusion throughout the entirety of a small town has that effect. Ronnie and Leslie helped Preston into the car and left all of Leslie's equipment out to freeze in the early hours of the morning except, of course, for Sasha. Leslie was sure to stick her prized possession in the trunk. She'd come back for the rest later.

Ronnie's repaired lungs savored each breath. He was forever changed. Once a kid who nobody saw, then the kid everyone knew for surviving a freak accident, he had embraced his small yet profound renown as the gatekeeper of Karnalaxe, Demon Ruler of the Underworld.

It had been a quiet ride to the hospital as Ronnie processed the events that transpired. It wasn't unlike his experience driving away from the woods with Preston and Leslie earlier that week. But while that was the moment they knew they had stumbled into something terrifying and bigger than themselves, this drive held an air of victory, and Ronnie was too tired to cheer.

They agreed on a lie. Preston was mugged, simple as that. He couldn't sleep and left the house for a late-night run and was snatched off the street in a van. Leslie and Ronnie had been driving by and happened to see him being beaten. When they ran out to help him, the attackers ran away.

"You didn't tell me you were gonna die, dick," Leslie said to Ronnie after a long stretch of silence in the hospital lobby. They faced out toward the lobby window, which displayed a well-lit, half-full parking lot and a quiet road that Ronnie had nodded off to. It was way too early and they had gone too long without sleeping. "What does this make you? Like... a ghost? Or a revenant? A phoenix?"

"Magic, I guess," Ronnie said.

"You weren't even alive for my concert."

"Was it epic?"

"Like you wouldn't believe."

Ronnie tapped her leg. "You did real good."

They sat in silence a bit longer.

"Don't you ever die in front of me again, Ronnie Hendrix," Leslie said.

Ronnie chuckled. "I don't plan to."

It was a little past three in the morning when Ronnie gave his mom a call. The police had taken his statement regarding the mugging and there wasn't much left to do but wait. She picked up the phone, of course. When a mother thinks her son is missing, the ringer stays on. Ronnie hoped any goodwill of his phony rescue story would help ease the wrath of his mom's punishment. Things had happened to him in the past week that he could never tell her. Perhaps most prominent was that he had met his father, then witnessed him being smashed to bits by a giant axe.

Cynthia ran through the automatic doors of the hospital and squeezed him tight. On the ride back, he told her the truth of his absence. He was a teenager who realized his life was confusing and complicated and left home temporarily to learn who he truly was. When she asked through gritted teeth and bloodshot eyes if he figured it out, he simply said, "I guess."

He had a newfound appreciation for his mother. He realized how difficult it must have been to abandon her natural world, uproot her life, and start over with a mouth to feed in addition to her own. She escaped a dark environment of people who thought they were driven by divine purpose to save the world and destroy all evil. Cynthia likely saw freaks playing with tattered books of magic who had a tendency toward violence, not knowing their true intentions. They created a puppet to harness the power of demons. It was only because he had been raised by Cynthia and Cynthia alone that Ronnie didn't fulfill their plan. While a darkness inherited by Davion's magic surged through Ronnie in his times of anger and weakness, a soft, kind heart was the power Cynthia instilled in him.

Chapter Forty-Four

Monday morning started with the sound of an alarm after a long and uneventful weekend. Ronnie came out of a dream—a real dream—and was happy to be forced awake from a deep cycle of sleep. He went about his morning routine and made eggs and bacon himself, which he and Cynthia scarfed down quickly.

His mother was stuck in a hard position that weekend, needing to be the authoritarian who punished Ronnie for running away, but desiring to shower him with compassion, letting him know home was where he belonged. That he was loved. She took away Ronnie's phone and grounded him. She hid her surprise when Ronnie accepted the conditions of his grounding without argument.

Leslie arrived at the house early to pick Ronnie up, with the grin of a girl who had gotten away with something only she and Ronnie knew about. He grinned back. There would be no parade for them. Today they were back to reality. Boring, perfect reality.

Ronnie noticed a tin bucket in the backseat of Leslie's car. He didn't realize until they'd gotten to the empty school parking lot that the bottle rattling around inside of it was lighter fluid. Leslie took the can from the backseat and said, "Follow me, hero," then led him toward the woods behind the football field as the plastic lighter fluid bottle clanked side-to-side with each step.

Preston and Malleck were waiting for them in the woods. Ronnie was overjoyed to see them healthy and on their feet. After exchanging hugs with each of them, Malleck slid a sling bag off her shoulder. As she unzipped it, the dread-inducing sight of Ronnie's leatherbound notebook appeared beneath the zipper. Malleck pulled out the book and held it out for Ronnie, who clenched his fists anxiously, hesitating to take it from her.

"I think you should do the honors," Malleck said.

Leslie sat the tin can down and removed the lighter fluid bottle, excited to set something on fire.

Ronnie took hold of the book and stared at it long and hard, the darkness of his past self pulsing through it like a heartbeat. As he looked around him, surrounded by people he had died for just days prior, he was ready to bury the ashes of his darkest self.

"Preston, uh…" he struggled to speak.

"We're cool, Ronnie," Preston said reassuringly. "We're friends."

Ronnie smirked and nodded. "Yeah, we are, aren't we?" He placed the notebook in the can.

As soon as he stepped away, Leslie shot a clear stream of lighter fluid over top of it. She took a packet of matches out of her jacket pocket and plucked a match out. "Well," she said, flicking the match and drawing a flame, "to new beginnings."

"To finding friends where you least expect them," Preston added.

"To being a square peg," Malleck said.

"To all of you," Ronnie said.

Leslie held the match over the can and before she was able to drop it triumphantly, the flame disappeared. "Damn," she said. "That would have been so cool." She lit another match and dropped it, causing a flash of fire from inside the tin can.

The four of them watched the book burn, saying nothing, until the pages and the cover crumpled and caved and it wasn't a book anymore. Malleck took a water canister out of her bag and poured it over the remains, which sizzled as the fire died.

"See you in class," Malleck said to Ronnie before walking off.

Ronnie gave one last glance at the mangled cover of his notebook and said to Preston and Leslie, "As soon as I'm not grounded, let's hit The Rambler."

"We love you, Ronnie," Leslie said.

"Not to break up the reunion, but... could you give Leslie and me a minute?" Preston asked.

"Collinsworth," Leslie said, "we're a band. Anything you have to say to me you can say in front of Ronnie."

"Uh... Yeah, okay," Preston said.

This should be interesting.

Preston turned to Leslie. "So... I know we didn't leave things on the best of terms, but I want you to know I'm going to do everything in my power to... make things right—"

Leslie grabbed him by the collar of his jacket and put his lips against hers.

Ronnie turned away. "Didn't need to see that."

After a long kiss, Leslie whispered, "I know you will." Then she added, "That was a hell of a throw by the way."

"What?"

"The axe, dumbass."

Preston, dazed by the kiss, gave a goofy laugh. "And you throw one heck of a concert."

They kissed again.

"Really?" Ronnie said.

Later that day, after Leslie had dropped him off, Ronnie walked through his quiet living room, into the quiet kitchen, and through the quiet hallway. He opened the door to his room and ran his fingers against the spines of his paperback collection, remembering the worlds they had taken him to and wondering if such fantastical tales would ever spin up surprise and danger to surpass what he'd experienced.

His square desk at the edge of the room with a small stack of blank papers in one corner and a collection of colored pencils, erasers, and pens scattered above it. The accompanying chair sat at an angle, welcoming Ronnie to fill it.

Ronnie repositioned the chair under the desk.

He grabbed a paperback off the shelf at random and sat up on his bed, curious to see where a fellow creator would take him next.

Acknowledgements

Whoever you are, whether you're a friend, family, or a complete stranger, I want to give you a sincere thank you for lending your eyeballs to this piece of writing.

Reading for me has been a therapeutic stress reliever for a decade of my life, and I suppose writing this book was an extension of that. I set out to write this book shortly after my child was born, and finished the first draft of it just a few days before his first birthday.

You could probably guess that the themes in this book stem from very personal experiences related to my fatherless upbringing. Thank you, Mom, for the way you raised me despite all the obstacles in your way. I think I turned out okay...

Thank you to my Aunt and Uncle for raising me as well. They say it takes a village, and whoever "they" are, well... "they" were on to something.

I'd like to thank my alpha reader, creative partner, and twin Josh Powell for reading a very raw draft of this as I was writing it—typos and all—and complaining fairly little about how sloppy it was. Josh is a filmmaker and I love pretending to be other people with him.

Thank you to my wife Amanda, who's been a cheerleader from the jump. Unfortunately, she lives in the same space I inhabit and has to deal with me obsessing over editing, cover design, and formatting. I'd like to think I have a few ticks in the "Pros" column as well, but I'll let her be the judge of that.

Thank you to Danny Rosin, who taught me that you don't *find* time, you *make* time, which is probably the best advice I've ever received.

Thank you to Raelene Roth, who taught me to keep it weird, even in a business setting. I'll get my first tattoo someday, Rae…

Thank you to Jerry Falls, a devout horror fan who read an early draft of this and had wonderful things to say. Putting anything creative into the world is a very vulnerable thing and I needed that ego boost at the time. Remember giving me those big boxes of King and Koontz books when I was a teenager? Welp, this is what happened.

Thank you to my beta readers Kay Apple, Beth Raxlin, and Amber Campbell, who each provided invaluable feedback.

Thank you to my professional mentor Jeff Raxlin for helping me become a professional human.

Thank you to my star proofreader Marilyn Beaver. I take full responsibility for any mistakes.

Thank you to Sean Fletcher, an editor who assessed my original manuscript back when it had every mistake a new writer could make.

And to little baby Chandler: I hope you never have to face otherworldly threats, but if you do, please come to me for help. We'll have a blast.

About the Author

Joey Powell lives in Raleigh, North Carolina, with his wife, child, and many animals. He spends the majority of his days as a professional techie and the majority of his nights sifting through an ever-growing stack of books. In addition to being a devout consumer and creator of things spooky and weird, Joey has acted in several award-winning short films. Find him on Instagram via the QR code below.

@WOWCOOLJOEYWRITES